Edited by:
Lura Lee Genz
Mia Manns
Rachel Weaver

Avenstar Productions
ISBN: 978-0-9903314-1-4
www.markwaynemcginnis.com

SPACE VENGEANCE

A SCRAPYARD SHIP NOVEL

Written By

Mark Wayne McGinnis

Contents

Chapter 1

The Lilly sat on the Chihuahuan Desert, a little more than two miles from the Earth Outpost for the United Planetary Alliance. Jason and Admiral Reynolds exchanged nervous glances.

"Go for Captain," Jason said, acknowledging his NanoCom connection.

"What do you want us to do, Cap?" Billy asked.

"Well, how many Craing crewmembers are dead?" Jason asked back.

"There's a shitload of the little guys lying around here. Could be all of them. Hold on—"

Jason continued to look at Captain Dolom's limp dead body sitting across from him at the conference table. The ramifications of his unexpected death were nothing short of disastrous. They needed this Craing, this one last link to the ticking time bombs in their own heads, alive. Jason took in a long breath and tried to ignore his own relentless pounding pain. The one positive was that they still had what remained of the battered Craing warship. Ricket sat back and stopped poking and prodding the corpse.

"I'm back, Cap," Billy said. "I was wrong; it looks like there's a single survivor. By the looks of his medallion, he's one of the officers. I'm trying to remember ... what's silver mean? Is that like an XO?"

"I don't remember, either. Maybe. Do what you can to stabilize him. We'll be right over."

* * *

Jason and Ricket had flown the *Pacesetter* over to the crippled Caldurian vessel. Now, as Ricket examined the small Craing officer, Jason took in the vessel's bridge. From what he understood, this ship was at least one hundred years newer and, unquestionably, more advanced than *The Lilly*, but there were a lot of similarities. About one-third the size of *The Lilly*, she was definitely compact in comparison. The ship had the same 360-degree virtual display high up around the bridge and an array of other, smaller holographic displays at each of the various station consoles.

"Captain, I've discovered something interesting," Ricket said, kneeling at the side of the unconscious Craing.

Jason kneeled down as well. "What is it?"

"His nano-devices are still operational. Damaged, but still functioning. I'll need to do more tests to determine if there's still a self-destruct countdown."

Jason nodded. "Can you analyze what happened?" Jason tried not to sound overly desperate. It weighed heavily on his mind that his daughter, ex-wife, and every other crewmember on board *The Lilly* had less than fourteen days to live.

The Craing officer was coming around. When he saw Ricket looking down at him, his eyes widened and he tried to sit up.

"Do not move," Ricket said, putting a hand on his chest. He'd spoken Terplin and the Craing answered back in the same language. Their internal NanoCom devices provided a translation of what was being said. The Craing officer wanted to know whether he was dead. Was Emperor Reechet here to welcome him home to the spirit world?

Jason interjected, "Sorry, you're not dead yet. What's your name and what was your position on this vessel?"

He replied in broken English, "I am the second in command. My name is Mal-tee." He was craning his neck to look around the bridge. There were eight Craing lying dead on the deck and two others hunched over in their chairs.

Ricket was back to prodding at the Craing's cranium. Jason watched Ricket's face, where small gears, micro pistons and actuators silently moved beneath his near-transparent skin. He was making an expression Jason hadn't seen on him before. Over the last month, Ricket seemed to have evolved; he'd become more expressive, more humanlike. Billy entered the bridge and stood at their side.

"Is he going to make it?" he asked, obviously not overly concerned with the Craing officer's feelings on the subject of his life or death prognosis.

Jason shrugged. "Think so," he said as he noticed Ricket doing that thing with his face again. *Was that a smile?*

"What is it, Ricket?"

Ricket tilted Mal-tee's head back and looked into his large eyes. "Can it really be that simple?" he said aloud.

"What? What is it you're mumbling about?" Jason asked impatiently.

Ricket held up a finger, another new gesture for the cyborg. "Mal-tee, this is very important. What exactly did you do when you saw the other crewmembers dying next to you?"

Mal-tee thought for a moment, then held Ricket's stare. "I accessed and downloaded the medical practitioner protocols. They needed a medic; I was in the process of becoming one when I must have passed out."

Ricket stood up and went to the nearest console and typed something at the virtual input device.

While Ricket worked, Jason addressed the alien officer.

"Before we go any further, you will transfer command of this ship to me. I'm Captain Reynolds. Do it now!"

Mal-tee was instantly on edge and looked over to Ricket.

Billy, holding a multi-gun, pressed the muzzle to the Craing's large forehead. "We won't ask twice, little Craing!" Billy said, his Cuban accent adding an almost humorous quality to his ultimatum.

Mal-tee nodded, spoke a series of words and numbers, and then waited. The Caldurian ship's AI spoke aloud, his voice friendly and non-threatening. "Command transfer complete. Welcome aboard, Captain Reynolds, Ricket, and Lieutenant Hernandez."

Jason instantly liked the Caldurian ship's AI; *The Lilly*'s AI and her patronizing tone had always rubbed him the wrong way.

Ricket moved to another of the forward consoles. The wraparound display changed. "Captain, we have two Allied battle cruisers leaving the outpost."

Jason had known it was only a matter of time before the outpost would send ships to recover what was left of the Caldurian vessel. Looking around the bridge, Jason wasn't about to allow the U.S. military to get anywhere near this ship's highly advanced technology. In the past, *The Lilly* had been at odds with Jason's own government, and after what happened with Admiral Cramer and her militia's attempted coup to take control of the newly acquired Craing fleet—well, self-preservation dictated there was only so much technology he was willing to share at this point.

Jason hailed his father, Admiral Reynolds.

"Go for Admiral Reynolds," the baritone voice came back.

"Admiral, we've got two outpost battle cruisers en route—"

"Yes. They're following new outpost protocol. I can't get in the middle of it without bringing undue attention to myself. You'll need to handle things as best you can."

"We've talked about this before, Admiral; we don't want to surrender the Caldurian ship's high-tech into the hands of anyone, including the U.S. government. Remember, this ship's advanced technology may end up being our only link to figuring out the nano-tech issues."

"I'm not likely to forget. My head's pounding too, Jason. I'm walking into a meeting right now."

"So, you can't talk freely, you're saying?"

"That's correct."

"Understood. So you won't be surprised if this ship ... disappears?" Jason asked.

"Do what you have to do and bring me up to speed as soon as you can."

Jason cut the connection and looked over to the small alien, who was now sitting up and leaning against one of the bridge consoles.

"Ricket, what's the ETA on those cruisers?"

"Six minutes, Captain."

"Mal-tee, what is the range for phase-shifting this ship?"

Mal-tee looked confused, first looking at Jason and then at Ricket. Jason waved his hand dismissively and addressed the AI directly.

"AI, what is the range for phase-shifting this ship?"

"In your measurements, and as currently configured, approximately three thousand miles," the AI replied.

Jason was momentarily stunned at the phase-shift capabilities of this little ship compared to *The Lilly*, with its phase-shifting range of only three miles. He brought up his virtual tablet and studied the screen for several moments.

"Ricket, can you disengage the rear section of this ship, specifically the aft section with the damaged drives?"

Ricket thought for a moment and nodded. "It's possible if we use missiles or rail-gun ordnances from the *Pacesetter*."

"That could work," Jason replied.

Ricket moved to a nearby console and keyed something in. Billy was still watching the display. "Captain, those cruisers are now in orbit on the far side of the Earth."

Mal-tee looked confused. "Why destroy the aft section of my vessel?"

"You'll see soon enough," Jason answered.

"Captain, I've forwarded the phase-shift coordinates."

"Can you configure the move for that distance?" Jason asked.

"If the information the AI provided is correct, then yes."

"Wait a minute, it won't work," Jason said, frustrated. "I can't pretend to blow up this damn ship and still have Billy and his team miraculously survive ..."

"There's a shuttle on board. It's actually bigger than *The Lilly*'s shuttles," Billy offered.

"AI, does the shuttle on this vessel have phase-shift capabilities?"

"Yes, sir. The phase-shift capabilities of the shuttle vessel are similar to those of—"

Jason interrupted the AI mid-sentence. "Billy, help me get everyone on board that shuttle. You go too, Ricket, and take the Craing officer along with you. We need to move it: chop, chop, everyone!"

"Aye, Cap," Billy said, rushing from the bridge.

"Ricket," Jason said, heading off the bridge, "the timing has to be perfect. As soon as you're all on board the shuttle, go ahead and phase-shift to open space.

* * *

Back in the cockpit of the *Pacesetter*, Jason reviewed the targeting information Ricket had preloaded earlier.

"Captain, the two cruisers will have visuals on us in less than a minute," Ricket said. "They're hailing us, sir."

"I hear them. Just ignore them," Jason said.

"We're all on board and ready to go, Cap. We're phase-shifting to open space," Billy said.

A moment later, the Caldurian shuttle appeared within a mile off his starboard side.

Jason hailed Ricket via his NanoCom.

"Go for Ricket."

"Ready?"

"I'm ready."

With eight seconds before the two battle cruisers would have visuals on the Caldurian ship, Jason deployed the *Pacesetter*'s rail-gun. The gun charged and came alive with a series of short bursts, targeting the predetermined firing solutions—solutions that pinpointed key areas along the Caldurian ship's hull.

Small explosions ripped at the aft section of the ship until the mangled drive section spun off on its own trajectory. At that precise moment, the larger forward section of the Caldurian vessel shifted away. With three seconds remaining before the two battle cruisers came into view, Jason fired a low-yield missile into the floating aft section of the Caldurian ship. It exploded just as the two massive Craing battle cruisers came into view. There were sizable pieces remaining of the blasted vessel—enough to leave no doubt the Caldurian vessel had just been destroyed there.

Jason was hailed by Billy.

"Go for Captain."

"Cap, you do know they would have detected that missile you fired?"

"Just protecting myself. Seems that Caldurian ship had multiple defensive weapons targeting the *Pacesetter*. You saw it, right? Had no choice. Sure was a good thing everyone was able to get off the ship in time."

"Um, yeah, good thing."

* * *

What remained of the Caldurian vessel, the forward two-thirds of the ship, now sat one mile below the Chihuahuan Desert in a cavern adjacent to the one in which *The Lilly* was currently situated. Jason had earlier recalled that there was that second, smaller cavern close by to the first one, but he wasn't completely sure it would be large enough to hold the newly-disabled alien vessel. Apparently it was.

The *Pacesetter* sat next to the Caldurian shuttle on the now somewhat cramped *Lilly* flight deck. Ricket had one priority and one priority only—to find a solution that would prevent their nano-tech from self-destructing. Later, if there was a later, he could start retrofitting *The Lilly* with any and all new technology that could be scavenged from the younger ship. Especially the phase-shift components, which would allow phase-shifts to significantly farther distances.

* * *

Jason was not prepared for the deterioration of *The Lilly* crew's health. Apparently, the nano-tech issues in their heads were cumulative, and with that, painful headaches and nausea were the result. He waited while Nan was in the head, brushing her teeth. He'd decided to check in on her and Mollie as soon as he'd returned from space. The overhead lights had been dimmed and Mollie was in bed with a cold compress on her forehead. Jason stood in her doorway watching her sleep.

"What are you doing?"

"You're awake?"

"Dad, I can't sleep with my head hurting, and I feel like barfing."

"I know, sweetie. I'm sorry. And I know it's not fair that a little girl should have to go through this—"

"I'm not really a little girl anymore, Dad."

"You'll always be my little girl, even when you're ninety years old," Jason said with a smile.

Nan joined Jason at his side. She'd touched up her makeup since he'd first arrived several minutes earlier.

"Any progress?" she asked.

"Ricket's working on it. But not really."

"How often are we going to put Mollie in jeopardy like this? I mean, what little girl goes through this kind of bullshit?"

"You said a bad word, Mom," came Mollie's soft voice.

"Sorry, honey. I thought you were asleep," Nan said, frustrated.

Then Nan put a hand to her mouth. "Oh, God." She turned and ran for her bathroom.

* * *

The XO was waiting in the corridor for Jason as he left Nan's quarters.

"Captain. We have a visitor."

Jason still hadn't gotten used to Lieutenant Commander Perkins' altered Caldurian appearance, and he hesitated before replying.

"What do you mean? Here, a mile underground?"

"Looks to be one of the indigenous tribesman, sir."

"Where is he? What's he doing?"

"Nothing. I mean, he's just standing there at the bow

9

watching us. To be honest, it's kinda creepy."

The first thing Jason noticed as they entered the bridge was the watch crew's inactivity. All eyes were on the overhead display and the solitary figure standing motionless. He was tall, wrapped in what appeared to be animal skins, and holding some kind of long wooden staff.

"Sensors have been picking up the close proximity of life forms for some time now. When we flipped on the running lights we noticed this guy directly in front of *The Lilly*," Perkins said.

"Lilly, zoom in on his face," Jason commanded the AI.

The tribesman's face filled the forward segment of the display. Similar in looks to Perkins, the tribesman was evidently a Caldurian too. As if knowing he was being watched, he slowly lowered his thick fur hood and smiled. With his free hand he pointed a long finger, then waved in a gesture to come out.

"What's he doing?" Perkins asked.

"Looks like he wants to talk to us. Suit up, XO, we're going out there."

Perkins, who had yet to go on a mission away, didn't respond at first.

"Hello? Battle suit ... XO? I imagine the pressure out there is quite a bit more than we're used to."

Seemingly nervous, Perkins was already scurrying out of the bridge.

"Aye, Captain. I'll, um, I'll get ready."

The XO nearly tripped over Ricket on his way out.

The cyborg drew Jason's attention; he looked worn out. "You look terrible, Ricket," Jason said. "No doubt what you're doing up on 4B is crucial, but you need to pace yourself. You don't want to end up like Dolan, do you? Go ahead and suit up. Let's take a few minutes and meet with this guy."

Chapter 2

With the forward gangway deployed, Jason, Ricket and Perkins made their way toward the bow of the ship. Jason's head was throbbing and, more than once, he felt like he might be sick into his helmet. He also felt that carrying on a conversation with this indigenous underground tribesman would be an act in futility. First, he would have to apologize for parking two space vessels in what well could be sacred caverns. And how could he even explain what a space vessel was? Would Ricket be familiar with the ancient language and dialect needed to speak with this tribesman? The thought of having to carry on a conversation through elaborate hand gestures made his aching head throb even more.

The tall tribesman calmly watched as the three *Lilly* crewmembers approached.

This guy's smiling again, Jason thought.

The tribesman spoke: "Welcome." His smile broadened and he raised his bushy eyebrows as if he'd contemplated their surprise.

Jason and the two others hesitated in their tracks.

"Thank you. I'm Captain Reynolds, this is Ricket, and this is Lieutenant Commander Perkins."

The tribesman looked at each of them, but spent a few additional moments inspecting Perkins.

"Now, aren't you an interesting looking one?" he said, stepping in closer to look into Perkins' visor.

"It's a long story," Jason said flatly. "Excuse my abruptness, but who are you? I take it you're not an indigenous tribesman living here, a mile into the Earth's crust?"

"Please, call me Granger. Phonetically, that's about as close as you'll be able to come to the actual pronunciation of my name."

"So, who are you, Granger, and what exactly are you doing here?" Jason asked, regretting how his bluntness must sound to the alien.

"Well, I guess you could say I'm here for you, Jason. I'm what you'd call your welcoming party."

Jason didn't reply, just waited for him to continue.

"As you may have assumed, I am what you would call a Caldurian. These vessels of yours are both products of Caldurian ingenuity."

Jason, head still throbbing, and normally more amicable to this kind of chitchat, was feeling anything but normal. He took in Granger's appearance, his furs and long wooden staff. Jason guessed he was around fifty, but in truth he could be a little younger or older. What distinguished him from the other Caldurians he'd seen, such as the bodies found on the Crystal City, or even Perkins, was a full head of salt and pepper hair and striking blue eyes. Two characteristics he hadn't seen before in a Caldurian.

"May I call you Jason?"

"That's fine. I have questions that need answering and I have no idea if you are the right person to ask. Why I'm standing here, a mile deep into the Earth's crust, and talking to an alien who seems to speak English better than I do is the first one that comes to mind."

Granger didn't answer right away, seeming to weigh his response before speaking. His eyes held on to Ricket. "My people have survived for hundreds of thousands of years. As with humanity, our civilizations have come and gone numerous times. The things I will be discussing with you may be difficult to comprehend."

"I'll do my best to keep up," Jason said sardonically.

"You wish to help your crew, and your family, survive the impending destruction of your internal nano-devices. You want to see your daughter live longer than fourteen more days. Perhaps it's best to put sarcasm aside, yes?"

Jason bristled, speechless that this strange being already knew all about him, as well as their predicament.

"Let me start by saying something you will undoubtedly not want to hear. Within the next fourteen days you, your crew, and even your daughter will all cease to exist."

"You're telling me we're all going to die? There's no way to reconfigure the devices—"

"No."

"But one of the Craing officers—"

Granger was already shaking his head. "A short reprieve. The counter on his neuro-based nano technology has merely been extended for several days. He too faces the same inevitable end."

Ricket, moving his weight from one foot to another, seemed agitated. "You aren't simply here to relay this dire prognosis. Did you give this same information to inhabitants of the Crystal City?"

"Yes."

"Well, whoever you are, thanks for ... the information," Jason said and turned—already heading back to the ship—when Granger replied: "Jason, I want to show you something. I want to show all three of you something."

Jason started to turn away, ready to let Granger go back to where he'd come from, but the look on the Caldurian's face was not what he'd expected. There it was again, that same damn smile. *What the hell.*

"Now? You want us to do what, follow you?" Jason asked.

"If you would indulge me, I think you will find it worthwhile to do so."

Granger headed in the direction of the commandeered Caldurian vessel hull. They maneuvered in between several natural rock columns and crossed over into the smaller cavern. For the first time, Jason had the opportunity to inspect its colorful wall murals up close. They were beautiful. Nothing like the ancient monotone cave drawings of early man, or those of the Neanderthals. These drawings were akin to colorful Egyptian murals. The figures depicted here were clearly Caldurian, with their angular heads, shorter torsos, longer limbs, and extended tapered fingers. Jason caught up to Granger.

"So, is Earth your, the Caldurian, home world?"

Granger turned and looked up at the painted walls. "These murals were made recently. Within the last fifteen thousand years. Caldurians have existed for hundreds of thousands of years. I, myself, am well over two thousand years old. What you're seeing here is the work of primitive relatives, an offshoot of our people, who did not embrace technological advancement. They're still around, underground. We leave them alone and, for the most part, they leave us alone." They skirted the disabled Caldurian ship situated in the middle of the second cavern and ascended the rock-carved stairs where the area dimension slightly narrowed. Ricket was slow to bring up the rear, stopping periodically to inspect this or that—usually a rock, or something else he found interesting.

They followed a dirt pathway that snaked between immense boulders. Only the light generated from their helmets illuminated their way and faintly silhouetted Granger's footfalls up ahead. Jason wondered how Granger could navigate through the darkness, moving over the rough terrain with more agility than seemed possible. They walked in silence for twenty minutes before the path veered off to the right, though Granger abruptly turned left and climbed down onto a rocky plateau of sorts. They were within another cavern, one much smaller than the others. Above their heads was nothing but vast open space—space that was swallowed up by utter, and complete, darkness.

Granger waited for the others to catch up before moving on. He took three quick steps and stopped inches from a solid rock wall. He placed a hand on a rocky protrusion about the size of a softball and slid it sideways to expose a familiar-looking virtual keypad. Ricket wedged himself in front of Jason's and Perkins' legs to get a better look at what the Caldurian was doing. Granger's long fingers flew over the keys until there were two audible beeps. A glowing green frame, approximately ten feet wide and just as high, outlined a now visible portal window— similar to the portals found within *The Lilly*'s Zoo, or the ones on the planet Halimar. Jason took in a rapid breath. What they saw through the portal window was so unexpected that no one spoke for several moments.

"Where is this?" Jason asked.

Granger smiled. "At the center of a distant asteroid." He gestured for the three of them to follow as he stepped into the portal. Only Perkins hesitated, first looking toward Jason and Ricket, then quickly glancing back, as if contemplating whether or not he should return to the ship.

"You'll be fine," Jason said to Perkins, somewhat irritated by his nervousness.

They crossed over through the somewhat illumined portal. It was the sheer immensity of space that struck Jason first. The plateau they stood upon was high above a cavern of immense dimensions. Jason calculated it to be twenty to thirty miles in circumference. On first impression, it reminded him of Grand Central Station in New York City, but on a much grander scale.

Massive portal windows, hundreds of them, filled the walls across, below, to their sides, and even above them. Space vessels slowly moved from one portal to another. In the vacuum of space their powerful drives had an eerie soundlessness.

Jason spoke first. "These ships. They're moving throughout the universe?"

It was Ricket who answered. "Not the universe, Captain. The multiverse."

Granger smiled down at Ricket and nodded. "Continue, Ricket."

"We've discussed this before, Captain. But seeing it manifested like this is something else entirely ... There are infinite layers or membranes of separate universes that exist and coexist in time and space simultaneously."

Granger added, "Where we are standing is actually located in a multiverse membrane that depicts events in six dimensions, versus your three dimensions. What you're looking at is a multiverse way station."

"So, you're saying this isn't actually the sixth dimension?"

Granger answered, "No, this is only a three dimensional representation of the sixth dimension. The sixth dimension takes place strictly in the realm of math, not physicality."

Ricket nodded approvingly. "I take it those ships are Caldurian vessels moving between multiverse layers?"

"That is correct."

Jason's brow furrowed. "Wait. There must be thousands of ships here. From what I understood, the Caldurians were all but destroyed hundreds of years ago by the Craing." Granger smiled at this comment. Gesturing at what stood before them, he continued. "Does this look like an extinct civilization?"

"No, it doesn't," Jason replied. "But why—"

"For millennia, Caldurians have been plagued by other

civilizations that desired their technology as well as their advances in the natural sciences. More and more resources were needed for defensive purposes to the point where our actions became no different than those of our aggressors. Then the breakthroughs started happening more frequently and, with those breakthroughs, the ability to travel the multiverse."

A behemoth-sized ship was slowly making its way across the void below, crossing over to an adjacent portal on the far side. Jason shook his head: "That ship there ... it's massive."

"One of our newer vessels. We call it the *Minian*."

Easily as big as a Craing Dreadnaught, it had similar visual characteristics to *The Lilly*.

"So, I understand that you have progressed. Your civilization has risen above fighting petty turf wars and you live in different realms, perhaps more peaceful ones. What about you personally? Some sort of Caldurian emissary?" Jason asked, ready now to cut to the chase.

"Yes, that would be a good analogy. This membrane, this particular slice of the multiverse, is our home. We care what happens here. We care how societies will eventually migrate into the multiverse themselves. We've been watching you closely, Jason."

"Really? How have you been watching me? I haven't exactly been sitting around idly on Earth."

Granger seemed to be contemplating how much he wanted to say, then continued, "Your ship, *The Lilly*, has tremendous capabilities, developed well after our society had made inroads into the physics of multiverse travel. The DeckPorts, the phase-shift capabilities, and the phase-synthesizer unit, which, by the way, is being far underutilized, all deal with facets of the multiverse. You're protective of the technology. You keep it at arm's length, even from your own government, realizing it could cause an imbalance of power on your planet, as well as in space."

"And how do you know these things?" Jason asked, feeling uncomfortable that this stranger knew so much about him and *The Lilly*.

"Because I've walked beside you numerous times. Often as one of your less familiar crewmembers. I appear from any one of your DeckPorts, or the habitats, from an alternative multiverse location. I have an unlimited selection of whom, or what, I can represent myself to be."

"Seriously? Why the hell would you bother? You must have more important things to do than spy on what must seem to you to be a primitive race of people."

"How your society develops toward working with the multiverse will affect us all. We think of it more as an investment than as spying. With that said, I apologize for the subterfuge."

"So, what do you want from me? Again, what's this really all about?"

"You have a problem. You're all going to die very shortly. Soon, the weaker of your crewmembers will find the pain unbearable. Some will resort to suicide. Some will lash out, perhaps even killing others."

"You've already made it clear you cannot repair the nano-devices in our heads. So what are you getting at?"

"There are two primary factions of Caldurians. Those like myself who have embraced life living among the multiverses, and those who have set limits as to how far they will venture in that regard."

Ricket had started to pace as he listened, then interrupted. "You die."

Granger paused and assessed the small cyborg. "Yes, we've chosen to die. Many times."

Now Jason was totally lost. "What do you mean, chosen to die?"

Ricket responded. "When you travel between DeckPorts, or phase-shift from one location to another, your physicality, the *you* part of the equation, for the most part, stays intact. What Granger and his faction of Caldurians routinely do is leave one existence for a nearly identical but completely new one as needed."

"So how does that work?"

"You move through a portal," Granger replied, "much like those vessels are doing now, and you walk out through another one feeling and looking as if nothing has changed."

"And the thousands of people we found dead within the Crystal City?"

"That faction of our people, typically referred to as the *originals*, were not comfortable with the prospect of phase-shifting out of their original bodies."

"And your people?" Jason asked.

"We're referred to as *progressives*. For hundreds of years we've been perfecting the process. By utilizing interface constructs such as this, that speak to the multiverse via the sixth dimension, changing form has become a routine occurrence."

Granger paused again, then spoke in a softer, more gentle voice. "Right now, somewhere within the multiverse, there is another Mollie. She's lived an identical life in every way. She is exactly the same person with one exception. This other Mollie's nano-devices are not defective. This other Mollie is not curled up in bed next to her mother, writhing in pain."

"So let me try to understand. You're offering us this process. But the downside is we have to voluntarily die in order to carry on as a new person in another body?"

"Both you and your counterpart walk into a portal at the same time. One person emerges."

Jason, Perkins, and Ricket all took in this last bit of

information, but it was Perkins who spoke up first.

"I understand why *our* Mollie would want to walk into the portal, but what about that other Mollie? If she does not have the defective nano-devices, why would she even—"

"The other Mollie has another, completely different reason to want to go through with the process. She too will leave that issue behind. The two Mollies come through as identically merged, with the sole exception that each has left behind an undesirable condition, or aspect of herself," Granger answered.

"There's something you're not telling us. What's the downside? If there's a faction of your society that opposes this technology but accepts all the other technological advances, there has to be a reason," Jason said skeptically.

"In the beginning, before the process had been perfected, there were anomalies. Very rarely, but with any new technological breakthrough there's a learning curve. That should be expected. The *originals* were not comfortable with the early results. They broke away, choosing to take a different path."

"Could I use this process to revert back to looking human again?" Perkins asked.

"Yes, possibly, but you have other options at your disposal," Granger replied.

Jason watched the Caldurian. What Granger was saying made sense, but there was something else ... Jason just didn't know if he should trust him.

Chapter 3

Jason sat in the command chair reviewing the crew roster on his virtual tablet. He looked up and saw Orion at her station running battle simulations, while Ensign McBride at his station simply sat holding his head, both elbows resting on the console before him.

Gunny, looking frustrated, turned and addressed Jason. "We have to do something, Captain. I'm not unaccustomed to dealing with pain, pushing my body to its limits. But I've reached my limits. God knows how the rest of the crew deals with the pain. If you want my opinion, I say we undergo the procedure."

McBride, head still in hands, nodded his approval.

Jason had spoken to most of the crewmembers earlier one on one. He wanted it to be an individual choice, but a unanimous decision would make things simpler. From the initial responses he'd received back, there was no question they were more than willing to undergo the procedure—anything was better than living like this. But hadn't the inhabitants of the Crystal City had the same choice while dealing with the same pain?

Jason closed down his tablet and stood.

"Made a decision, Cap?" Orion asked.

"A partial one. I'll test it on myself; if I'm found to be medically sound and have no adverse effects, then I'll let others choose for themselves."

As Jason headed for the DeckPort he noticed Granger, wearing a standard spacer's jumpsuit, now walking in stride at his side.

"Where do we set this thing up?" Jason asked.

"I've taken the liberty of placing two portals within the ship's forward hold area."

"You never had any doubt that I'd acquiesce to this, did you?"

"Not really. When people are given the choice to live or die, most will opt for living. There's no secret motive or agenda here, Captain. It is a good thing. Nothing more than another tool made available in an extraordinary, technologically-advanced age."

Jason didn't respond to that. He then stopped and looked at Granger. "Let me make one thing perfectly clear. Anything adverse happens to my crew or my family, and I'll hold you personally responsible. You don't want me as your enemy. And one more thing—you pop into my ship unannounced again, I'll shoot you where you stand. Is that clear?"

"Quite clear, Captain," Granger replied with that same damn smile.

* * *

Both Ricket and Dira were waiting in the forward hold and turned as Jason and Granger entered. No one else had been informed why they'd come. Dira's eyes brightened as Jason approached and she rushed forward and hugged him.

He felt her arms around his neck pulling him in close, and it felt good. She brought her lips up to his ear and said, "I don't care if anyone sees us like this or not. I needed to be in your arms, Jason. If this is the last time I have to tell you—"

Jason gently pushed her away and looked into her eyes. "It won't be, Dira. I promise."

He smiled at her and kissed her forehead. The last thing Jason wanted was mixed feelings about going ahead. The more he had thought about it, the more nervous he'd become. But no matter how he approached it, he was about to kill himself. The person who would reenter the world would no longer be the same Jason Reynolds who had left it—was he truly prepared for that? And there were other concerns—would he still be able to captain *The Lilly* effectively? What type of man would he be?

In the middle of the hold were what looked like any two of their seven-foot-high, four-foot-wide DeckPorts, although these two were both framed in a bright glowing gold color.

"Ricket, if something goes wrong, don't let anyone else try this."

"Captain, there is something I'd like to show you before you enter the portal."

"What? Can't it wait?"

"No, sir. I don't think it can." Ricket then walked over to the portal on the left and stepped inside, disappearing from sight.

"Ricket! What the hell did you do?" Jason turned and glared at Granger, then back at the portal. "Well? Where is he?"

"Sometimes it takes a moment," Granger replied nonchalantly. Ricket came through the portal on the right. He stopped and turned to look back from where he'd just exited. "Quite amazing, Captain."

"What happened? Where did you go?" Jason asked, his anger somewhat abated seeing Ricket alive and unhurt.

"I will have to play back the process to analyze things more closely. But I simply walked into one portal and came out the other."

Dira knelt down at Ricket's side and held a small scanner to his head.

"Well, your nano-devices seem to be operating nominally. Any pain?" she asked.

"No pain. My own internal sensors tell me everything is as it should be."

"Do you feel ... any different? Do you feel like you?" asked Jason.

"I don't feel any different. Yes, I feel like me, Captain."

Jason started to move toward the portal, then stopped and turned toward Granger. "How does it know what to do? How does it know if I want my nano-devices repaired or if I want two heads?"

Granger smiled and shook his head. "How do DeckPorts know which level on the ship you want to travel to?"

Jason didn't answer.

"Intention," Granger replied. "Intention is real, quantifiable and measurable. What you're doing here, what you're all doing here, is evident. With that said, have a clear intention before you enter the portal."

Jason stepped up close to the portal and hesitated. He turned and looked back, noting the concern on Dira's face. He took a breath and stepped through. Like when phase-shifting, he experienced a flash of light and then immediately reentered the hold of the ship. The first thing he noticed was the complete lack of pain in his head. He felt wonderful. As far as he could tell, he was still the same person he had always been. At least he felt he was. Jason looked down at his arms, his legs—nothing seemed out of place.

Dira stood at the portal smiling. She raised her eyebrows as if to say: *well, should I go?*

Jason nodded. She stepped inside and was gone. Several moments later she re-emerged. She, too, was smiling and obviously relieved that the pain in her head was gone. She looked at Ricket and Granger, but not at Jason. She let out a deep breath and walked over to her small medical pack and started to place items back into their appropriate compartments.

"How do you feel, are you okay?" Jason asked, kneeling down next to her.

"I feel fine, Captain."

Jason nodded and smiled.

"If it's all right, I'll start moving the crew and your family through the portals right away, sir."

"That would be fine, Dira."

As he looked into her beautiful eyes, with their flecks of violet and amber, he realized there was something different in the way she looked back at him.

Chapter 4

Traveler entered the camp with his quarry draped over his shoulder. No one was in sight and there was a stillness in the air that raised the small hairs on the back of his thick neck. Up ahead three furry carcasses hung from a low-hanging branch. The tree, similar to a large oak, stood tall and dominated the center point of the rhino encampment. Blood pooled, thick and viscous in the soil. Traveler, tired from a two-day hunt in the forest alone, stood silently before the large tree. As he watched the three magnificent Furlong Bear carcasses sway in the late afternoon breeze, first shame, then guilt, and then anger filled his thoughts.

Eventually, with Captain Reynolds's blessing, they had been allowed to hunt whatever they needed—with one exception, the Furlong Bear. *Why do this now?* he wondered. There was plenty of other game. Traveler had given the ultimate oath—one based on his prowess as a male warrior, the Oath of Strength. To deviate from this oath required an offering of something most precious—one of his testicles. Instinctively, he reached down and cupped his maleness in one hand.

He turned and slowly surveyed his surroundings. Large mud-packed domes encircled the camp. A fire blazed nearby; soon, it would be hot enough to cook the Furlong Bear. Four large rhino-warriors emerged from the largest of the domes, domicile of their leader, the one called Three Horns.

They approached slowly and spread out. Dressed for battle, they wore thick leather breastplates and gripped heavy hammers in their fists. No energy weapons were strapped to their wrists. A large buck was still draped over one of Traveler's shoulders. He made no effort to move. Three Horns stopped ten feet in front of Traveler; the others also stopped.

"Your hunt was successful, my friend?" Three Horns asked, though it was more of a statement than a question.

"Yes. Though there already seems to be more than enough meat available here."

"We now hunt the Furlong Bear, Traveler. For too long we have succumbed to the wishes of the humans."

"Humans that saved us from the Craing. Humans that gave us a home," Traveler said.

"And at what price? How many of our kind must die for their cause? Are they so different from the Craing? And now, where we once were thousands, a mere one hundred and seventy of our warriors are left. It is time to go home, return to our mates and offspring. We will leave this habitat and take control of the space vessel. Will you join with us?"

"I will speak with Captain Reynolds."

"No, you have aligned yourself with the humans. Gone so far as to give an Oath of Strength to those puny beings. I am the leader here, Traveler. For too long I have let you speak for our warriors."

"No one has stopped you from being a leader—other than yourself, perhaps."

The breeze stopped, as if on command; smoke from the fire hung thick and dark in the air. Traveler let the carcass around his shoulders fall freely to the ground. Blood stained his broad shoulders and glistened in the afternoon sun. His own heavy hammer still hung from a leather thong at his belt. The four rhino-warriors charged at once.

Two of the rhino-warriors came at him low, heads down, with horns leveled at his lower extremities. The other two charged with hammers held high, going for his head. Behind him, the fire raged, making a retreat backwards impossible. Traveler barely skirted the first of the low-charging beasts, who, unchecked, was carried by his own momentum forward headlong into the fire. Red-hot embers filled the air as the fallen rhino thrashed about, attempting to get back to his feet. Simultaneously, Traveler ducked down as a heavy hammer missed his head by inches. With both hands, Traveler grabbed at a low oncoming horn. With his outstretched arms locked, Traveler turned his body sideways and brought the attacker onto his back. He reached for his own heavy hammer, but felt a crushing blow to his back, delivered by Three Horns. He staggered, but managed to stay on his feet. Traveler pulled his own hammer free, raised it high, and brought it down with all his strength. The rhino at his feet died instantly, his cranium crushed. With one rhino dead and another one still unable to escape from the flames of the cook fire, Traveler was able to move about more easily.

Three Horns and Great Hunter crouched low, poised to attack. The remaining rhino-warriors had come out from their domes and encircled them. But they would not enter this fight.

Great Hunter charged, feigned using his hammer, then struck out with an uppercut to Traveler's jaw. It connected, a blow hard enough to bring Traveler to his knees. Great Hunter pulled back and swung his hammer. Although there had been stories, more like tales or fables, of warriors catching heavy hammers mid-flight, no one there had ever actually seen it done.

Traveler caught the broad head of the hammer in the palm of his outstretched hand and held it there, to Great Hunter's astonishment. His expression quickly turned to fear as Traveler regained his footing and proceeded to pummel Great Hunter into the ground with his own heavy hammer.

Traveler then turned to face Three Horns, ready for him to make his move. But there was no need for Three Horns to do anything at all. From behind, finally able to extricate himself from the fire, the first of the rhinos to attack Traveler, the one called Black Tooth, connected a solid blow to the back of Traveler's head. His body fell to the ground. Near death himself, Black Tooth stumbled and fell back into the burning embers.

Three Horns signaled to several nearby onlookers. "You two, throw Traveler's body on the fire." Turning to the others, he continued, "We will feast tonight and we will prepare for battle. Tomorrow we leave this habitat."

Chapter 5

Jason was there when both Mollie and Nan entered the forward hold; both were nervous and held each other's hand tightly. He still was uncomfortable with either of them going through this life-altering process. They both moved toward Jason. Mollie, hunched over, wiped tears from her cheeks and tried to smile. They looked at Jason but soon their eyes were drawn to the standing portals, like two beckoning monoliths, in the middle of the hold.

Jason's heart was heavy and he was reluctant to speak, afraid his voice might betray him. In minutes the Mollie he knew and loved would cease to exist. She would be walking to her own death.

Nan scowled. "Oh, for God's sake, Jason, you seem to have come out of it all right. Pull yourself together. Now, what are we supposed to do here? Enter one of these portals?"

Jason didn't expect to laugh, but he couldn't help it. Leave it to Nan to be the eternal pragmatist. She smiled and headed for the two portals. Looking back over her shoulder she pointed to the one on the left, and Jason nodded. She stepped through and disappeared.

Mollie watched with eyes wide open. Jason could tell she was holding her breath. Then, she let it all out as Nan reappeared through the other portal. Nan smiled and held her arms out wide as Mollie ran to her. They embraced. Nan looked up and winked at Jason. She kissed Mollie on the forehead and ushered her over to the left portal. Before stepping through, Mollie gave a little wave toward her father, smiled excitedly, and was gone.

Now it was Jason's turn to hold his breath. When she reentered through the other portal, Mollie was all smiles and giggles. Jason relaxed his shoulders and smiled. She seemed more than happy to be a little girl again, with nothing all that important to worry about.

Jason turned to see his father, Admiral Reynolds, entering the hold. He, like the other crewmembers, looked ill and tired.

"It seems you're ... you all are ... feeling much better?" Admiral Reynolds asked, attempting, and failing, to sound upbeat.

Mollie rushed to give her grandfather a hug and looked up at him.

"Let me tell you how to do this, Grandpa."

"Okay, what is it I'm supposed to do here, Mollie?"

"You need to think about what you want to happen. It's called indention."

"Intention," Nan said, correcting her.

"Yeah, intention. Anyway, you walk into the portal on the left and you'll come out of the one on the right feeling a whole lot better."

The admiral walked to the portal and hesitated. Looking at Jason and then at Granger, he asked, "You sure about this?"

Jason shrugged. "No, not really. But I didn't see there were any other viable options."

The admiral stepped through the portal. A moment later Jason saw his father reappear as he stepped through the second portal. Jason asked him how he felt.

"Much better, thank you for asking. I feel like I can actually think clearly again." The admiral walked over to Granger and held out his hand. Granger shook his hand and they spoke quietly for several minutes. Other than the occasional word here and there, Jason couldn't make out what was being said.

A line had formed and Ricket and Dira were directing people

into the left portal. The relief on their faces when they exited the portal told Jason he'd made the right decision. He felt life could finally get back to normal. The admiral was back at his side and he put a hand on Jason's shoulder.

"Son, I want to thank you." He gestured towards the portals. "I'm not so sure I would have lasted much longer."

Son? Jason couldn't remember the last time his father had called him that. "Well, it's really Granger you want to thank. This setup was his doing."

"That's not exactly what he says, but just the same, thank you." The admiral changed subjects. "We have visitors coming in tomorrow morning. I need you to be at the outpost."

As Jason left the hold he looked back one more time. Not once since she had come through the second portal had Dira looked his way.

* * *

Jason awoke early the next morning and was again relieved to feel back to normal, and still human. He'd been pinged several times already with reminders that there was a morning meeting at the outpost and not to be late.

But this morning was all about Mollie. He'd had little time to spend with her lately and nothing was going to stand in the way of him having a little dad and daughter time.

She'd arrived at his cabin with a hundred questions, but Jason kept mum to where they were going or how they were going to get there.

"What should I bring?" she asked, looking for a hint in the way he was dressed.

"Nothing. Here, hold this for a sec, I packed us a lunch." Jason finished putting on his shoes.

Molly looked in the small satchel to see what he'd brought.

"Why are you being so secretive? I hate surprises."

"Yeah, sure you do."

"I'm supposed to go to work today; Jack will be upset."

"I've cleared it with Jack."

They left the cabin and headed astern. At the DeckPort Mollie scowled. "If you don't tell me, I'm not going."

"Okay, I guess I'll have to go by myself."

When they emerged on the flight deck her expression changed from frustration to confusion. The *Pacesetter*, already prepped, was sitting in the middle of the bay with its canopy open.

"Wait, we're going in that?"

"Is that okay?"

"Yes, that's okay. That is more than okay!"

Mollie sat in the forward seat. Her helmet was a little big on her but she didn't seem to notice. All strapped in and the canopy secured, Jason entered the coordinates. After a quick conversation with his XO, they phase-shifted to the Chihuahuan Desert above.

"Ready to go?" Jason asked.

"Stop asking me that, Dad—wherever we're going, let's just go already!"

With that, Jason steered the *Pacesetter* off the ground and headed south, then nearly vertically straight up, toward the stratosphere. Mollie screamed. Quickly, her fear turned to excitement, though the screams continued. The edge of the stratosphere changed from light to blackness and then back to light again as they descended. Jason watched as her helmet spun this way and that as she took it all in. When they reached near-ground level again, the world had turned white. Miles and miles of white. Skimming the Antarctic planes at two hundred miles an hour, Mollie became quiet. The landscape, barren and beautiful, demanded it. They approached a coast of jagged white cliffs—contrasted against small inlet pools the color of aquamarine. Fifty feet below, too many penguins to count shuffled here and there as they swam and romped around.

"Oh my God! They are soooo cute!"

They phase-shifted to an open area below. Jason climbed down the ladder first, telling Mollie to sit tight for a moment. Stowed away in the *Pacesetter*'s storage compartment were sub-zero coats, snow pants and boots. The cold was almost unbearable. Now properly outfitted, with teeth chattering, Jason pulled a thermos from the compartment and poured Mollie and himself a steaming cup of hot chocolate. They headed off to play with the penguins.

* * *

Four hours later, with Mollie back with her mother, Jason used the *Pacesetter* to phase-shift back up to Earth's surface and then flew on to the outpost. After requesting permission to land, Jason made a complete circuit around the perimeter of the outpost. Below was a flurry of activity. Troops were moving from one location to another. Equipment was being transferred out of the belly of a C5 U.S. military transport plane from origins unknown. The outpost's fleet of two hundred plus Craing warships was in the process of being painted over—from a drab brown color to battleship grey, navy blue, or stark white.

Jason set the fighter down at a designated field location near one of the two runways. The last time Jason landed here, he'd been greeted with an armed militia. Now, a small contingent of five men, apparently a mixed bag of Army, Navy, and Marine military services, stood at attention and waited for Jason to join them. They saluted and Jason couldn't help but notice they were all excited and holding back smiles. This is how he'd initially imagined the outpost—a place where the best of the best could serve their country. Some would be among the elite few who'd travel into the far reaches of space.

"Welcome, Captain Reynolds. I'm Sergeant Matheney; we'll be escorting you to your meeting with the admiral and the Joint Chiefs."

"Thank you, Sergeant."

It was then that Jason noticed the top of the closest flagpole. A new flag fluttered there in the afternoon breeze. A striking red, gold, and blue design for the Earth Outpost for the United Planetary Alliance—the EOUPA flag. Each of the men had a matching EOUPA patch on the upper arm of his uniform as well.

Jason fell in step with the group as they headed for the larger of the two outpost buildings. Before entering, he stopped and turned toward the right-most flagpole. At the top of this pole was the flag of the United States of America. Jason stood a bit taller and saluted the flag. He turned to join the others and entered the building.

* * *

The admiral's office, or, more accurately, his suite of offices, took up the complete top floor of the Outpost Systems and Command Building. Military police were positioned at the ground floor elevator, as well as at the elevator exit on the top floor.

A ruckus came from the end of the hall. Jason instantly recognized his father's deep voice, as well as the voices of several others. He entered the admiral's large wood-paneled conference room. Apparently, someone had just released the punch line to a funny joke. All of the five men present were laughing so heartily they hadn't noticed Jason's presence. The first to look up and see Jason was Secretary of Defense Ben Walker. The laughing subsided and the others, General Brian Carter, Vice Admiral Harold Brightman, and General Eric Slayton, acknowledged Jason with somewhat subdued politeness. The room was thick with cigar smoke and the smell of expensive Scotch. Jason saluted them and the five men stood and returned his salute.

Jason moved toward the open chair near his father's, situated at the head of the table. Before sitting down, he shook the men's outstretched hands.

It was Ben Walker who spoke first. "Captain Reynolds, Jason ... we all owe you a great debt of gratitude."

The room had become quiet and each man, now serious, had his eyes locked on Jason.

"Thank you, sir. I'm sure you've noticed I've made my share of stumbles along the way."

"Oh, we've noticed," General Slayton chided.

"All right, let's all sit and get down to business," Admiral Reynolds said, taking his own seat. A tumbler with several fingers of Scotch slid across the mahogany tabletop, stopping right in front of Jason's right hand. Jason nodded his appreciation toward Vice Admiral Brightman.

"Although we're all pretty much up to speed, why don't you give us a quick synopsis of the course of events that occurred over the last few weeks, up to the destruction of the three Caldurian vessels?" Admiral Reynolds said.

"Three? I thought it was only two Caldurian vessels that were destroyed," the Secretary of Defense muttered, confused.

Admiral Reynolds raised his hand. "We'll get to that. Jason, go ahead."

Jason stared at the table for a moment, trying to organize his thoughts on everything that had happened over the last few weeks. He then began to speak: first relating the meeting he'd had with the three Craing overlord prisoners at the outpost, and learning from them two important factors. "First," Jason continued, "In response to our unexpected victory, defeating five hundred Craing vessels on the outskirts of our solar system, the Craing readied their response. They had three Caldurian vessels of their own. Called the Emperor's Guard, these newer, more technologically advanced warships were being readied to assault Earth. Second, we learned of the Craing's ability to use something called the Loop. By way of a stabilized wormhole they had created close to their home worlds, they were able to move about and dominate other civilizations throughout the universe. The bottom line was something needed to be done, right there on their home turf, to even the odds. But even with FTL technology, a trip to Craing space would take over one hundred years. We then came up with another idea on how to get there, but it would be risky."

Jason paused and took a sip of his drink. The room was quiet and he had their full attention. "You're all familiar with the Zoo on board *The Lilly*. Well, it just so happens that one of the habitats there is on Halimar, which is one of the Craing worlds. The habitat, which we call HAB 12, is out of phase from our own perspective, so once in there, we needed to find another portal to access the Craing planet. We had less than a week to find the portal, destroy the Loop and stop the Craing from sending the Emperor's Guard. After losing a substantial number of our team, we made it onto their planet and destroyed the Loop. We were unsuccessful at stopping those three Caldurian ships from entering the wormhole, though. While all this was going on, *The Lilly* was en route to another star system to deliver the three overlords to discuss asylum for their people. With minimal crew and security forces, *The Lilly* never made it there. Tricking *The Lilly*'s crew with a phoney distress signal on a space freighter, and assisted by a traitor crewmember on board *The Lilly*, the pirates boarded the ship and took hostages."

"Yes, we read in your report that your ex-wife was held by their leader, um ... what's his name?" General Slayton asked.

"Captain Stalls. A real piece of work and someone we'll need to keep tabs on. He has no less than two hundred warships at his command—any one of which could wipe out millions here on Earth. We re-entered the ship from HAB 12 and regained partial control of *The Lilly*. It was more of a stand-off, really, which lead to Stalls and his band of pirates releasing the hostages and abandoning the ship."

"So, we not only have the Craing to deal with in open space, we have this band of killer pirates, as well?" Vice Admiral Brightman asked.

"Afraid so. Anyway, once we made it back here, Earth was already engaged with the three Caldurian ships of the Emperor's Guard."

"Now, let me stop you there, Captain. They weren't actually attacking us outright," Brightman said.

"That's correct; they were looking for something or someone. Caldurians had, or have, access to what amounts to unlimited wormhole travel. While the Craing were able to utilize their Loop wormhole to access a limited number of outpoints throughout the universe, the Caldurian technology has no such restrictions: travel seems to be instantaneous to anywhere. The Craing had limited information about that kind of capability and were desperately looking for answers to acquire it. Somehow, they got the idea that the answers lay deep here, within the Earth's crust."

Jason was willing to provide only so much information about

this subject, and wanted to evade the current line of questioning. "Anyway, when we entered Earth space, we engaged the three vessels. Although the ships were somewhat more advanced than *The Lilly*, the Craing crews seemed to be inexperienced with the technology. Two of the vessels were destroyed and the third was disabled. We boarded that vessel and took control, but within hours the Craing crew, all at once, started to die. It was then that we discovered that we, the crew of *The Lilly*, also had the same defective nano-tech devices in our heads, and we too had very little time left to live."

Jason saw that the others around the table were exchanging glances. This time it was Ben Walker who interjected. "So, tell us again how that one remaining Caldurian ship was destroyed? Seems we have conflicting reports about this aspect of your story, Captain. The vessel was extremely important; the loss of its technological advances is tremendous." Walker was clearly agitated and made no attempt to hide it.

"As I mentioned, sir, the Caldurian ships were highly advanced. From what we've been able to piece together, the ship's AI had triggered defensive actions and fired at one of our approaching vessels. We returned fire and were lucky enough to destroy the ship before any more of our people were killed. It was then that the two outpost battle cruisers rendezvoused with us."

Jason was perfectly aware they were skeptical of his accounts. They probably had suspicions that the Caldurian vessel was still in one piece, hidden somewhere. Jason's father stood and walked over to the small minibar on the other side of the conference room.

"Who needs their drink topped off?" he asked, taking some of the tension out of the room. Each of the men, including Jason, nodded. The admiral took extra time pouring from a cut glass decanter. Jason wanted to avoid the inevitable ongoing discussion of bringing *The Lilly* under the U.S. government's purview.

"I do have something more of interest to add about the Caldurians," Jason said. "I'm not sure how much the admiral has already shared." Jason saw his father's alarmed expression and instantly regretted speaking up. Jason continued, "The same technology the Craing were so desperately trying to uncover here on Earth—actually, below Earth's surface—apparently does in fact exist. Perhaps in time we'll have access to this technology. What I'm talking about is unlimited wormhole travel."

The admiral replaced the decanter on the sideboard table with enough noise to stop Jason mid-sentence.

"Jason, getting everyone's hopes up at this stage would be ill-advised. It's premature for us to count our chickens before they're hatched."

Ben Walker looked from the admiral and then over to Jason and held up both hands. "Wait just a minute; we're not talking fucking chickens here, we're talking military capabilities that could alter the ongoing strategic balance of power in space. Who the hell are you, Admiral, to make the decision whether or not to disseminate or withhold that crucial information?"

The admiral quickly shot another irritated glance at Jason as he sat back down at the head of the table. Jason felt for his father—he really did—but he was relieved, even temporarily, to be off the hot seat.

"Relax, Ben! We were hoping to have a full report to you within the next day or so," the admiral said. "Jason can provide more of the details, but we've met with a Caldurian representative. Apparently, they have been watching us for some time now."

Jason continued on for his father. "They are on the fence about our intentions. Their fear is of putting this technology in the wrong hands, such as the Craing, which would, beyond doubt, unbalance planetary co-existence to the far reaches of space. The Caldurians are not a warring society. If we approach them solely for our own military aspirations, in their eyes we're no different than the Craing. It's for these reasons we have kept this delicate stage of negotiations more informal. Please understand, this representative approached me personally, not the U.S. government."

This seemed to appease Walker, and he mulled over Jason's comments. Jason saw that his father had relaxed somewhat.

"Let's give it a day or so and see what Jason and this Caldurian come up with. What's his name?" the admiral asked.

"He goes by the name Granger," Jason replied.

"Okay, let's give Jason some time to work with Granger and see what inroads can be made. But Jason, this technology needs to be shared, is that understood?" Walker said in a stern voice.

"Yes, sir."

"All right, we need to change gears, Captain," Walker said. "As I'm sure you've noticed, the outpost has come under the reign of the U.S. government. Each of the military branches—Army, Navy, Air Force, and Marines—are now an integral part of this installation. I know you don't approve, but that's the way it is."

"And you are dividing up the Craing warships we have into those separate divisions?" Jason asked.

"The lion's share will go to the Air Force to support our efforts and defense of Earth space. The remaining crafts will supplement the Army, Navy and Marine's defense efforts here on Earth."

"You do realize that diminishing the size of the fleet, even by a few warships, could render catastrophic results for us going up against potential enemies in space?" Jason asked, trying to keep calm.

"The admiral has already made that argument; it's been

noted. Although I tend to agree with the two of you, there are other political forces at work here," Walker replied.

Jason sat back in his chair, amazed how little had changed in Washington. The only two officers present who'd actually had deep space combat experience were being indiscriminately discounted.

"That's not what we need to discuss with you right now, Captain," Admiral Reynolds said flatly. "I had thought what remained of the Alliance would still be in shambles, but they've reached out to me via FTL transmission. It seems they're rallying again. Pooling what forces they have left, and now, other planetary systems have asked to join the Alliance."

"Why? Why now?" Jason asked.

"As we all know, several months ago the Craing annihilated the Alliance fleet. The Craing, with a fleet of two thousand warships, moved on with virtually no losses. Five hundred of those ships broke off and headed straight for Earth. We defeated them at the outskirts of our solar system. We had hoped what remained of the original Craing fleet, some fifteen hundred warships, had returned to the Craing worlds. Unfortunately, we've recently discovered that was not the case. With the destruction of the Loop, those ships were indeed marooned here and all indications are they're now heading back toward Alliance space."

"How much time do we have?"

"A week, maybe two."

Jason thought about that. "You mentioned the Alliance is rebuilding. What are we talking about? How many vessels?"

"Maybe five hundred, give or take," the admiral replied.

Jason looked back at his father and then at the others around the table. "Against fifteen hundred Craing warships, three of which are Dreadnaught class vessels?"

Ben Walker ground the stub of his cigar into an oversized ashtray. "Captain, this is an all or nothing situation. If we can defeat them here, we'll rid Alliance space of the Craing well into the next century. What we need is your input on how we can accomplish this."

Jason knew exactly what they were asking of him. They wanted *The Lilly* back in the fight. "Even with *The Lilly*, we're in no position to take on that fleet."

"We were already counting on *The Lilly*, Captain. We should also make every effort to acquire the new technology that Granger and his people possess. That could be a deciding factor, no?"

"Perhaps we can make it worth their while; what can we offer them?" Vice Admiral Brightman asked.

"There's little the Caldurians seem to need from us. Although their disdain for the Craing is evident, I can't say to what lengths they'll go to help us. I'm sure I'll be seeing Granger again soon. I'll keep you all up to date on what transpires."

Jason had the feeling that the men in this room were under the illusion that they'd be able to muster an adequate defense. He pushed his chair out to stand, then added, "The truth is, I think we need to be prepared for the worst. With fifteen hundred warships, even with help from the Alliance, I'm sorry but I don't see how we can defeat the Craing. Not this time."

The room went quiet, the men obviously sobered by Jason's comment.

Jason's father added, "If the Craing are victorious, we should be prepared. They'll be heading for Earth wanting to finish what they'd started. My suggestion—contact other world leaders, tell them to prepare as best they can for an alien incursion."

Chapter 6

The smaller of the two rhinos, Walks With Limp, grabbed Traveler's feet and hefted them to his midsection. Rustling Leaves, one of the rhino warriors that had been watching the battle from the side-lines, now stood at Traveler's shoulders, hesitated, and then bent down to inspect Traveler's wound. It was serious, but his friend was not dead, at least not yet. Rustling Leaves had watched Traveler take down three of the strongest warriors, only to be struck with a cowardly hit from behind.

Three Horns watched from across the camp. His irritation was clearly evident by a growing number of snorts and huffs—a misty spray of snot shot in Rustling Leaves' direction.

"You will do as I say or face his same fate," Three Horns barked.

Rustling Leaves did not acknowledge the older rhino's words. Instead, he looked to the others. Slowly, one by one, making eye contact with each. Nearly imperceptibly, each conveyed their intention with the slightest movements of their large heads. Each had nodded toward Rustling Leaves—each agreed to stand at his side. The tribe of rhinos converged on the leader.

Three Horns' death was quick and honorable. His heavy hammer would be saved and given to his offspring. His body was thrown onto the fire and prayers were spoken aloud.

Rustling Leaves knew Traveler had little chance of survival. He would need help from the strange-colored being, the one called Dira.

"Take Traveler to his dome," Rustling Leaves said. "I will bring help."

* * *

Jack and Mollie were having one of their many heated discussions. Jack wanted her to finish her daily chores in the Zoo, while Mollie would have preferred to go into HAB 4 and play with Alice, her *drog*, a dog-like creature brought back from HAB 12. Impertinent, hands on hips, Mollie was making a stand. But it was Rustling Leaves' shadow farther down the corridor that caught her attention. Jack turned to see what Mollie was looking at, then scurried over to see what the large beast wanted. Jack was reluctant to unlock the portal into the habitat without Captain Reynolds' permission, but something was wrong. The rhino needed help. Jack input the necessary keystrokes and the portal opened.

"We need the one you call Dira."

"What's wrong? Who's sick?" Mollie asked, looking up at the large beast in front of her.

"It is Traveler. Hit in the head with a heavy hammer."

* * *

In addition to Dira, both Ricket and the captain had been notified. The three now moved quickly into the rhino encampment. At the entrance to one of the large mud-packed domes, Rustling Leaves waved them over. Jason was the last to enter the dome and it took several moments for his eyes to adjust to the dark. A small fire burned in the middle of the room, its smoke leisurely rising up, disappearing into a small opening high above. Dira and Ricket were kneeling at Traveler's side and speaking in hushed voices. They went to work.

Jason approached Rustling Leaves. "What the hell happened?"

"Our leader, Three Horns, and three others attacked Traveler."

"Why? I thought Traveler was respected—"

"Three Horns feared Traveler and no longer wished to be confined in a habitat. Time to return home to mates and offspring. Was planning to take ship back home."

"Why didn't Three Horns, or any of you, just come to me? I know it's taken longer than I'd hoped, but we will get you home. I've promised that much."

"At a high cost, Captain. Few of us remain. But Three Horns lives no more."

"Was that your doing?" Jason asked.

"Yes. Traveler should have been our leader long before this. But Three Horns was not entirely wrong, either."

Ricket stood up and joined Jason and Rustling Leaves. Dira, still at Traveler's side, continued to attend to the rhino's wound. Now, up on all fours, she reached across his chest, wiping blood from his face. As if knowing Jason was watching her, she glanced back over her shoulder. She furrowed her brow at Jason and quickly moved to the rhino's other side.

"Oh ... No, I wasn't looking at—"

Dira wasn't listening, busy wrapping gauze around Traveler's head.

Embarrassed, Jason felt his face flush. *She can't believe I'd be checking out her backside; not at a time like this*, he thought. *Or was I?*

"Captain," Ricket said, taking his attention off an awkward situation.

"Yes, um, what's going on with Traveler?"

"His wounds are serious. He's hemorrhaging into his brain."

"Is there anything we can do? Perhaps take him to Medical?"

"He is far too large to fit into a MediPod. That would be his only chance of survival."

"Can you make a bigger MediPod, one that would fit a rhino?"

"I've already thought of that. The rhinos' physiology is not contained within *The Lilly*'s medical database," Ricket answered.

They both spoke at the same time: "The Caldurian ship!"

"Yes, I will check. Ensure his head remains stable, the environment quiet." Ricket hurried from the dome.

"I must attend to my duties, Captain," Rustling Leaves said. With that, Jason was alone with Dira and Traveler. He watched her work. With her eyes looking down, her long lashes were even more accentuated. He was staring again. He quickly looked away. It was obvious. Dira, this Dira, was no more in love with him than she was with Ricket or Traveler. Jason quietly cursed to himself ... that damn portal. What the hell was he supposed to do now?

"Can you hand me my kit, Captain?"

Startled, Jason looked down at his feet and found the medical bag she'd brought with her. He handed it to her. "I'll leave you alone. Let me know if you need anything."

Jason stood and turned toward the dome's entrance.

"How's your research going?" she asked, her voice no more than a whisper.

Jason stopped, but didn't turn around. "Research?"

"Uh huh."

"I'm not following."

"Courting a Jhardian girl? Or perhaps you've forgotten."

"Oh, I see. You've been fucking with me."

When he left the dome, he didn't need to turn around to know she was smiling.

* * *

Jason entered Deck 4B via the DeckPort. It was where *The Lilly*'s phase-synthesizer unit churned out a myriad of things, from weapons armament munitions to new technological prototypes—all of which were pulled from alternate slices of the multiverse. And it was here that Ricket spent much of his time when not on duty.

The phase-synthesizer was doing something, and making more than a little noise in the process. A new MediPod device, significantly larger than those in Medical, stood off to the side. It looked to be nearly complete.

Expecting to see Ricket alone sitting at his workbench, Jason was surprised to see both Granger and Ricket sitting at the bench together, with a 3D hologram of something floating several inches above the bench.

Granger's expression changed when he saw Jason approach. "I did not drop by uninvited, Captain."

Ricket momentarily looked up, then continued with what he was doing. "Captain, development of a new, substantially larger MediPod was far more involved than I had estimated. With the help of Granger, not only did we produce the necessary MediPod configuration, but he has offered to assist in the overall retrofitting of *The Lilly* with the more advanced technology found on the Caldurian ship."

Jason tried to keep his face neutral, keeping his growing irritation and distrust hidden from the tall Caldurian. "I still would like to know ahead of time when non-crewmembers are coming on board," Jason said sternly.

"Yes, Captain, that was my mistake," Ricket replied, now looking up at Jason.

Jason turned his attention to Granger. "Don't interpret this as my not being appreciative of any help you can offer us. But I'm still not clear what your motivations are."

"Only time will tell, Captain. Rest assured, though: defeating the Craing is paramount to both our people's wellbeing. As you learned while meeting with the Joint Chiefs and Secretary of Defense Walker, you have little time to prepare for the approaching Craing fleet."

How would he know that? Jason thought to himself. His mind flashed back to the smoke-filled conference room. There had been a junior officer standing in the wings, refreshing drinks and lighting cigars.

"Do I have to put a bell around your neck, Granger? What don't you understand about uninvited eavesdropping?"

"You were specific to this vessel; you never mentioned anything about the outpost," Granger said innocently.

Jason knew there was little he could do to keep the Caldurian representative from prying where he wasn't welcome. The fact of the matter was the Caldurians were substantially more advanced, and keeping them at arm's length was probably an act of futility.

"So what are we doing here? What is that thing?" Jason asked, gesturing toward the virtual object hovering above the bench.

"This is what the Craing have been looking for. What they referred to as the source, but we refer to it as the *interchange.*"

Jason moved in closer, but stood back again when Granger simply expanded the virtual model out several more feet.

"That looks more organic than any kind of technology."

"What you're seeing is only one small aspect of the interchange. Constantly moving, it spreads itself across the multiverse, having the ability to keep a foot in multiple-time references and phased-dimensional realities at once."

"You talk about it as if it's a being. So it's not technology based?" Jason asked.

Granger smiled at this. "You'll find that the lines

differentiating things technologically- developed and things that are organically produced become more and more blurred with advanced cultures. To be honest, we don't know what this *interchange* truly is. We do know that it doesn't eat and drink or sleep like typical organic beings. We do know it builds relationships and provides access to wormhole travel to those with whom it has connections."

"What does that even mean? Like to its friends?"

Granger smiled. "For hundreds of years now my people have moved about the universe through the aid of the interchange. Most definitely ours is a symbiotic, friendship-based relationship."

"How does that work? What does the interchange get in return?"

"When the time comes, when you wish to build your own relationship with it, that will be made apparent. But as part of our agreement, it is not something I am free to discuss."

"Seriously? I find this all a bit hard to believe ..." Jason said.

Granger did not reply and simply nodded his head.

"Okay, so how do you contact it when you want to utilize the wormhole capability?"

"A simple request. One that is formatted specifically with the desired in-and-out point coordinates, along with other crucial information. The request is sent through something similar to— but much more efficient than—your FTL-type communications. In this case, it's instantaneous. Just one of the locations, among many, where this information can be directed to is here, deep within Earth's crust."

"I guess that explains why the three Caldurian ships, the ones appropriated by the Craing to form the Emperor's Guard, were scouring our planet. Seems they already knew much of this."

"They were wasting their time. The interchange is quite particular about who will be allowed access. The Craing have proven to be brutal and selfish. Not unlike governments on your own planet."

"So we are to be denied access to—"

"No, Captain. Although you have exhibited a higher degree of violence than the interchange, as well as the Caldurians, would prefer, the simple fact that you yourself have withheld certain technologies from your government speaks volumes," Granger said. "So, with the Caldurians acting as a go-between, I have little doubt you'll be granted access to the interchange."

Ah, so there it is, Jason thought. Granger, and the Caldurians, would be acting as a go-between, which really meant they could maintain control.

Granger continued, "One more thing, Jason. You are under the assumption that the Craing Loop has been destroyed. That the Craing worlds will no longer be sending their fleet of warships to these sectors of the universe."

Stunned, Jason didn't respond.

"I'm sorry, but you are mistaken. In less than three of your months, the Craing will again have the capability to travel to the far reaches of the universe. Even without access to the interchange."

"No. That's not possible. I witnessed it myself; those sub-stations on Halimar were totally destroyed."

"What you didn't know was that their science had already progressed to the point that soon they would no longer need those archaic planetary sub-stations. In fact, the Craing had already started tests on a significantly smaller, more powerful, and far more accurate space-based laser platform system. Your actions merely accelerated the testing and production of their new Loop program."

Feeling defeated, Jason's shoulders sank. So many had died in that mission across HAB 12 and onto Halimar. Was there truly no way to stop the Craing?

"And what of the rebellion, the uprising on the Craing worlds?" Jason asked.

Granger's expression, if possible, looked even more dire. "After your attack on Halimar, the Craing Empire's military mobilized. Anyone suspected of taking part in the rebellion, and I'm talking many thousands here, were publicly executed."

Jason's mind flashed to Gaddy, the young, idealistic Craing dissident who had helped transport them on Halimar. Had she and her friends been among those executed?

"So, yes," Granger continued, "the rebellion has been quelled for now. But discord is building. More than ever the people of the Craing worlds yearn for the kind of independence they see exists here on Earth. Another uprising is coming, Jason. Will it triumph? It's hard to say."

"So what do you suggest we do now?" Jason asked.

"The Craing Empire is on the precipice of even greater, unparalleled dominance throughout the universe. We cannot allow that to continue. Providing you, your government, and its military factions access to the interchange, and the ability to move about the universe with far more accuracy than the Craing, will somewhat level the battlefield."

Jason continued to look at the virtual image hovering over Ricket's bench. As it slowly turned on its axis, another aspect of the interchange came into view. And with that, Jason realized he was looking at something familiar.

Chapter 7

Several rhinos helped lift and position Traveler onto a waiting hover cart. A circle had formed around Dira and Jason. Uneasiness was in the air. The rhinos, now without a leader, watched as Traveler, whom many considered to be their true leader, would soon be carted off onto the human's ship. Jason brought his attention to the murmuring crowd of rhinos.

"We will do everything possible to return Traveler to you shortly. Some of you are questioning whether you should be helping us at all. Truth is, I'd probably feel the same way. But we must continue to fight the Craing Empire. Do not forget, this is the same empire that has enslaved your home world. Your mates and your offspring are still at their mercy. That scenario has undoubtedly been repeated countless times across the universe, with other warriors, other species. Now, the Craing's ability to move across the universe has been disrupted. But many Craing warships are still close. None of us will be safe until we rid ourselves of their last remaining fleet. We need your help. I need your help this one last time. I cannot force you to fight. You must decide amongst yourselves which course of action is best for you. Whatever course of action you choose, I consider you my friends, and I thank you for all you've sacrificed."

Jason stepped in closer and walked the perimeter of the circle, his eyes meeting theirs one by one. "We leave here shortly. Our fleet of Craing warships will join with other fleets in the Alliance, and perhaps others will join the fight as well. We will make this stand against the Craing—this last stand together. We'll rid ourselves of those bastards once and for all."

Rustling Leaves stepped forward and raised his heavy hammer. He did not speak. One by one, each of the rhino-warriors also raised their hammers. Then the rhinos lifted their heads toward the sky and howled. A strange mix of noises, not unlike the howl of a wolf, an animal they had recently come to admire here in the habitat. Soon, heavy hammers were smashing together high in the air—the resulting sound so loud Traveler was even brought back to consciousness, briefly.

* * *

The new MediPod, nearly twice as large as the others, had been moved into Medical. Ricket stood at the device's new interface. The clamshell commenced closing. Traveler, unconscious, lay quietly, his head bandaged. Several moments later, a vacuum-seal *thump* indicated the MediPod was indeed tightly closed and ready to begin.

"Captain, as with the other MediPods, this process utilizes the introduction of nanites into the rhinos' physiology. We also have the option of installing a full set of new-generation nano-devices as well," Ricket said.

Jason thought about it. NanoCom was a frustrating intrusion to say the least. But it had saved his life more than once.

"Go ahead. Do it."

Jason left Medical and headed for the DeckPort.

* * *

Jason found Nan and Mollie taking another self-defense class in the gym. Orion was in the process of throwing Nan over her shoulder. He cringed as Nan hit the mat with a loud *thud*.

"Good!" Orion yelled. "See how you broke your fall using

your other arm? Now let's try some kicks. You too, Mollie. Front and center."

Sitting down, Jason leaned against the bulkhead and watched while Orion put Nan and Mollie through various front, side and back kick drills. Within minutes, all three were sweating profusely. But what impressed Jason the most was Mollie. Never a complaint—no whining. She was eating this stuff up. Orion looked up and saw Jason and smiled. But that two second distraction cost her; Mollie connected an impressive side kick to her abdomen, while adding a loud *Kia!* in the process. Orion bent over holding her stomach, then gave Mollie a rueful smile.

"Okay, let's take a ten minute break," Orion said, clearly still hurting.

Nan, spotting Jason, walked over and sat down beside him. "The rumor mill has it that we're heading back into space soon."

Jason nodded. "We're retrofitting *The Lilly* right now. As well as making changes to the rest of the fleet. So, yeah, sometime in the next few days."

"I think Mollie and I should stay here on Earth. I need to put Mollie back in school. She needs to be around other kids, Jason. I want to go back home to Los Angeles."

"You know if the Craing make it past our fleet, there's a good chance they'll head straight for Earth. The major metropolises, including Los Angeles, will be targeted first."

Nan shook her head. "I don't know what to tell you."

"I'd feel a whole lot better if you stayed in San Bernardino."

"You mean at the scrapyard house? Why on Earth would we want to stay there?" Nan asked, looking disgusted.

Jason laughed. "Come on, it's not that bad. The main thing is at least there you can hide, and if necessary get to the base below ground."

"Oh God, really? You know I'm still the legal envoy between

the EOUPA and a slew of allied governments around the world, not to mention Washington. I need an office; I need fast Internet access. Do you even have running water at that place?"

Jason rolled his eyes, but then remembered the infiltration of subterranean roots into the house's plumbing. "Of course I have running water. Look, according to Ben Walker, the U.S. government wants to provide me with reparations for the two fighter jets that crashed into the yard. Plus, there's a bonus amount for above and beyond services rendered. It's fairly substantial—"

"I don't know," she replied.

"It's close to three million dollars."

"Three million dollars!" she repeated, her interest level suddenly heightened.

"Yeah, go hog-wild; fix up the place ... if you want."

Chapter 8

The Lilly had returned to San Bernardino to the underground base beneath the scrapyard. *The Lilly's* two holds were temporarily reconfigured into one larger hold compartment. A tight fit, they'd phase-shifted the salvaged hull from the damaged Caldurian vessel into *The Lilly's* hold prior to leaving the Chihuahuan Desert.

Now, a flurry of activity continued. Under the joint direction of Granger and Ricket, ten Caldurian workers had spent the last few hours retrofitting *The Lilly*. Moving back and forth from various DeckPorts, the men transported both small and large pieces of equipment that were being installed and configured at various locations throughout the ship. Jason's primary stipulation before getting started had been that nothing was to be installed without at least a rudimentary explanation of how each of the changes would affect *The Lilly*. It turned out the staff on Granger's workforce, both male and female, were exemplary in that regard. *The Lilly's* section heads were individually brought up to speed on the new modifications added to their areas: Dira received a wide array of new medical equipment; Orion and the Gunnery in general benefited with updated weapons and tactical components; and Jason and the XO with a completely new bridge configuration, including the one hundred years more advanced consoles and a significantly higher-resolution 3D wraparound overhead display. Granger had also furnished new large drive components from somewhere for Chief Horris and his group. The installation and subsequent hands-on instructions continued for seven straight days.

Jason sat in the command chair reviewing the progress.

"Captain, the last of the modifications have been completed, with one exception," Ricket said. He was wearing his LA Dodgers baseball cap and a tool belt around his hips.

"And what's that?"

"The AI."

"Yes. I've been thinking about that. I'd like to talk to you in private, without the AI listening in."

Ricket moved to a side console for several moments, then returned. "The audio input for the AI has been disabled here in the bridge. You can talk freely."

Jason looked around the bridge, unsure if he believed that was actually true. "Here's the thing, Ricket. As much as our current AI can be annoying, she's always come through for us. So I don't want her completely removed. Is it possible to keep her, say, as a backup, if necessary?"

"Two artificial intelligence systems?"

"Yes."

"There is plenty of core storage space available. The new AI will take over from the original one. If ever the need arises, she can be reinstated—although she may not be as adept with some of the newer technology now installed. Would that be acceptable?"

"That should work. Also, how many are there of the newer droids—the ones that were on the Caldurian ship?"

"There are three, Captain."

"I'd like to repurpose one of them to stay here to provide security, and to help Nan if anything comes up. From what I understand, they have defensive capabilities and can pilot any of our vessels. So I'd also like to keep one of the original shuttles here underground."

"Yes, Captain." Ricket nodded once, then scurried off the bridge.

* * *

Nan was in the kitchen showing Mollie how to put together a salad, while Jason manned the BBQ on the back porch. He checked the hamburger patties and saw they were just about ready. He added a slice of cheese to each and closed the grill again.

Jason took a pull of his beer and looked out at the acres of junk cars. The sun had set and he noticed there was a bit of autumn chill in the air. Laughter was coming from the kitchen. It had been a while since they'd all been back together like this, like a family. It felt good. It was bittersweet, though. Although the subject hadn't been breached, and nobody had said the words, this little party tonight would be their last opportunity to be together for an indefinite period of time. In truth, it was more than likely he would not return home at all. For that reason, he'd provided a stack of documents for Nan to sign, giving her power of attorney over his funds and anything to do with the scrapyard property.

They had dinner outside under the stars. A radio was on somewhere in the house and the soft overhead lights from the yard gave the night a soft, pleasing atmosphere. Jason glanced across the table and caught Nan's eyes. She held his stare a moment and then nervously looked away. She was obviously thinking about the same thing he was. Earlier, an hour before dinner, he had unintentionally walked in on her just as she was getting out of the shower. Like an idiot, he'd just stood there, staring at her—taking in her nakedness, the absolute perfection of her body, and the flush of her skin as she grabbed for a towel. And then she yelled at him to knock next time and get the hell out.

"What's so funny?" Mollie asked, looking at the two of them.

Nan made a bewildered expression. "Nothing's funny, it's just a nice night. That okay with you, Pumpkin?"

Mollie turned her attention to her father, who'd also been smiling, but now just shrugged.

"You guys are weird."

Nan looked out at the scrapyard beyond. Jason turned to see what she was looking at.

"It kind of grows on you, doesn't it?" Jason asked.

"I guess. Everything here is so ... old. Even the house is falling apart," she said.

"I've thought about rebuilding. Maybe start from scratch. Put up a new house."

"That would be a start, I guess," Nan replied.

"A start?"

Nan ignored the question, and passed Mollie a plate, "Hey, kiddo, help clear the table?"

With exaggerated movements, Mollie held out her arms like a robot. Jason and Nan stacked the dinner plates onto them with the silverware on top.

"You got all that? Careful now, don't drop those," Nan said.

Mollie, still acting like a robot, slowly walked back into the house. A minute later they heard water running and the sounds of the plates being rinsed off in the sink.

"She's a good kid. You've done well with her, Nan."

She nodded, looked as if she was about to say something, but then didn't. She glanced his way again, smiled, and looked out toward the scrapyard. He noticed she was biting her lip. A nervous habit when she felt uncomfortable. She really was lovely. More so right now than he could ever remember. Her small upturned nose, the little dimples on her cheeks when she smiled, like now.

"Okay, you really need to stop doing that."

"I'm staring, aren't I?"

"Yes. Again! You tend to do that, you know?" She shook her head and smiled. "What the hell are you doing, Jason?"

Mollie, back for the glasses, sang along with the radio but seemed to make up her own words as the music played. Once she was gone, Jason reached over the table and took Nan's hand. She didn't pull away.

"To be honest, I have no idea what I'm doing. But what I do know is that it feels right," he said.

"Well, knock it off. You're not only confusing me, you're confusing your daughter." She pulled her hand away and stood up. Before she walked away she smiled down at Jason and tousled his hair.

"Oh, come on, don't look so distraught. It's not like it's the end of the world." When she walked toward the kitchen, she too began singing along with that same damn tune on the radio.

Later, when the dishes were dried and put away, the three of them played far too many hands of Go Fish. Mollie was put to bed in Brian's old bedroom and Nan went to the master bedroom at the end of the hall. Jason retreated to the same small bedroom he'd slept in as a kid. He tried to get comfortable but his feet hung over the end of the bed by nearly a foot, and memories of the house, of his youth, filled his thoughts, until he heard his bedroom door open and then close again. When Nan slid in next to him on the small bed, she was naked.

"I couldn't sleep, how about you?" she asked, right before kissing him on the mouth and pulling him close.

* * *

When Jason awoke the next morning, he was alone in bed.

His thoughts immediately went to Nan and their late-night lovemaking. Now, in retrospect, it only complicated things. His mind then went to Dira. *Why do I feel I've been unfaithful?* Jason knew why ... Because that's exactly what he was.

Someone was yelling at the back of the house. It was Nan. No, Nan and Mollie. He quickly pulled on his jeans, opened the door, and ran down the hallway into the den.

It they hadn't looked so scared, the scene would have been funny. Nan was holding a floor mop ready to strike and Mollie was ready to swing the old Louisville slugger.

"Get back! Get out of here!" Nan yelled in the direction of the front door. Jason couldn't see who they were screaming at. As he stepped around the corner and into the room, he understood. It must be one of the new droids, specifically the one Ricket had repurposed to stay behind.

"It's okay, it's one of ours," Jason said, holding up his hands to fend off an attack from either of them.

Turning to the droid, Jason was surprised by its appearance. It seemed the Caldurians had made an effort to humanize, or more accurately, Caldurian-ize, its appearance. But there was something menacing, dangerous about it. As tall as Nan, the drone was an iridescent white, had a head and two arms, a long angular-shaped torso and it was legless—it hovered several inches above the floor. It had a cold, intimidating face with a somewhat downturned mouth, which Jason guessed was strictly placed there for appearance's sake, without being functional. It moved with aggressive purpose.

"What the hell are you doing in here?" Jason scolded.

"Captain Reynolds identified. Nan Reynolds identified. Mollie Reynolds identified. Drone allocation 724 security perimeter circuit in process."

Mollie's eyes were wide with fear and never left the hovering droid.

"Relax, both of you. It's here for your safety; really, it's okay," Jason said, trying to sound calm.

The drone moved forward into the house, passed by Jason, and turned down the hallway toward the bedrooms.

"Oh no, that thing is not going to be floating around this house like a frigging ghost while you're gone."

Mollie nodded her head in agreement, eyes still wide.

Jason knew Nan well enough to know that laughing would be a bad idea.

"This is my fault. I should have mentioned the drone. But it's here for your protection. We just need to set up some parameters."

"You think?" Nan barked. Then she gestured for Jason to look behind him.

Startled, Jason jumped back. The drone was hovering mere inches from his back.

"Get away from me!" Jason yelled.

This brought nervous giggles from both Nan and Mollie.

"Seriously, Jason. That thing creeps me out. Tell it to stay outside. And maybe it can make some noise once in a while," Nan said.

"Yes, absolutely." Jason held two fingers to his ear and hailed Ricket.

"Go for Ricket."

Chapter 9

Bristol had contemplated leaving—but where would he go? Pirating had been the way of his family, their clan, for hundreds of years. Truth was, it was all he'd ever known. If nothing else, he supposed he was loyal.

Bristol watched as his brother sent another backhand toward Brian's already red and beaten face. Usually, he was not one to feel much in the way of sympathy for anyone, but this new round of beatings was taking things a bit too far. Fuck, the guy had already lost an eye to his brother's fury.

Brian, a bloodied makeshift patch covering his now empty right eye socket, moved to protect his damaged face. But he was too slow, or too weary to fend off the blow.

A week had passed since Brian had been chained to a post below ground in the bowels of this ridiculous fortress monstrosity. Made of stone, and virtually all the available timber on this Godforsaken planet, Bristol's brother's lair was more like a castle.

"Generalities are useless. So exactly where will I find them?" Captain Stalls asked, his voice stern but hushed.

Bristol had to give Brian his due; he'd still not given up the specific location on Earth for Captain Reynolds or his family. And he knew his brother well enough not to intervene, but the continual torturing of Brian didn't seem to be working very well.

"Just tell him what he wants to know, Brian," Bristol said. "Come on, you're going to tell him eventually anyway."

Captain Stalls hesitated. "They always do, don't they, little brother?" Stalls replied, with a quick glance and smile toward Bristol.

"I haven't lived on or even visited Earth in years. I have no idea where Jason or his family would be living now."

"So, let's start with the last place you saw him. How about that?" Stalls asked.

A virtual image of Earth hovered in the air close by. Brian watched as it slowly rotated. Stalls pointed a finger toward North America. "Let's start with the continent and work our way down from there."

Stalls knelt down next to Brian and put an arm around his shoulder. Somewhere along the line Stalls had pulled a knife from his sleeve and now held it in front of Brian's one remaining eye. "Remember this? Silly of me, of course you do. I imagine it was quite uncomfortable, losing an eye that way. Plucked from your head like a plum from a jar. You have plums on your planet, don't you?"

"We have plums."

Now seated, Stalls used his hands to virtually expand North America. "Where?"

Brian hesitated, then gestured his head toward the left. The western states of the U.S. magnified. The knife was back in front of his eye.

"San Bernardino. We grew up in San Bernardino, Central Valley Scrapyard. That's the only place I know where he may still go."

Stalls got to his feet, then gave Brian several pats on his head. "Release him into the dunes. It'll give the hoppers something to play with tonight."

"Why don't you just kill him? You've gotten everything you need from him," Bristol asked, immediately regretting he'd opened his mouth.

"Oh, so now you want to tell me how to run my business? Perhaps you think you're ready to lead the clan yourself? Be my guest ... but be forewarned, it's far more trouble than it is worth. You've seen it. Nary a day goes by without someone evoking the *clan challenge*, thinking they are strong enough or cunning enough to take my place at the top. It has not been easy, little brother. The many scars on my body are a testament to that, no?"

"I'm just saying it seems senseless to keep tormenting him. Why not just kill him and be done with it?"

Stalls contemplated that for a moment, then shrugged. "No. Strip him down and deliver him out on the dunes. Do it now and let's not speak of this again, understood?"

"Yes, okay, whatever." Bristol watched as his brother rushed across the stone floor and ascended the long stairway.

"What are hoppers?" Brian asked, his one eye still on the stairway.

"Best if you don't know ahead of time."

Chapter 10

As of that morning, the modifications to *The Lilly* were finally completed and put through an exhaustive regimen of tests and virtual combat scenarios. Jason reluctantly said his goodbyes to Nan and Mollie and wondered if he was doing the right thing leaving them behind. But in the end, he'd left them with the droid, a healthy stock of energy weapons, and one of the older shuttles, parked in the cavern below the scrapyard. With luck, they would be fine and even have some semblance of a normal life again, at least for a while.

The Lilly made her approach to the Allied outpost in the Chihuahuan Desert. Jason, who had been sitting at the desk in his ready room for the last two hours, needed to get his head back into the game. He'd been working and reworking a strategy to deal with the Craing fleet, but each plan of approach came up short. Simple math revealed the problem: fifteen hundred Craing vessels against eight or nine hundred Allied warships. Even with *The Lilly*'s advanced capabilities, the Craing fleet, with their three massive Dreadnaughts, would be nearly impossible to defeat in any kind of conventional space battle. Although no one had used the words, it was obvious the upcoming confrontation would be all or nothing. A defeat by the Craing fleet would certainly result in the total subjectification of all the Allied worlds, including Earth.

As the Allied Forces Commander, Jason's father Admiral Reynolds was in command of the EOUPA fleet, as well as its ragtag forces now assembling in space. The logistics alone had become an overwhelming nightmare for the admiral, and Jason had seen and heard little from his father over the past week. In lieu of that, the admiral was adamant that his commanders come up with better, more effective strategies than those proposed thus far.

Jason entered the bridge. The wraparound display, showing the outpost below, was a vision to behold. Freshly painted, the fleet of two hundred and thirty destroyers, light cruisers, and heavy battle cruisers shimmered under the midday sun. Each vessel bore a large U.S. flag at its aft section. Looking at the warships on display, Jason became more cognizant of another potential complication. The vessels' pilots were mostly Craing, and out-and-out bribery had been used to entice those same Craing prisoners to join the Allied fleet. But it was the threat of being sent back home to the Craing worlds that worked best. Dishonored by a defeat against significantly fewer ships at the edge of the solar system, the captured Craing crewmembers faced public humiliation and inevitable execution if they ever returned home. Jason wondered if they would hold to their new Allied allegiance during intense battle situations ... or would their previous loyalty to the Craing Empire re-manifest itself?

Jason gave the order to set down at the designated landing zone, but to keep all systems active and at the ready.

* * *

The admiral had assembled his fleet commanders in the outpost mess hall and Jason took a seat just as Admiral Reynolds moved to the front of the room.

"The Craing will most assuredly be ready for us. The same unconventional methods used by Captain Reynolds and *The Lilly* crew to defeat the Craing at the edge of our solar system will be expected and, if tried again, could be used against us."

Heads turned in Jason's direction. He felt scrutiny from the other officers as they assessed him. Not only was he the admiral's son, he had defeated an overwhelming force and virtually saved their planet. There wasn't a man or woman present, Jason thought, who didn't want to prove they were just as capable, or even more so, than he.

The admiral continued. "With that said, we have been studying the combat vids from that battle and have uncovered several potential weaknesses within the Craing defenses." The admiral proceeded then to talk specifics, including the use of drone fighters, combined centralized attack formations, and better utilization and distribution of shields.

Unfortunately, Jason thought to himself, none of that was going to be enough. Perhaps he should have pushed Granger and the Caldurians harder to upgrade the weaponry on the outpost's fleet and not just on *The Lilly*. But Granger had been fairly clear that the Caldurians weren't ready to go that far. It seemed the last thing the Caldurians wanted was an imbalance of military might in the universe, and a force, perhaps, to contend with further on. Simply put, they did not trust us yet. So ... the one technological advancement they were given access to would have to be enough.

"With the detection of the Craing fleet on long-range scans," the admiral continued, "I've had numerous enquiries as to how we'll even reach the Allied systems in time to make a difference. But there have been some new and, quite frankly, exciting developments in that regard. Captain Reynolds, please come on up and give your report."

Jason made his way to the front of the room where the thousand-plus seated officers silently waited for him to take the podium.

Jason pointed out the large floor-to-ceiling windows to the airfield beyond and the hundreds of warships sitting at the ready.

"What if each one of those vessels had the capability to reach virtually anywhere in the universe—and do so in the blink of an eye? This technology may soon be available."

Expressions of disbelief were followed by low murmurs. This was all about instilling some semblance of *hope.* Jason maintained an expression of confidence, while in truth, he had no illusions that defeat by the returning Craing fleet wasn't possibly imminent. He raised a hand. "Hold on, everyone. Let me bring you up to speed: first, about the race of people who call themselves the Caldurians, and then about an alien being simply known as the *interchange.*"

Chapter 12

Brian was less concerned with his nakedness than with the cold. The cold, and his pounding, aching, head. And there was something wrong with his internal nano-devices. Repeatedly, a countdown timer had appeared. Apparently, something was going to happen in the next few days. He didn't want to think about that right now. And the pain emanating from his open, oozing eye socket was worse than ever.

They'd left him alone for several hours in the dark dungeon below Stalls' fortress. When they'd come for him, a part of him hoped his death would be quick; he hated pain. Let others play the hero. He knew his limitations. But they had other plans for him. Two of Stalls' men released his bonds and dragged him up the stone stairs and out to a waiting hover ship. More like a cart. By the looks of things—some dried blood, several errant bone chips—he was keenly aware others had taken this same joyless ride. An hour or so later, they reached a shoreline—perhaps of an ocean or large lake. They secured him to another pole. Again, someone mentioned hoppers. The two men seemed to be in a hurry. Perhaps that was why they'd only secured his hands and not his feet. At least this way, with his arms wrapped around the pole, he could turn and see what was around him. *What the fuck is a hopper?* The tide was coming in and small waves lapped several yards from his feet. In the early morning dawn, more and more of the beach became visible. Squinting his solitary eye, Brian could see other poles off in the distance. And there, past several empty poles, was a figure tied to another one, and by the looks of him or her, the body was long dead.

"Shit!" He closed his eyes, unable to believe Stalls had turned on him like this. He'd certainly made their relationship worth Stalls' while. The business he'd brought him with the Craing was highly profitable. Truth was, Brian knew perfectly well why things had turned out badly. Jason. Jason had humiliated Stalls in front of his own men. No, it was more than that. It was that woman, Nan. Jason's ex-wife. Stalls wanted her for himself. Brian had learned long ago that love and business don't mix.

Movement. Brian jerked his head and then spun his body around the pole. Subtle, but there was definitely movement close by, off to his left. There it was again, near where the lapping waves met the sand. They all seemed to arrive at once, as if an early morning bugle call had summoned the troops forth to assemble.

"Holy mother of God! Get the hell away from me!" Brian screamed, while repeatedly kicking out with his bare feet at the approaching monstrosity. Wet and bulbous, the thing moved toward him backward, propelled by four crab-like legs covered with hundreds of knife-like spikes. It seemed to have trouble moving. He saw why. Hanging down from its belly was a large translucent sack. Inside it were four bright orange balls, which jostled around as the creature repositioned itself. Brian figured they were probably eggs.

"Terrific, soon there'll be four more of these fucking things."

Brian heard a series of rapid clicking sounds and something else. Actually, he *did* hear something else—talking. Two more of the eight-foot-long, crablike creatures emerged from beneath the sand. With their arrival, more clicking, and more talking. *Crap*, his nano-tech was deciphering their clicks. From the sound of things, they were hungry. They were looking at him. They were portioning out his body—*Good God, they were deciding who would get what to eat!*

"Get back!" he yelled, kicking sand in their direction.

The three crab creatures then turned and were facing him—maneuvering to get in closer. Large rubber band-like mouths gaped, each with a series of tiny fine teeth. Rows and rows of teeth. Brian pulled back against his bonds and looked behind him for anything that could help.

Ahh, now he knew what the pirates were referring to when they spoke of the *hoppers*. Hundreds of them appeared, jumping ten, twenty feet in the air. They came from the dunes behind and were making their way towards the crabs. Breakfast time.

A hopper landed atop one of the craps directly in front of Brian. Man-like with two arms and two thick legs, it was green and scaly. With three thick fingers, each with long, extended talons, it ripped and pried at the crustacean's back plates. Brian grimaced as the hopper drove a hand beneath the shell and pulled out a handful of wet white meat and brought it up to his mouth.

"That's truly disgusting," he said, but he spoke aloud in a foreign language: the language the hoppers spoke. Aided by NanoCom, Brian was used to the nano-tech in his head utilizing this capability, but the hopper certainly wasn't. It stopped chewing and looked over at Brian.

"How do you speak our language?"

Not sure honesty would be in his best interest, Brian hesitated before answering. "I have a device in my head that lets me talk to other species."

"Your own kind has turned against you. Why do they do such a thing?"

"They only look like my species. They are not."

"It insults us, leaving these imprisoned carcasses here as if we would feast on them. For the most part, we leave them for the *shells* to eat." The hopper gestured toward the crabs, which were quickly scurrying backwards toward the shoreline. Then the hopper did something unexpected. He reached in and brought out another handful of meat, stopped, and held it out to Brian.

"You will eat."

Brian's eyes went to the still-twitching crab held securely beneath the hopper's muscular thighs. He hadn't eaten in days. How different could this be from regular crabmeat, or even lobster for that matter?

Brian nodded and let the hopper place a large chunk of the white meat into his mouth. It was surprisingly good. He didn't hesitate for the second mouthful.

"Thank you," Brian said. "Why did you—"

"Eat," the hopper said.

"One more thing. Can you help me get off this pole?" For the first time in years, Brian wanted to go home. Back to Earth.

Chapter 13

Ricket requested a private meeting with Jason and the admiral. In itself, that wasn't unusual, but its location made Jason curious. Ricket wanted to meet on the far side of the moon. Jason had almost forgotten about the crippled Craing Dreadnaught—the principal massive warship that took point in a fleet of five hundred. For a short while it had been placed in high orbit around Earth and used as a base for their fleet and for training exercises in space. But it was a battered, war-torn vessel. Several chunks had dislodged and careened into other ships. Then another even larger section broke off and headed directly toward Earth, but fortunately it splashed down somewhere in the Pacific Ocean. Deemed too dangerous to be allowed to maintain orbit around Earth, the Dreadnaught was hauled away by several of the larger battle cruisers and placed in its current orbit around the moon.

They picked up the admiral at the outpost and flew *The Lilly* over to the moon. Once the Dreadnaught was within sight, they phase-shifted into the mammoth ship's primary corridor, which ran the length of the vessel. Once close to the Dreadnaught's bridge, they headed to *The Lilly*'s armory on Deck 2, where they readied themselves.

"So what is this thing?" the admiral asked with a furrowed brow. Orion continued to secure a phase-shift belt around his midsection.

"The belts will transport us to the Dreadnaught's bridge," Jason replied. "But we can walk, if you'd prefer. Probably take us fifteen or twenty minutes by foot."

"No, I'll give this a try," the admiral replied with a shrug. "Hell, it's not like this is the first time you've used them, right?"

"Right. We couldn't have made it across HAB 12 without them."

Not wanting to suit up into combat suits, they each were fitted with a wristband interface. One by one, Ricket double-checked each of their phase-shift coordinates.

"We are ready," Ricket said.

"Sure you don't want me to join you, Cap?" Orion asked, looking uneasy that they were leaving without a security detail.

"We'll be fine. There's no one on board—it's a deserted ship. But you can phase-shift over if we run into any kind of trouble, that work?" Jason replied.

With Ricket's help, the first one to phase-shift over was the admiral; Jason went next, then Ricket.

The Dreadnaught's sprawling command center was eerily quiet. The three of them stood near the officer's section of the bridge. Jason looked out at the rows of unmanned stations.

"It's like a ghost ship."

"And that's what I wanted to speak with you about, Captain," Ricket said. "I am not convinced the Craing crewmembers, even working alongside our own people, can be fully trusted."

Ricket walked over to the command chair, sat down, and accessed a small viewing screen and interface device. "This isn't common knowledge. I discovered it purely by accident."

"What's with all the secrecy, Ricket? What's going on?" the admiral asked.

The largest of the display screens mounted on the bulkhead came alive.

"What is that?" Jason asked.

The image on the display was barely visible. Ricket keyed something else in and overhead lights came on. It was a ship's hold of immense proportions. Stacks and stacks of mechanical equipment filled the screen and faded into the distance.

"Build and repair tractor drones," Ricket said. "These were not listed on the ship's inventory database."

"So what? What's a build and repair tractor drone and why is this significant?" Jason asked.

Ricket looked over at Jason, then walked toward the display. "Captain, these are the types of mechanical tractor drones that were used to build this Dreadnaught in the first place, as well as all the other vessels within the Craing fleet. Depending on whether or not they have the necessary programming, they could repair this vessel. And with the right materials, they could build others."

That got the admiral's attention. "Wait just a minute. Are you telling me we have the capability to manufacture additional warships? And repair this one? What kind of timeframe are we talking about?"

Ricket entered something on the input device. The display changed again, this time to another hold area.

"These are spare parts. There are also several holds that contain raw materials. I believe the Craing were going to set up a remote manufacturing base on another planet, or even on a space platform. This Dreadnaught holds everything needed to outfit a dry dock."

"So why the secrecy?" the admiral asked.

"I know why," Jason interjected. "If the Craing knew we had discovered these supply holds, they would come straight for Earth and bypass the Allied worlds completely."

"I believe you are correct, Captain. One subversive FTL transmission from here to the Craing would put our planet in jeopardy. Other than the three of us, no one else knows; this information is secure."

"That's good, right?" the admiral asked.

Ricket hesitated, and checked several more screens before answering. "I don't believe we can proceed without the help of key Craing personnel. The drones need parameters set—variances to their programming on a daily, sometimes hourly, basis."

"Can't our people learn—"

"I do not believe so, Captain. It would take many months, if not years, to bring your personnel up to speed," Ricket replied, looking up at Jason and then to the admiral.

"How many key Craing personnel are we talking about?"

"My suggestion would be to develop a dry dock on the surface of the moon ... here on the dark side, away from Earth's view. We will need no fewer than twenty Craing personnel who have the necessary programming skills."

"Why do I get the feeling you know exactly who those twenty Craing crewmembers are?"

"I have a list of thirty-five potential candidates; they have the proper educational and skill-level credentials, Captain," Ricket replied.

"So we vet the Craing personnel down to twenty ... maybe a few more as extras. How long does it take to repair a Dreadnaught?" the admiral asked.

"To put this vessel back into a fully-operational status will take approximately thirty-eight days."

"Well, that won't work. The Craing fleet will have swept through the Allied worlds way before then," Jason said dismissively.

"The drones work surprisingly fast. If we repurpose them to concentrate only on the major systems, such as the drives and on weapons repair, that timeframe could be significantly reduced."

"By how much?"

"One week, Captain. This Dreadnaught could be ready for battle in one week."

Jason and his father looked at each other.

"Can we wait that long before heading to the Allied worlds?" Jason asked.

"At their current FTL speeds, we calculate the Craing fleet will arrive there in just over nine days."

"Okay, Ricket. Let's get this started. And I want to be a part of the vetting process of your proposed Craing team. We select the wrong people and we're screwed."

"Yes, sir."

Chapter 14

Nan was up early and headed for the shower. She'd tossed and turned most of the night, and with that damn drone bumping into things every few minutes, she was already running on a short fuse. She turned on the hot water and let it run a second before climbing in. She screamed and threw herself against the far shower wall. The water was ice cold. In seconds, the drone crashed into the bathroom. A weapon protruded from a center panel.

"Halt movement! Security verification in process ..."

With that, the shower door was ripped from its hinges and Nan, naked, trying desperately to avoid the still icy cold water, was held at gunpoint. Trying to keep her voice calm, she spoke in an even tone, "Get-the-hell-out-of-here-right-this-fucking-second. Do-you-understand-me?"

* * *

Nan found there was little in the fridge for breakfast. She discovered a frozen box of Eggos in the freezer and an unopened bottle of syrup in the pantry. She placed the plate of toasted waffles down in front of Mollie.

"What's this?"

"What does it look like? It's your breakfast," Nan said, sitting down across from her and resuming her search through the classified section of the local paper.

"I know that. But where is the butter? And these are old."

"How do you know how old they are? They're probably not

that old."

"I was with Dad when he bought them."

"They were frozen. Those things are meant to last forever. Eat. You need to get ready to be at the bus stop in fifteen minutes."

"Where do I go? How do you know where my bus stop even is?"

"Enough with the twenty questions! Eat your breakfast. I spent two hours at your school yesterday, remember? I know where your bus stop is. I also know who your teacher is and that you're expected to play an instrument this year."

"You mean like a trombone or something?" Mollie asked, making a face.

Nan didn't answer. She'd found something and was circling the ad.

"Did you find a car?" Mollie asked, with a mouthful of syrupy waffles.

"Maybe. A 2003 Jeep Cherokee."

"There's a Jeep Cherokee in the yard."

"Well, I need one that works. One that's safe. Not a junker from the lot."

The security drone was back in the room.

"Teardrop's back," Mollie said, watching the drone hover its way forward.

Nan had suspected it was nearby. Probably eavesdropping, she thought to herself. She glared at it as it moved closer. Mollie had named it Teardrop since that's what it 'kinda' looked like to her. A pearly-white teardrop, with a head and two arms.

"Good morning, Teardrop. Don't you know it's polite to say good morning?" Mollie scolded.

"Good morning, Mollie Reynolds," it said in a very humanlike male voice.

"You don't always have to say my last name. That sounds retarded."

"Mollie, I don't like that word," Nan said, looking up from her paper.

"Good morning, Mollie," the drone repeated. It moved forward and opened the sliding glass door to the back porch. Before exiting it turned toward Nan.

"I have located the coordinates of a Jeep Cherokee. It is currently non-functional. I will attempt to repair it to within manufacturer's safety parameters."

The drone was out the door and halfway into the junkyard before Nan could respond.

Mollie giggled. "That thing's weird, Mom. But kinda funny."

Nan walked Mollie to the bus stop on West 59th street, several streets away from the scrapyard. They waited together for the bus to arrive. With a kiss to her forehead, Mollie was off and running for the bus. Nan's smile was gone as the bus disappeared down the street. Looking above a nearby grove of orange trees, the sky was bright and cloudless. She wondered if Jason would be successful in deterring the returning Craing fleet. Or was it just a matter of time before Craing warships landed here again? How would she protect Mollie?

When Nan returned home, she immediately headed for the back porch. Teardrop moved quickly, lighting fast. One moment it was at the far end of the lot, only to show up at the tool shed a moment later. At some point, using its two clawed arms, Teardrop had lifted an automobile from the middle of the lot and maneuvered it closer to the porch where Nan, feet up on the stacked wheel-rim table, sat and watched in amazement.

It was in fact a Jeep Cherokee. The navy-blue body was in pretty good shape, except for the right rear quarter panel. The drone had replaced it with a dark red one from another jeep somewhere in the yard. The front hood was now up and the drone rushed back and forth, in and out of the yard, scrounging for needed parts. Soon, a loud air compressor blared from inside the tool shed. Teardrop, pulling an air hose behind itself, began to fill each of the tires. Several moments passed and Teardrop positioned itself behind the steering wheel. Nan heard something click a few times. Teardrop left the car and returned to the scrapyard. It came back with another battery. Once the battery was swapped, Teardrop was back behind the wheel. The engine started on the first try and idled as smoothly as a brand new car.

Having an operational vehicle would be a good start. Looking out over the scrapyard, Nan still felt uneasy, vulnerable. She needed to do more.

Chapter 15

They'd spent another four days behind the moon. The new, much faster Caldurian shuttle was used to ferry the Craing crewmember candidates back and forth from the outpost. Several Craing officers had proven themselves competent over the last few weeks at the outpost, and now were assisting with the vetting process of the others. It seemed to Jason the Craing were inherently distrustful. Even the officers they counted on to help with the vetting process needed constant reassurances. In the end, though, there were no loyalists to the enemy Craing forces. None of the crewmembers wanted to return to the Craing home worlds, and none seemed to have any moral issues helping those who were declared mortal enemies of the Craing Empire.

When Jason emerged from his cabin and entered the bridge, it became obvious to him Ricket had made substantial progress with the Dreadnaught's reconstruction effort. The wraparound display was segmented into multiple outside views of the crippled Dreadnaught.

Ricket was waiting for Jason and stood by the command chair. "Captain, I've deployed the tractor drones. They were already pre-programmed and so far only need new repair configurations."

"Where are the Craing programmers?" Jason asked, watching one of the shuttle-sized tractor drones dislodge a large segment of the outer hull, while another tractor drone placed a new section in its place. Then, crablike, they moved on to another damaged section of the hull.

"They are working on Deck 2. We've provisioned an unused

section of the ship as a bullpen for the programmers. It's close to their quarters."

Orion rushed onto the bridge. "Captain, what are those Craing doing on Deck 2?"

"Programming the drone tractors, why?"

"Because they never shut up. Whoever provisioned that part of the ship didn't take into account that Gunnery is right across the hall. I can't think straight with their constant chattering."

Jason looked down at Ricket. "I take it you didn't add a door to the section of the ship you provisioned?"

"No, Captain."

"See what you can do, Ricket. In the meantime, Gunny, try to put up with a temporary irritation. Your bridge shift starts soon anyway."

"Aye, Cap," she said and slid into her chair at the tactical station.

"Captain, we're being hailed by the outpost. It's the admiral," Orion said.

His father had taken the shuttle back to Earth the previous day. A new segment feed displayed and the admiral's face filled the screen.

"Admiral," Jason said.

"Seems our timetable has just been moved up."

"What's happened?"

"The Craing fleet has reached the outskirts of Allied space. They're now systematically annihilating every planet in their path. Probably those they suspect are part of the Alliance. They'll reach Trumach within the next three days and Jhardon a day after that."

Jason's heart sank. He remembered that Trumach was the rhinos's home world and had been attacked several times over the last few years, subjugating its populace. And Jhardon, of course, was Dira's home planet.

Jason knew that confronting the Craing fleet before they were fully prepared would result in their own decisive defeat. Every new battle scenario, such as those including their own operational Dreadnaught, now offered them some semblance of hope.

"I know your strategic plans, your logistics, rely on *The Lilly*'s presence as an integral part of the fleet when we attack."

"Most definitely. Jason, we can't break up our forces to accommodate two alien worlds when the Allied forces' very existence is at stake. You do realize that, I hope," the admiral stated.

Jason didn't answer for several moments. "There's no way I'm letting those two planets be discounted as mere collateral damage."

"It's really not up to you, I want you to—"

"Let me propose something else then," Jason interrupted his father.

"Like what?"

"That I agree *The Lilly* will be in formation when the Allied forces make their stand, just as you have planned."

"And?"

"But until the fleet arrives, we'll be there stalling their progress and making their life miserable ahead of time."

"The problem with that is there's a very good chance you'll be destroyed long before we get there. The risks are too great."

Jason's temper flared. "Fine, then I'll let you be the one to tell Dira that aiding her home planet doesn't fit into your strategic plan!"

Now it was the admiral who didn't speak for several beats. "I need your word you'll not go head to head against the Craing fleet. Perhaps playing cat and mouse, causing enough havoc to slow them down could work. But everything changes. Hell, the location of the battle could be thirty light years away, in a completely different sector."

The admiral looked away—he was thinking it through. Jason could see he was considering all options. Then he looked up again and frowned. "Come up with a plan and submit it to me by the end of the day. And wipe that smile off your face, Captain."

"Aye, sir," Jason replied.

* * *

Jason had several stops to make this morning, and first was Medical. He didn't want Dira to hear about the approach of the Craing fleet and the jeopardy Jhardon would be in from anyone other than himself. He entered Medical and found a group formed around the new MediPod. He joined Chief Horris, at the back of the group, who jostled his ample frame over a few steps to let the captain get in closer. Dira was helping someone out of the new MediPod.

"What do we have here, Chief?"

But Dira's voice interrupted the chief's response. "It is my great honor to present to you the new, recognizable, Lieutenant Commander Perkins."

Surprised to see the XO back in human form, Jason joined in the round of applause as

Perkins, now all smiles, stood and casually waved a hand to his friends. When he noticed Jason, he stood up straight, saluted, and said, "Everything's back to normal, sir."

"Good. Good to have the old you back again, XO. You all right to handle your next watch?"

With a quick glance and a nod back from Dira, Perkins said, "Aye, sir. Ready for duty."

Chief Horris leaned in: "Um, Captain?"

"Chief?"

"Would you come by Engineering sometime this morning? Have something I wanted to ask you. Actually show you."

"No problem, give me a few minutes," Jason replied, and he made his way over to Dira.

"Why hello, Captain," Dira said, stepping in close enough for him to smell the light fragrance of her shampoo.

"What brings you to this part of the ship today?"

"First of all, good work with Perkins," Jason said.

"Thank you. So, what's with the sour face?"

Jason placed a hand on her shoulder. "Let's go in here," he said, gently guiding her into the hospital section of Medical.

Once one the other side of the bulkhead, Jason turned to Dira. "It's no secret the Craing fleet is headed for Allied space, but they're not taking a direct route."

Dira's face lost all color. Eyes opening wide she said, "No, not Jhardon! Please tell me they haven't attacked Jhardon." She brought both hands up to her face, covering her mouth.

"No, they haven't. Not yet. But you need to be prepared that it's a distinct possibility. I didn't want you to hear about this from someone else."

"Oh God, Jason, we have to protect them. My planet has virtually no defenses; they're not a warring society. They hate violence."

Dira leaned back against a bulkhead, her hands still up to her face. Jason rushed forward and put his arms around her. She buried her face in his chest. "Just tell me you'll do something."

There were guarded stares from other crewmembers in the area, but Jason didn't care. He hated seeing her like this. He wanted to protect her, keep her from ever feeling sad again. And then he realized the truth. His heart belonged to Dira.

He replayed making love to Nan just days before, and guilt and remorse flooded his mind.

"I'll do what I can, Dira. But I need you to be strong right now. The coming days will be hard on all of us. All our home planets are in jeopardy."

Jason felt Dira nod as she stood back, tears falling down her cheeks. "You're right, I'm sorry. But know this: even though violence is not the *Jhardonian* way, I want to destroy those little fuckers. You put a weapon in my hand and I'll kill every last one of them."

Jason gently wiped the tears from beneath her eyes with his thumbs. "It may come to that. But in the meantime, I promise we'll do everything we can to save Jhardon." He kissed her and enveloped her in his arms.

A long moment later she pushed him away and looked into his eyes. "I'm okay. Thank you, Jason." With a self-conscious smile, she looked around Medical. "Oh god, everyone's looking at us."

He shrugged and smiled. Jason left Medical wondering if he could actually keep that promise. He made his way over to the DeckPort, remembering Chief Horris wanted to show him something.

During his last visit to Engineering, it had been undergoing retrofitting by the Caldurians. The first thing Jason noticed was the addition of several new consoles, but there was something else different. Engineering seemed substantially smaller.

"Captain, thank you for coming by," the chief yelled down from a catwalk above. "It's up here, sir."

Jason climbed the steps and met the chief on the catwalk.

"What do you have for me, Chief?"

Chief Horris pointed in the aft direction of the ship, toward the two massive drive systems, across the open four floors of Engineering.

"What the hell is that?" Jason asked, leaning forward over the railing.

Chapter 16

Bristol sat on the bridge of the command ship next to his brother with nothing to do. He hated being there. He felt awkward and out of place and would have much preferred to be tinkering on his latest invention back in his makeshift laboratory. Just like his brother's pretentious castle, his latest vessel was another extravagant, flamboyant testament to his ever-growing ego.

Once an interstellar luxury liner, where only the wealthiest could afford her premium price tag, he had renamed the ginormous vessel *Her Majesty*. She had been commandeered into Captain Stalls' fleet. With literally a shipload of wealthy hostages, and all too willing family members agreeing to pay outrageous ransoms, the pirate clan sat pretty, their coffers brimming at higher-than-ever levels. Now, meticulously retrofitted with defensive shields and the latest armaments money could buy, *Her Majesty* dominated virtually any ship with which it came into contact.

"Why do I need to be here?"

"Because you're an officer on *Her Majesty*. How are you going to learn anything hidden away in some dark hole in the middle of the ship?"

"Um, first of all, what's this about me being an officer? You know we're just pirates, right? I certainly didn't sign up for any kind of military position."

"You'll show proper respect while you're on my bridge. Don't expect differential treatment just because you are my brother," Stalls said in a lowered tone.

Bristol rolled his eyes, but held his tongue.

"The last fourteen vessels have joined the fleet, sir," one of Stalls' newly appointed officers announced.

Bristol looked over at Pike, the grey-bearded elderly pirate manning the Comms station. Bristol shook his head; the guy had to be seventy-five years old, if he was a day.

"The Leister Clan," Stalls said with a smile. "And that brings our armada to three hundred and twenty vessels, if I'm not mistaken."

"Three hundred and four," Bristol corrected.

"Whatever! There's not a fleet in this sector that can touch us." Stalls stood and walked over to the ornate casino table that now supported a large logistics display. He waved his brother over to join him. Yellow icons representing the pirate armada, with *Her Majesty* leading the pack, dominated the left side of the display. Stalls changed the zoom level and concentrated on a planetary system three sectors over. He leaned in on his elbows and stared at a bright blue solitary planet.

"Earth. I've heard good things about this planet. Three days from now, she'll be mine."

Bristol looked down at the display and shrugged. "Let me guess ... that woman. Nan something or other is there. There's better quarry right here in our own backyard. You're making a mistake. You're thinking with your cock again, big brother."

"Watch your tongue. Vengeance will be mine."

"Just saying. Next time it may be more than a few toes you lose."

* * *

Freed from his bindings and the tall wooden pole, still naked, Brian shivered against the chilly sea air. The hopper, for some unknown reason, continued to help him.

"I'llneedclothes.I'mgoingtofreezetodeathifIcan'tgetwarm." The hopper, which was also naked, turned its head sideways and appraised the small human. "You are truly a weak being. How has your kind survived this long?"

"We wear clothes. It's not that big a deal." He turned and looked down the beach toward the figure still secured to a pole. He figured it was about a hundred yards and started walking in that direction.

The hopper watched and made a series of clicking sounds. "You move slower than a shell. Get on."

It made a series of small hops and positioned itself in front of Brian. "Seriously, like a piggyback?"

"I do not know what piggyback refers to. You will get on my back."

Feeling a bit silly, Brian did as the scaly green hopper asked. At first he didn't know what to do with his arms: should he wrap them around its shoulders? Or its neck? Either way it felt peculiar and overly intimate. In the end he held on to its neck and said, "Okay, let's go."

In three hops they reached the pole and the corpse affixed to it. The smell alone caused Brian to turn away and retch. Taking in a deep breath, Brian looked over at the hopper's confused face.

"You don't smell that?"

It shrugged. "The ripe smell of the dead, so what?"

"Nothing. Just help me get these clothes off him."

The dead human wore pants, shoes, a thick sweater and, most importantly of all to Brian, a jacket. But none of the clothing items were retrievable as the body's hands and legs were secured around the thick wooden pole.

"Just like you helped me, can you hop up to the top there? Pull this guy off the pole?" Brian asked.

Without hesitation, the hopper leapt ten feet to the top of

the pole and pulled on the corpse by his arms. Brian watched as the limp body jerked and flailed about like a rag doll. Once freed, the body fell and landed on the sand several feet away. Now, under closer inspection, Brian could see the body had started to decompose. There was a wet glossiness to the guy's skin. And that smell! Holding his breath, Brian got busy undressing the body.

The shoes weren't a perfect fit—but close enough. He figured in time, hopefully, the smell would fade, or he'd get used to it. Brian found several things in the man's pockets; the most curious was a small cylindrical electronic device about the size of an automobile key fob. A series of colored buttons populated the circumference, with a small circular display screen integrated into the top. He pressed a few buttons to see what would happen and eventually a menu appeared on the screen. Brian accessed his own internal nano-devices and brought up the visual translation settings. Seeming bored, the hopper wandered off to find shells to eat closer to the shoreline. Thirty seconds later Brian could move up and down the device's menus and various input prompts with relative ease. The screen that caught his interest most was something called *Retrieval.*

That sounds promising, Brian thought. He pressed the corresponding key combinations, but nothing happened. The hopper was back, its mouth full of shell meat. It handed Brian a wet handful. Brian took the offering, again curious why the creature would help him. The hopper's head jerked up with a start. Brian followed its gaze and in the distance saw a small speck of something in the air approaching them in the distance. As it neared, it was visibly a transport shuttle. It slowed and paused in midair. Then, quietly, it landed on the beach within twenty yards. A small gangway extended from the aft part of the shuttle, but no one disembarked. Wavering from a rising fever, cold, and not liking the way the other hoppers were looking at him, Brian stumbled into the awaiting vessel where he fell to the deck, unconscious.

He awoke sometime later and found himself sprawled on the deck within a large compartment on board a different vessel. With the hopper still along side of him, he spun around to assess their situation.

Brian counted six humanoids, each one pointing some kind of energy weapon in their direction. One of them stepped forward, but then dropped back again.

"What the hell is that smell?"

Chapter 17

By the time Jason entered the habitat and made his way into the rhinos' encampment, the sun was already setting. Two rhinos, both dressed for battle, intersected his progress.

"Is that you, Captain Reynolds?" the taller of the two rhinos asked.

"It's okay," Jason answered. "It's just me, Rustling Leaves. Looks like you've added a bit more security."

"It's not for you, Captain."

"Then who?" Jason asked, bewildered that anyone would even consider attacking a camp full of several hundred seven-foot-tall rhino-warriors.

"Our new leader, Traveler, has had a vision. We will be attacked."

Jason didn't reply to that, but gestured toward the largest of the mud domes. "Is he there?"

"I will see if he can be disturbed." Rustling Leaves hurried off and disappeared into the dome. Several seconds later, Traveler appeared in the doorway, then quickly walked toward Jason. Rustling Leaves attempted to keep up but only managed to stay several strides behind.

"Captain Reynolds, it is good to see you."

"Good to see you, too. You certainly look to be in better shape than the last time I saw you."

"I am strong with nanites. And I am smarter with this nano-tech in my skull."

"I understand you had a vision?" Jason asked.

"As clear as I am talking to you now. They will come from the heavens. We will be prepared."

"That is why I've come here, Traveler. It is not here that you will be attacked. It's Trumach. What remains of the Craing fleet has returned. They'll reach your planet within several days."

"Yes. The vision makes more sense now. We must return and defend our mates and offspring." As if expecting resistance, Traveler expanded his chest and stood taller.

"I will take you directly to Trumach, if that is what you wish. You certainly deserve that much and a lot more. But please, hear me out first."

A burst of steamy snot blew from the rhino's snout. It was obvious Traveler didn't like the direction Jason was taking.

Jason went on anyway. "You are a warrior, no? So let me ask you a simple question, warrior to warrior. Is it better to wait and defend against your enemy's advances, or to take the initiative, be the aggressor—attack them when they least expect it?"

Traveler slowly nodded his large head. "In my vision we fought against the mightiest of adversaries. There could be no bigger dishonor than having our mates taken by others. We will fight this battle your way, Captain, but afterward, those of us who survive must return to Trumach."

* * *

Jason's last stop for the day was back at the outpost. He'd left *The Lilly* at the far side of the moon where the Dreadnaught's reconstruction efforts continued to make steady, albeit slow, progress. Jason took the opportunity to get behind the stick of his favorite fighter, the *Pacesetter*. He'd brought along Gunny Orion for a meetup with Billy Hernandez and several others. Over the last few weeks *The Lilly*'s crew and SEAL forces had been dangerously downsized due to reassignments and in training other fleet personnel. Jason would not make the mistake again of being caught unprepared in deep space.

The first thing Jason noticed as he and Gunny approached the outpost and prepared to land was the dismantled Craing prison camp. That was the Craing's primary condition for returning to full duty within the Allied fleet. Rightfully, they demanded more equality, which meant an end to prison-style housing and all ill treatment.

Billy had spent the last few days looking for the remainder of the original *Lilly* SEAL team. Some had been reassigned to other ships; others were assisting with combat training geared toward the particulars of space fleet tactics. It would be up to Jason, and ultimately Admiral Reynolds, to process the necessary paperwork to bring them all back together again as a unit.

Flight training was in full swing, with no fewer than a dozen Craing warships in the air at any one time, practicing landings, take offs, and an assortment of other essential maneuvers. Troops were being assembled—mostly from the Navy and Marines, but the Army was represented, as well. The smallest of the reconstructed Craing light cruisers was still twice the size of *The Lilly*. The ships would accommodate a fighting force of hundreds.

Jason wondered why so many of what looked to be ground forces were being trained here. Were they really being specifically readied for space missions? That seemed unlikely. Interstellar engagements involved close-quarter combat. Hell, they'd be stumbling over each other.

Jason and Orion pulled their duffle bags from the *Pacesetter*'s storage compartment. They heard a familiar voice in the distance. Looking up, Jason saw the admiral, who was jogging across the open quad in their direction.

"Your father's a spry old guy, Cap."

"He certainly is." Jason gestured toward the goings-on around them. "This is what he lives for. He's a born leader. I think preparing for what could be considered the ultimate military engagement, well, that only spurs him on more. And the last time he went up against the Craing fleet he was defeated—humiliated. This is redemption for him." The admiral slowed to a walk and joined Jason and Orion in front of the *Pacesetter*.

"You're late," the admiral barked, but kept a smile on his face.

"Sorry, seems I've been putting out fires since I saw you last," Jason replied. "Hey, what's with all the troops? You don't think they'll be tripping over each other up there?"

"They probably will be. But it's becoming more and more evident that our forces will be needed on the ground as much as in space. Even if they're not, we want to be prepared," the admiral said.

"I've been caught short-handed several times now, so I certainly can't fault your logic. Which reminds me, we need to reassemble our original SEAL team. Any possibility you can flex your military-command muscles and help expedite that? Billy's been making the rounds and has a list of who is where and under which command."

"Get me the list. No promises, but I'll do my best," the admiral answered. "Talk to me about our Dreadnaught. What's the progress?"

"As of two hours ago, breaches to the outer hull have been repaired. The tractor drones are currently working on various weapons and armaments. Getting the drives online is another story; seems we're coming up short with replacement parts."

"I guess we can't just order up a new set of parts from the Craing Empire, huh?" the admiral asked, looking disappointed.

"Ricket thinks he can fabricate most, if not all, of the parts with the phase-synthesizer. He's up on Deck 4B now. I told him not to show his face until he's gotten the parts made."

"Oh, that reminds me," the admiral said, turning to his left. "The Caldurians arrived several hours ago and left us these."

Jason saw the glowing portal opening and a small mountain of crates.

The admiral continued, "Guess we're getting a special delivery: two hundred and thirty-five toaster-sized devices. We're not completely sure what we're supposed to do with them."

Jason squinted in the direction of the crates.

Orion was already on the move. "I'll bring one back."

In less than a minute, Orion ran there and back, returning with one of the devices in her hands. Turning it end-over-end, she shrugged and handed it to Jason. "Sorry, sir, I have no idea what it is either," she said apologetically.

"That's all right, Gunny. I think I know." Jason looked over the seamless white cube, then tossed it over to his father.

The admiral caught it, but made a face. "Hey, I might have dropped it, you know. What the hell is it?"

Jason shrugged. "We knew they were coming. Our ticket for moving unrestricted across the universe. I suspect this is how the fleet will communicate with the interchange. Most importantly, this device provides ... at least some hope that we can go up against the Craing."

"I'm still not comfortable placing alien technology aboard our fleet vessels. We have no idea what these fucking things really are. Hell, even if they're the real deal, the Caldurians could turn them back off on a whim. We've talked about this, Jason. We're still not sure what the Caldurians' true motivations are."

"You're preaching to the choir, Dad. But, in for a penny, in for a pound ... right? Truth is, the fleet is comprised of one hundred percent alien technology already. It's piloted, for the most part, by alien crewmembers. So now we're going to put a stake in the ground? And stop using alien tech?"

"Don't be a smart-ass," the admiral snapped back. "I know all that. We've already integrated Caldurian wormhole travel into our strategic planning. Obviously, without those devices we'd miss confronting the Craing fleet entirely. I'm just saying I'm not comfortable with it."

"I'm not either. The prospect of having these things on *The Lilly* and the rest of the fleet gives me the willies," Jason replied.

"So, how do we even install these things? Where do we put them?" the admiral asked.

"That's a question for Granger, but I imagine somewhere on the bridge," Jason said, unsure.

As if waiting for this opportune moment, Granger stepped from the portal opening, followed by twenty other Caldurians right behind him. Granger spotted them and made his way over to join them.

"We would like to assist you with installation."

Jason looked to his father. "It's your call, Admiral."

Chapter 18

Billy did a good job rounding up their scattered SEAL teammates, as well as their original fighter pilot crew. With very few exceptions, the admiral had made good on his promise to help get *The Lilly*'s military people reassigned back where they belonged.

Jason entered the mess hall back on board *The Lilly*. In his frantic rush to prepare for the impending Craing fleet engagement, he'd only been able to catch sporadic sleep and was missing more than a few meals. Feeling anxious and hungry, he forced himself to get out of his ready room. Now, looking around the crowded compartment he realized it had been some time since there'd been this many crew on board at any one time. At last count, the ship's military complement was up to two hundred and sixty-three. He had three full shift rotations in every department. Additions had been made to the SEAL security forces, now sitting at seventy-two men, as well as to the fighter squadron, now totaling sixteen pilots.

"Hey, Cap, I hear we have some new tech on board," Rizzo said from the other end of the table. "Can you tell us anything about that?"

"Well, I don't know, Mr. Rizzo; it's all pretty secret ... If I tell you, I'll have to kill you," Jason replied with a wry smile. Rizzo smirked and was jeered at by several of his friends.

"Yes, in all seriousness, we have significantly upgraded multiple areas of the ship. Medical has a new ginormous MediPod, and other departments have had their databases updated. And as you already know, we have the latest nano-tech in our heads. Tactical has undergone significant changes as well. Our four plasma cannons have been replaced by newer and more effective versions of the same. We have three new gimbal-mounted rail-guns, in addition to the two we had before. The third new one deploys from the top of the ship. Each of these guns takes better advantage of the JIT ordnances. *The Lilly*'s shields, which were already impressive, have been strengthened. We also have the ability to phase-shift up to three thousand miles, with more precision and accuracy than before. This same phase-shift tech carries over to our missiles and other ordnances as well. Our drives have been … no better way to describe it, turbo-charged. Increased nearly a third in size, they provide a thirty percent increase in thrust. And faster-than-light travel has increased by a factor of three. But perhaps our biggest advancement, one that is yet to be tested, is our ability to call up a wormhole on demand and transport to virtually anywhere in the universe. Thanks to our new Caldurian friends, the entire fleet shares this added ability."

"Is it true we'll be heading through Allied space alone to face the Craing?" another crewmember asked from across the room.

"Who am I talking to over there?"

"Seaman First Class Bigelow, sir."

"I'm not ready to discuss specific strategic or tactical information, Seaman Bigelow. What I can say is we will be leaving Earth orbit at 0600. At some point in the near future *The Lilly* and the Allied fleet will engage the Craing. By anyone's measurement, this will be a decisive turning point in the war against the enemy."

"But you think we'll defeat the Craing, right, sir?"

Jason didn't answer right away, not wanting to quell anyone's enthusiasm. "We're doing everything we can to be fully prepared this time. Keep in mind, the fifteen hundred Craing warships headed for Allied space are but a fraction of the Craing's total forces. We have our work cut out for us." Jason became less serious. "Listen, each and every one of you will need to put on your superman cape and be a hero to those we're fighting for back on Earth. Can you do that?"

"Aye, sir. I can do that," Bigelow replied.

Jason looked around the mess, which had become quiet. All eyes were on him. Then several of them repeated the seaman's words: "Aye, sir. I can do that." Then more of them said it, a little louder, and finally everyone in the room repeated the same words again, "Aye, sir. I can do that!"

* * *

Ricket met Jason as he headed out of the mess. "Have you been waiting for me?" Jason asked.

"Captain, I'd like to discuss something with you. Something on a personal level." They continued on together toward the DeckPort. Jason couldn't remember Ricket ever wanting to speak to him on a personal level. But then again, since he'd met the cyborg months earlier, Ricket had changed, evolved: his speech patterns were more relaxed and his mannerisms more humanlike.

"What is it, Ricket?"

Ricket seemed uneasy to the point that he turned and verified they were truly alone. "I wish to make an adjustment, a change with my status on this vessel."

Jason's mind reeled. The mere thought of commanding this ship without Ricket at his side was unthinkable. Could he even manage that? What had happened? Had he discounted or trivialized Ricket in some way?

"I don't understand. I thought you were happy here,"

Jason asked.

"I am happy here. And I am not talking about leaving the ship."

Jason was relieved and his face must have shown it.

"Captain, as indicated by the transformation experienced by Lieutenant Commander Perkins, it is evident that one's physical form can be dramatically altered."

Jason stepped through the DeckPort and waited for Ricket. When Ricket joined him on Deck 2, Jason said, "Let's make this conversation more private."

Once seated at the conference table in the captain's ready room, Jason asked Ricket to continue.

"Captain, as you know I have been through what is called the *transformation of eternity*. My body is no less than two hundred years old, but it was only from the point when your father and Gus discovered me half-buried beneath rocks and dirt that I have any recollection of life. In a sense, that was my birthday. This body of mine, half organic half mechanical, has always felt strange or foreign to me."

"Ricket, Perkins' body was totally organic, he wasn't a cyborg. Separating—"

"Understand, Captain, I would not approach you with this if I had not conducted the necessary investigative research. Reversal of the *transformation of eternity,* at least to my knowledge, has never been attempted. The technology was not available. But now, with the latest Caldurian MediPod upgrades, I believe it is."

"And the downside? How dangerous a procedure is this?"

"In my estimation, my odds of mortality are approximately fifty percent."

"Are you so unhappy that you're willing to risk your life for no better than fifty-fifty, the flip of a coin, odds?"

Jason watched Ricket contemplate the question. Looking

small, in some ways childlike, he removed his LA Dodgers ball cap and placed it on the table in front of him. The micro-mechanical devices moving beneath his skin only emphasized his point. With the ship's added Caldurian technology, the constant movement of gears, actuators and tiny pistons now made Ricket's appearance seem anything but high tech.

"Captain, there is enough of me that *is* organic to know I am not *truly* alive. Not really alive."

"So, what would be the next step? If you went through this process."

"A complete reversal, separating organic from mechanical, as you put it, would not be possible. Much of my cognitive faculties rely on components that are non-organic."

"So what are you proposing?"

"A next-generation set of nano-devices. Obviously customized for my physiology. My core memory and multi-processors will migrate into the new nano-device, with room to spare. With the help of Granger and his scientists, I have already provisioned the necessary device from the phase-synthesizer."

"And the mechanical parts of the rest of your body?"

"That is actually the most difficult aspect of this procedure. This body will be discarded. Using my original DNA, a new body, one that is totally organic, will be synthesized via the new MediPod."

"The timing of this, Ricket, could not be worse. Can't it wait until we've dealt with the Craing fleet?"

"Precisely why I have come to you now. If the Allied forces, *The Lilly*, were to fall to the Craing, you and the rest of the crew would, in all likelihood, perish, Captain. My body is uniquely robust. In all probability, I would survive as I am now, as a cyborg, perhaps for hundreds, if not thousands of years."

"I do see your point."

Chapter 19

Nan was afraid to look in the bathroom. For two straight hours there'd been constant noise. The house shook with the sounds of wood splintering and pipes being cut and pulled out from God knew where.

With Teardrop's success rebuilding the Cherokee from the scrapyard, Nan had asked the drone if it could make household repairs, as well. Scanning through walls seemed to be one of its attributes, and with delivery of the necessary replacement parts, Teardrop was confident the old house's plumbing problems could be alleviated.

As Nan watched the drone silently hover down the hall, into the den, then out into the yard, she marveled at its wherewithal to complete any task put before it. With Jason's bank debit card information on hand, Teardrop had accessed Home Depot's website, ordered the necessary tools and supplies, and even arranged for their delivery to the front gate. Nan couldn't help but wonder if she was thinking too small. Teardrop was back and carrying several long metal pipes in one of its clawed hands.

"Teardrop, can you provide me with a Wi-Fi connection for my laptop?"

The drone didn't even hesitate. "Yes, I have implemented a connection for you, Nan."

She brought up her browser and logged into Jason's bank checking account. His password was the same as it used to be when they were still married, *Mollie123*. Several keystrokes later she was looking at his account information. Sure enough, there was close to three million dollars, just sitting there. Her mind flashed to Jason's words, "*I've thought about rebuilding. Maybe start from scratch. Put up a new house.*"

She brought up Google and did a search for complete modular home construction sites. Selecting the link, a website loaded and displayed a full-page image of what looked to be a high-end luxury home. Scrolling down the page, one floor plan caught her attention. It was a sprawling four bedroom, three bathroom ranch-style home. Everything, from land surveys, the permit process, even getting assistance with installation of the various modular components, if needed, was included!

"Teardrop? Can I show you something?"

* * *

Brian raised his hands and gestured for the hopper to do the same. The hopper looked confused by the strange act, but followed his lead. They were on a large vessel. If he was to speculate, it was some kind of freighter, a cargo ship. From bulkhead to bulkhead was easily seventy-five yards across. And even above the smell of death on his apparel, there was a predominant odor of grain.

"Who are you?" a slender humanoid with colorless eyes asked. He was dressed in clothing similar to Brian's, and continued to point his weapon at Brian's head.

"Um, I'm Captain Brian Reynolds," Brian said, exaggerating his rank.

"Why are you wearing our captain's clothes?"

"Look, I've been held hostage by space pirates. Only with the help of this creature was I able to escape. I'm sorry to say, I took these clothes from a dead body. Evidently that of your captain."

The hopper made a series of clicks and hisses. Brian looked over to the hopper and shrugged. "I'll see," Brian replied.

"The creature, the hopper, wishes to be returned to his home."

110

"The best we can do is let it out here," the humanoid said.

Brian glanced out the largest of the nearby portholes—nothing but the blackness of deep space surrounded them.

"We're in space."

"Exactly. We would be happy to throw it out of an airlock. You, on the other hand, will be brought back to face charges for the murder of our commanding officer."

"I didn't murder your captain. He was tied to a pole, same as I had been."

"So you say."

"Back to where you will be taking us, exactly?" Brian asked.

"I'm done answering your questions." He looked to the others. "Put the two of them in the brig. Kill them if they resist." Brian figured he was the man in charge, since he was the one giving orders. Brian staggered. Between the loss of his eye and the continual throbbing pain in his head, he was on the verge of blacking out. Going from a dungeon beneath Stalls' castle to a prison on another planet wasn't going to happen. Using his NanoCom, he produced his own series of clicks and hisses in the direction of the hopper.

The hopper sprang—so fast, in fact, that it took Brian off guard. With its three-inch claws extended, it drove one of its arms deep into the commanding officer's torso. It wasn't dissimilar to how it had dug meat from those crab creatures back on its own planet. Stunned, the others in the group stood paralyzed. Brian rushed the closest of them and pulled the energy rifle from his hands. Getting a better grip, he then drove the butt of the rifle into his forehead and the crewmember fell unconscious to the deck. These people certainly weren't military-trained, he thought. Brian pointed the weapon back around at the remaining four crewmembers. They were still frozen with fear.

But they weren't looking in his direction. Brian turned and

understood. The hopper, fingers dripping blood, was casually eating the dead commander's heart.

Brian stepped forward, getting their attention. "Who here is now in charge?"

The four of them looked at each other. The one woman in the group, short and pretty, if somewhat ordinary-looking, spoke. "I guess I am."

"What's your name?" Brian demanded.

"We don't have names. We go by numbers, or abbreviations of our numbers."

"Well, what's your number then?"

"My abbreviated number is 56567."

"I won't remember that, so you're now called Betty. How many crewmembers are on board? Lie to me and I'll kill the lot of you."

"Twelve, including us. Listen, we're a simple freighter outfit out of the Durainium sector. Unless you're looking for a shitload of grain, there's nothing of value for you here."

"Just for the record, the story I told you about your captain was true. I didn't kill him. That was the work of a pirate named Captain Stalls."

The crew exchanged quick glances with each other.

"You've heard that name before?"

"We've had run-ins with him and his clan before. Most freighters moving through this part of space simply pay his tolls. He makes a quick example of those that don't."

"You're taking me to Earth; after that, you're free to go where you want."

"What is Earth?"

Brian waited for another wave of nausea to subside and his head to clear before speaking again. "Take me to your bridge; I'll give you the specific coordinates." Brian gestured with his weapon for them to all get moving. The hopper followed.

To Brian, it seemed as though they had walked miles. He could tell Betty was watching him, had seen him waver and rub his aching head.

"What's wrong with you. You sick?"

"Don't worry about me. Just worry that I don't accidentally pull the trigger on this weapon. All of you keep going."

Brian's NanoCom was working overtime: first, with the hopper's constant hissing and clicking—the creature wanted to go home—and now, translating the back and forth murmurs between the crewmembers.

"Stop talking, all of you."

They made their way through a maze of intersecting corridors and finally entered the freighter's small bridge. Brian found the navigation station but had no idea how to access it. He nodded toward Betty and she reluctantly stepped in and entered a code. Several small displays filled with numerical information and another one that showed icons of their own sector, as well as a nearby planetary system. Brian sat down at the station and within several moments was able to pinpoint their current location and its relationship to Allied space, which was relatively close, as well as to Earth in the far away Sol solar system.

"We don't have the propellant for a trip like that," Betty said.

Brian looked at her in disbelief.

"Sorry! But we're on the return leg of a three-month, thirteen planet circuit."

"Can you make it here, over to this sector?"

Betty looked at the screen and chewed at her lip. She leaned in over Brian's legs to access the input device. Her chest lightly brushed against Brian's arm and she became flustered. She adjusted her stance and leaned in again to enter the coordinates. She stood back and shrugged. "Probably could make it."

Chapter 20

Jason thought about Ricket's request overnight. As much as he wanted to acquiesce, the needs of his crew and Earth itself had to come first. Ricket would have to take his chances with the rest of them. If they were successful at dealing with the Craing fleet, he'd be open to discussing the matter further. Jason found Ricket up on Deck 4B and delivered the disappointing news.

"I understand, Captain. I apologize for proposing the procedure at such an inopportune time."

"Let's see how we do against the Craing. We'll talk about it again after that."

"Yes, Captain."

Jason looked down at the bench top. There was a myriad of high-tech looking devices at different levels of assembly. Jason picked up one of their standard battle helmets and noticed the HUD visor was active. "What are you working on here?"

"Something I'm calling a phase-time-comparator circuit. Or PTCC."

"What's it do?"

"It is just about ready for implementation, if you decide it's worthwhile. Go ahead and put on the helmet."

Jason did as Ricket requested.

"What it will do is allow for playback of previous timeframe visuals based on current optic references. For example, I have set the parameters for exactly thirty days in the past. Now, as you look around viewing the current timeframe, either a smaller window or a direct visual overlay will display the corresponding visual timeframe of thirty days ago."

Jason slowly turned and surveyed the room. A smaller window was activated and seemed to show the exact same visuals. "Oh, wait," he said, turning back in the other direction. "That's really cool. I actually see you in the little window. You're doing something with the phase-synthesizer. And you're not wearing your Dodgers cap. I'm impressed. To be honest, I can't really think of an application I'd need this for today, but if it's not too much trouble—"

"No, not at all. It will be uploaded into our next battle suit design."

Jason took off the helmet. "Can this PTCC thing be added to our wraparound bridge display? Perhaps a way to rewind and fast-forward through visual time?"

Ricket took the helmet from Jason and thought about it for a moment. "Of course. That's a good idea, Captain."

* * *

Jason entered the bridge and heard the new AI's male voice announce: "Captain on the bridge."

He hesitated. "So this is what it looks like when every station is manned, huh?"

There was a whirlwind of activity as the bridge crew prepared for disembarking from the far side of the moon. Above, the Dreadnaught filled most of the wraparound display.

"Aye, Captain," the XO replied, now standing to his right. Like insects, hundreds of tractor drones scurried about the Dreadnaught's outer hull.

"Captain, we have a problem," Perkins said, concern in his voice. "One of the tractors is misbehaving."

Another video feed was added showing a close-up view of a tractor drone caught in some kind of frenetic loop. Its clawed arms whipped and flailed spastically as sections of the Dreadnaught's hull tore free. In less than thirty seconds the tractor drone had burrowed itself into the hull and was out of sight.

"I can't even imagine the kind of damage that thing is causing," Jason said.

Perkins stood up, watching the display with two fingers to his ear, then nodded.

"Captain, apparently it was a programming glitch. It's been brought back under control. It was halted before there was any serious internal systems damage."

Jason let out a breath.

Changing the subject, Perkins said, "The outpost's come up with a name for the Dreadnaught, Captain."

"And what's that?"

"The *Independence*."

"I like it. Seems appropriate. What's the latest status of the *Independence*?"

"All systems are now operational. We needed to retrofit replacement parts coming out of the phase-synthesizer," Perkins replied. "They're shuttling over some crewmembers as we speak. It'll still seem like a ghost ship, but we'll have enough crew there to keep critical systems alive."

"Good. According to the admiral the rest of the outpost fleet is ready."

"Yes, sir."

Jason brought his attention back to the bridge and the small white cube sitting atop the Comms station. "And we're ready to test this thing?"

"Aye, sir. Everything seems to be properly installed and configured. The Caldurians synchronized the equipment—and tested that it talks to the interchange. I think we're good to go. Ready to jump across the universe, whenever you're ready."

"That, or get stranded a thousand light years from home. Let's hope we don't lose favor with the Caldurians, or worse, the interchange. Seems we're not only putting our own lives at stake, but those of the entire fleet."

"Having second thoughts, sir?"

Jason shrugged. "We either attempt to use this technology, or stick with FTL and show up in Allied space several weeks from now. Two options, and lives are at stake either way."

"Aye, sir."

Jason saw one of the Gordon brothers, Michael, at the Comms station.

"Opening a channel with the interchange, sir. Connection established and in-and-out coordinates have been relayed."

Thirty seconds later, space distorted and a spectrum of colors emanated from an irregular opening.

"McBride, ready a long-range probe and deliver it into the mouth of that wormhole. I want to see what we'll be dropping into on the other side."

"Aye, Captain."

All eyes turned to the display.

"Probe's away, sir," McBride said.

The probe was at the mouth of the wormhole. It seemed to hesitate, then was quickly swallowed up into the blackness at its center.

"We're receiving a signal from Trumach space, sir. Must be our connection through the wormhole," Gordon added.

"Yes, that goes without saying, Seaman," Jason replied.

The wraparound display came alive with new visuals.

"It's got to be from the Craing fleet, sir!" Orion said from Tactical. Three drab brown Craing battle cruisers were holding stationary. Further away, three more warships were firing missiles in the direction of a blue, Earth-like planet.

"Trumach," Jason said aloud.

"Seems they've just arrived, sir. Minimal damage indicated. But that will change with that latest missile barrage."

"How many warships are in the vicinity?"

"Medium-range scans indicate ten. The rest of their fleet isn't far, though. Looks to be en route to the next system," Gunny replied.

"Captain, two of the cruisers are maneuvering to set down on the surface."

"Helm, new coordinates. Change our outpoint to the far side of that planet. And somebody get down to the Zoo. Find Traveler and tell him to prepare his warriors for battle."

"Outpoint reconfigured, sir."

"Make the announcement for general quarters, XO," Jason said. "Deploy the rail-guns; hell, deploy everything."

"Aye, Captain."

"Helm, phase-shift us to the mouth of that wormhole."

"Aye, sir."

The bridge flashed white as they phase-shifted into position. Then, poised at the mouth of the wormhole, *The Lilly* hesitated briefly and was drawn in.

Chapter 21

They'd traveled sixty light years in an instant.

Trumach filled the forward section of the display.

"She's beautiful," Orion said aloud. "We're undetected, sir."

Jason agreed. It was similar to Earth but different, too. No polar icecaps, less ocean, larger and greener continents.

"Where do we stand, Gunny?"

"Long-range sensors indicate the entire Craing fleet, which is more like two thousand vessels than fifteen hundred, has already moved past us by Trumach space and is about to leave this sector. Ten warships are still here in Trumach space and no more than five light minutes distance. As indicated earlier, three light cruisers look to be patrolling open space, while two of their large heavy cruisers have now set down at one of Trumach's major population centers. The Craing have destroyed Trumach's capital city, as well as key communication hubs around the planet."

"Two thousand? Somehow they've added five hundred additional warships. What about the heavy cruisers on the ground? What are they doing?"

"Unloading, Captain. I'm seeing a large deployment of troops from both vessels," Orion replied.

Jason's orders had been fairly explicit: don't directly engage the Craing before the rest of the Allied forces arrive.

"Gunny, those troops. Are they Craing?"

"No, sir, different physiology. My guess is they are rhinos," she said.

Traveler's voice bellowed from behind and filled the bridge. "Different rhinos," he said, striding over to Orion and looking at her display. "Those are Reds."

"Reds?" Both Orion and Jason repeated simultaneously. Traveler huffed.

"How many, Gunny?"

"Between the two groups, close to one thousand."

"Who are Reds, Traveler?" Jason asked.

"An inferior breed of rhino from our sister planet, Mangus. Less intelligent. Physically larger than Greys."

"Greys?"

"Our kind—we are Greys."

"I'm picking up weapons fire, sir," Orion said.

Jason knew that Traveler, once he became agitated, was a force to be reckoned with and right now he was on the verge of wrecking the bridge. He stood up tall, fists clenched on hips. "Why have you not landed your ship? Our kind are dying."

"We can do a lot more damage from the air, Traveler. Our fighters can—"

"No, we fight with honor. You must land now, Captain." Traveler stormed off the bridge.

At the helm, McBride looked back over his shoulder with his brows raised.

"Get us in position to phase-shift, Ensign. Put us right in between them," Jason said and then hailed Billy.

"Go for Billy, Cap."

"Be ready to deploy in two minutes."

"We're ready now. Rhinos and SEALs are lining up at the airlocks. Overflows assembling in the mess hall."

"How many SEALs have you left us?" Jason asked.

"Twenty, including Rizzo."

The bridge flashed white and they were on the ground. Jason took in the scene and was surprised by what he saw. Hundreds of dark red-colored rhino-warriors were rushing down the gangways off both Craing ships. It seemed Traveler had somewhat trivialized the Reds' size. They were easily ten feet tall. Dressed almost identically to the Greys, they carried similar heavy hammers. Energy weapons were holstered on their hips.

"Deploy both gangways, Gunny; show those cruisers what you can do with our rail-guns."

"Gladly, sir."

Jason watched the display screen as *The Lilly*'s rail ordnances blasted the Craing cruisers on both sides.

"That was quick. Their shields have already failed, sir."

Remembering his father's last command to not engage the enemy fleet, Jason realized it had been a promise he shouldn't have made. The truth was the bulk of the Craing fleet was still light years away. But certainly engaging these enemy warships here was not something that could be avoided. Hostile aggression from the Craing was not something he was willing to simply observe from the sidelines.

The upgrade to their guns seemed to provide a bit more kick, Jason thought, and he noticed more vibration coming up through the soles of his boots. Both cruisers began to return plasma fire.

Hundreds of Red rhinos, now fully deployed, continued on toward a city of mud domes several miles away in the distance.

First one, then the second Craing cruiser stopped firing altogether. Their outer hulls almost simultaneously disintegrated under the continual hail of explosive rail munitions. In seconds, little of the mammoth-sized vessels remained.

Jason answered another hail. "Go ahead, Billy."

"Cap, seems our rhino friends ... actually Traveler ... don't want our help. Something about it's not our place to protect the virtue of their mates. The problem is, though, without our help they look to be outnumbered three to one."

"Captain, the three Craing cruisers are entering orbit," Orion said.

Jason went back to Billy. "Follow them. Get in as close as you can and set up a perimeter. But hold fire and keep me apprised of the situation."

"Aye, Cap."

Jason watched the display as Traveler led two hundred-plus rhino-warriors and headed after the Reds. Several moments later Billy and his SEALs assembled at the base of the forward gangway. Within a minute they'd broken into multiple ten-man teams, spread out, and followed behind their Grey compatriots.

"Incoming!" Orion yelled. "Twenty-seven high-yield nukes. Enough to level half the continent."

"ETA?"

"Less than a minute, Captain."

"Seems they've cut their losses here. Better to just level the planet. Do we have a lock on those nukes?"

"Aye, Captain."

"Ready fusion-tip missiles; fire at will, Gunny."

"Twenty-eight missiles away, sir. I threw in one extra just in case," Orion said.

Perkins leaned over from the tactical station next to Orion, then stood. "Captain, the fleet, their entire fleet, has changed direction."

"Good! That's what we're supposed to do here. Hold up their progress. Keep their attention."

Jason heard McBride snicker from the helm station.

"You have something to add to that, Ensign?"

"Well, aye, sir. We're like rodeo clowns, Captain."

"Come again?"

"Back home. Any good rodeo has clowns. You know, to keep the bulls at bay and off the cowboys until they're safe."

"Captain, now all seven of the remaining Craing cruisers are either in, or entering into, Trumach orbit," Orion said. "They carry Craing signatures, but three of them are nothing we've come across before. Actually, they're similar to the three Caldurian ships—the Emperor's Guard."

"All right, we need to get out of here for a while. XO, in our absence, let's get our fighters out there to protect our ground forces."

"Aye, Captain," Perkins replied.

Jason mulled over Orion's comment. Any Caldurian vessel, even one hundreds of years old, could have advanced technology they'd be unprepared for.

"Can you get me visuals of those three vessels?"

"Yes, on one of them. The closest one."

A segment on the overhead display changed to a different feed. Sure enough, it wasn't anything like the typical Craing cruiser. But then again, it didn't look like a Caldurian ship, either.

"Lilly, can you decipher the writing on the side of the hull on that vessel?" Jason asked.

"Yes, Captain," the new Lilly AI replied. "The writing originates from Carz-Mau, a planet some ninety light years from this location. Its people, known as the Mau, are rich with scientific and progressive technological advances; their society is not unlike that of the Caldurians, prior to their disappearance."

"Are those additional five hundred ships in the Craing fleet of that same origin?"

"Four hundred-six vessels are from Carz-Mau. The other one hundred ten are from different locations, in different sectors, in this part of the universe."

Jason was quiet for several moments. That intel definitely complicated things. A nearly impossible situation had just become a lot worse.

"AI, can you scan that vessel's life forms, the crew?"

"Yes, Captain. Ninety-three percent of the crew are a derivative of Mau. The rest are of Craing physiology."

Jason let himself smile. "It's my guess the Craing, probably with brute-force strength in sheer numbers alone, have brought the Mau along as unwilling combatants." He shook his head. "God forbid the Craing ever fight their own battles."

"Orders, sir?" Perkins asked.

"AI, what's the comparative size of that vessel to a Craing heavy cruiser?"

"Both have an approximate beam of three hundred yards. The Carz-Mau vessel, considered a destroyer-class ship, is rated at 48,000 tons, and the Craing heavy battle cruiser is just under 45,000 tons."

"I think I know where you're going with this, Captain," Perkins said. A new display segment was added, revealing a wireframe view of the vessel's insides. The ship was horseshoe-shaped and there were indeed two large hold areas.

"Captain, the rhinos have engaged each other," Orion reported.

"Put up the feed from Billy's helmet cam," Jason ordered.

Chapter 22

Traveler knew they were at a disadvantage; too few in number and they were smaller in size. The Reds had always depended on their brawn in confrontations such as this one. Unfortunately, Traveler was given little time to formulate a plan. His rhino-warriors reached the flanks of the Reds' position just as the Reds neared the outskirts of the city. With luck, only a few of the females had been beaten, or worse, raped. They came across a makeshift corral, with fifteen-foot-high fencing; he knew it was erected to hold captured young male rhinos. The terrain was open with little in the way of cover. The Red sentries saw Traveler's rhinos approaching and spread out in a circle around the football field-sized corral. Traveler counted fifty Reds. In the distance, coming from the dome city, frantic shrieks carried across the open plains. Their pillage spree had begun. Frustrated, Traveler knew that battling fifty Red rhino-warriors alone, with his limited army, could take hours. How many of their mates will ... His thoughts were interrupted.

Traveler was well aware Billy and his team had moved into position around them. Billy rushed forward and joined Traveler at his side.

"Hey, the Reds here are mere sentry guards, right? Not worth your time. Hell, they don't even have prisoners to guard. These are ass clowns. Why don't you let us handle these guys? That way you can continue the real fight, there at the edge of the city?"

Traveler snorted his disapproval, then started to pace. He looked toward the city one more time. With barely a glance, he nodded. Hammer held high in the air, he was off and running toward the distant domes. The ground shook as two hundred-fifty or so Grey rhino-warriors followed after him.

* * *

Billy finished updating the captain and closed the channel. He passed the information on to his men, via their comms, and they all moved back from the high fencing around the corral. Inside, looking triumphant, the Red rhinos snorted and shook their hammers in the direction of the retreating SEALs. Their celebration was short-lived as five sleek fighters suddenly dropped from the sky, encircling them. The fighters held their position, ten feet off the ground, with their forward rail-guns deployed. An eerily quiet standoff.

Billy gestured into the air with a quick twirling motion of his hand. The rail-guns erupted in a blaze. The corral fencing flew into pieces, then the ground below it was pummeled—sending dirt and small rocks high up into the air. The five fighters continued the barrage. The Red rhinos retreated, moving back toward center ground, until they were huddled back-to-back in a group. The guns stopped all at once.

Billy moved forward until he reached the edge of the newly-dug culvert: it was twenty feet across, twenty to thirty feet deep, and completely encircled the Red rhinos. The rhinos looked scared. He almost felt sorry for them. Billy held up a hand, hoping they'd recognize it as a gesture of peace and that the firing had ceased for now. One of the large Reds moved forward, away from the others, and snorted.

Each of the SEALs' battle suits had been equipped with the latest phase-shift belts. Billy quickly configured a jump distance through HUD settings, and phase-shifted to within three feet of the rhino. Startled, the Red rhino-warrior took a quick step back.

Billy put his hands up again, gesturing he was there to talk. He kept his voice even, non-threatening, and hoped his words would translate correctly.

"You've been brought here by the Craing, correct?"

The huge rhino looked down at Billy but didn't answer.

"It's what they do. They use their technology, their many warships, to conquer others. Your mates and offspring have been taken hostage; the Craing have threatened to kill them if you do not fight their battles for them," Billy said.

"How do you know that?" the rhino replied.

"The Greys. Same thing happened to them. We're helping them get their planet back."

"Yes, the Craing have killed many of our kind, taken our mates and offspring. But they have also given us powerful weapons to fight our enemies," he said, patting the energy weapon holstered at his side. "Soon, they will provide us with our own space vehicles so we can fight the Greys, destroy them once and for all."

"You will never be free of the Craing. Once you are no longer needed to serve the Craing Empire, you and your kind will be slaughtered."

The rhino looked to the others; they were all getting agitated and starting to pace.

"It seems to me you have three options. One, you make a stand here and fight. Unfortunately, it won't be much of a fight since those five fighters will cut you down in less than a second, and you'll all die. Second option, you'll surrender and we hand you over to the Greys, at which point you'll most likely be killed."

"What is the third option?"

"You join in our fight against the Craing. We will drive the Craing from this part of space and you can return to your mates and offspring, return to a free and independent home world."

"We cannot speak for the others. We are only a few; there are thousands more of us here and on the Craing vessels."

"Often a revolt starts with only a few. Do you have a way to contact the others? Those attacking the dome city?"

"Yes."

"Do it. Stop the killing before we use our fighters and vaporize every last one of you."

The rhinos spoke between themselves in low voices. Finally, one of them stepped to the far side of the corral, closer toward the dome city, and trumpeted a sound so loud that Billy felt it vibrate through his helmet.

A moment passed and a similar sound echoed back from miles away. The exchange continued back and forth for some time. Eventually, it ceased and the rhino returned to the pack.

"Well?" Billy asked.

"It took some convincing. A temporary truce has been declared between Reds and Greys. The Reds are on their way back."

* * *

"There's simply no way both Reds and Greys will agree to cohabit the same vessel, Cap," Billy said. "Where are you, anyway?"

Jason stood on the bridge looking at Billy's helmet cam feed of the planet below. "For now, we're playing hide-and-seek with the other warships. Phase-shifting from one location to another so they can't get a lock on us."

"How long can you do that?"

"Since the Craing fleet has made an about-face and are headed back here, not too much longer. Maybe a day. What we need is a second ship. A big one. Secure the area. If things go right, we'll be back to pick you all up in a few hours."

"Aye, Cap."

Jason brought his attention back to the bridge. Turning around, Jason looked for Ricket. "Where the hell's Ricket?"

"I think he's up on 4B, sir," Orion answered, not taking her eyes from Billy's helmet video feed.

"Gunny, is this going to be a problem?"

"Sir?" She pulled her eyes back toward Jason, then seemed to catch his meaning. "Sorry, sir."

Jason brought two fingers up to his ear and hailed Ricket.

"Go for Ricket."

"I need you on the bridge."

"Yes, I was already on my way, sir."

Jason wondered if something was up. He couldn't remember the last time Ricket hadn't shown up even before Jason realized he needed him.

Ricket arrived a moment later and headed directly for Jason in the command chair.

"Sorry, Captain, I was making some last-minute alterations to the PTCC software."

"You'll need to play with that on your free time, Ricket. Right now I need you to collect what's necessary for one of your remote piloting kits."

"Yes, Captain. For a Craing battle cruiser?"

"Not necessarily."

Chapter 23

It seemed modular housing was much more prevalent than Nan had first thought. Surfing the web, she discovered a manufacturing and distribution center right there in San Bernardino. She spent the morning taking her refitted Jeep in for a required smog-emission test, and then registered the vehicle at the local DMV. After that, she picked Mollie up at school and headed for Gillgood Modular Home Builders.

"How was our first day of school?"

"Hated it," Mollie said, looking out the side window.

"Care to elaborate on that?"

"What does that mean?" Mollie asked, not looking at her mother.

"Care to explain why you hated school today?"

"Everything I've learned you and Dad say I'm not allowed to talk about."

"You mean about things that have happened in space and on *The Lilly*?"

"That and other stuff. I don't fit in anymore, Mom. And I was so bored."

"Tomorrow will be better, you'll see."

"Where are we going? I'm hungry," Mollie said, looking at her mother for the first time.

"We're going to look at some modular homes."

"Why?"

"Because I don't like your Dad's house. Don't tell him I said that. I think it's creepy."

"That's not a very nice thing to say. I like the house just the way it is."

"Uh huh. Well, let's just take a look, okay?"

"I don't like shopping. I want a Big Mac, Coke, and fries, and hot apple pie."

"If you're good and don't whine ... maybe after," Nan replied with a smile.

"Is that where we're going?" Mollie asked, pointing a finger toward a large lot with sections of homes supported up on temporary pilings.

Nan pulled in and parked next to a mobile home trailer. A sign said Office above the door.

Both Nan and Mollie bypassed the office trailer and headed directly for one of the modular homes. Unfinished plywood steps led up to wide double front doors. The door was unlocked and Mollie was the first one in.

"Wow!"

Nan joined her and stood in the middle of what she figured was the home's open great room. Although the flooring consisted of plywood sheets, the walls were in and the adjoining kitchen was completely done, with granite countertops and stainless steel appliances.

"You'll have to go outside to see the other modular sections of this particular model," a man's British-accented voice informed them.

Both Nan and Mollie turned to see a salesman, wearing a yellow shirt and a broad brown-striped tie, standing behind them.

Mollie spoke up first. "Who are you?"

"I'm Jonathan, a representative here. And who am I addressing?"

Nan smiled and offered her hand. "I'm Nan Reynolds; this is my daughter, Mollie."

"Nice to meet you both. You're in the market for a new modular factory-built home?"

"Maybe. We're just checking things out. Looking at my options."

"Let me tell you a little about them. They are just as strong and reliable as any traditional, pad-built home. The loan process is the same and—"

"Sorry to interrupt, but I've already researched all the pros and cons, Jonathan. What's the size of this particular model?"

"Twenty-eight hundred square feet. The other sections include four bedrooms, three baths, laundry room, a great room, and even a three-car garage."

"And what's the minimum lot size for this plan?"

"Well, you're getting into specifics that come well down the line. But we suggest a quarter- acre lot, minimum—you know, so you can have an adequate yard."

Nan pulled a small notebook from her purse and flipped it open. Next door to Jason's current relic of a house there was an open lot. Teardrop calculated it to be a full acre.

"Okay, good. Um, how much do these modules weigh?"

Jonathan was taken aback by the question and furrowed his brow. "Ms. Reynolds, a typical crane will have no problem lifting, or positioning, the modules. Again, all that is well down the road after selecting your home plan."

"Generally speaking, then, just spitball it, how heavy are these things?"

"Ten to fifteen thousand pounds per modular unit. Let's say fifty thousand pounds, total weight. Of course, rigging and extraneous items would be added on to that number," Jonathan said, still confused.

"No, that's good. Rough numbers work." Nan wrote them down in her little notebook. Teardrop had been specific; lifting anything heavier than twenty thousand pounds was problematic.

"What's the price of this particular home?"

"There's no one set price, since they are all configurable to what options you'll want."

"How about this one?"

"Well, this is a model."

"Yes. How much is this one?"

"This is a quite complex, multi-roofed plan. No less than six modules. Let's say one hundred ten dollars a square foot."

Nan went back to writing in her notebook. "A twenty-eight hundred square foot home. Let's see, that comes to three hundred and eight thousand dollars, right?"

"Give or take. Now, that's complete: delivery, set onto the foundation, plumbing and electrical hookups, and all the detail finishes inside and out."

"Jonathan, I'm going to go look at the other sections, its other modules. When I get back I'd like you, or someone who is the decision-maker, to give me the full price for delivering this home locally, as it's currently configured, by tomorrow afternoon."

"You're serious?"

"Yes."

"That's not possible."

"I'll pay three hundred thousand dollars and you won't have to install anything. Just drop off the modules and be on your way. Are you the person to make that deal?"

"Um, no, but I'll find out. Take your time looking at the modules. This could take a while."

* * *

Teardrop finished clearing and then excavating the lot. It had found in the scrapyard several tractors, a Caterpillar backhoe, and an ancient-looking bulldozer. Both of the latter were soon up and running and, with Teardrop at the controls, made quick work of Jason's next-door lot.

The modules arrived at the Central Valley Scrapyard on six specialized wide-load flatbed trucks the following afternoon. Expediting a crane and the truck to carry it had been an extra cost. The modules were lifted and placed around the outside periphery of the open lot. There was still much to do before the modular sections could be moved and assembled. Since Teardrop had access to the house plans the previous day, it was able to order what was needed from local contractor supply stores with early morning deliveries. It had already configured hookups for the municipal water and sewer lines, as well as the underground utility lines.

Two jumbo-sized cement mixers were going non-stop and Teardrop had made the footings for the above ground foundation, as well as the back porch. The driveway would take a few days longer but had been staked out, and graded, forms and rebar positioned. Throughout the day, city and county inspectors showed up, requiring Teardrop to drop everything and hide. Nan hadn't believed it possible to get so many people moving with such short notice. But with her access to additional funds for discreet, under-the-table payoffs, local government officials were not adverse to making special arrangements, just this once.

Next door, Nan and Mollie sat out on the old porch eating grilled cheese sandwiches and watched as Teardrop tirelessly worked into the night. Nan marveled at the drone's ability to do what fifty, maybe even a hundred, men could accomplish—all in a fraction of the time.

She looked out over the scrapyard and beyond to the foothills of San Bernardino. This place would never be her first choice for a home. But life was different now. There were security issues to contend with, and Jason would never be far from *The Lilly*. That meant staying close to this old scrapyard and the hidden underground aquifer.

Even so, she thought that maybe she was pushing things. Well, no matter what, this old house was close to falling in on itself. If Mollie was going to stay here, even part of the time, something needed to change. And just maybe Jason would like the new place.

Nan saw Teardrop hovering nearby, holding a set of architectural plans. "Would now be a good time to talk about the added security items you've requested?"

Chapter 24

"We came out of FTL for this?" Stalls asked.

"It's taken more of a beating than I thought. From the looks of things she must have put up quite a fight," Pike said, admiration in his voice.

The bulbous, almost angry-looking vessel drifted and seemed to list to one side. Scorched and showing what could only be the result of repeated plasma fire, it was obviously dead in space.

"Destroyer-class, Captain. Eight rail-guns, multiple energy weapons and something else." Pike leaned in closer to the display on his station. "Ah, a toric-cloaking device!"

Captain Stalls impatiently looked over at the old bearded pirate, waiting for him to continue.

"I've seen these before, Captain. Ships with that kind of technology were more prevalent a hundred years ago, but sure enough, this ship can disappear and be totally undetectable by sight and sensors."

"Why am I just hearing about this now? Why doesn't every warship have this technology?"

"Three words: black zodium crystals. Can't be synthesized in a lab and the only source was on a planet the Craing destroyed a century ago. Oh yes, without a doubt an excellent bit of technology over there ... no doubting that."

Captain Stalls continued to look at Pike, then the edges of his mouth turned up.

"And no life forms detected?"

"Not that I can see; probably been drifting out here for years. Nothing more than scrap."

Stalls turned and found his younger brother asleep in his chair at the rear of the bridge. A new goliath-sized pimple had formed at the end of his prominent nose.

"Bristol! Bristol, wake up!"

His brother stirred and eventually looked up through half-opened eyes.

"What? What's with the yelling?"

"On the viewer. Ever see a ship like that?"

Bristol glanced up and shrugged. "I don't know. Who gives a fuck? It's a wreck, space trash."

Stalls walked to within several feet of his brother and stooped, hands on knees, leaning in closer. "Ever heard of a toric-cloaking device?"

That evoked another glance at the viewer. "Yeah, that technology went away sometime last century."

"Well, there's one on that ship over there."

Bristol, now awake, sat up and took a better look at the destroyer.

"Eston, are you serious? It's just a wreck."

"Don't call me by my first name."

"Whatever—it's a wreck, Captain."

"I know it's a wreck. Forget the wreck! Could you get me that device, retrofit *Her Majesty*?"

Another shrug. "Maybe, but why? Don't you have enough hell-fire with this monstrosity of a ship already?"

"You're going over there. I want you to join a team and evaluate if it's repairable. Can you do that for me?"

Bristol yawned in his brother's face and shrugged again. "I guess—whatever."

* * *

His environmental suit was a joke; nothing like the form-fitting battles suits worn on *The Lilly*. Bristol turned around and looked down at the back of his legs and the baggy extra material that seemed to hang off his ass. Annoyed, he stepped into the compact shuttle, joining three crewmen waiting for him.

"It's about time, Bristol," the leader and largest of the three men said. Bristol would never admit it, but he liked him. Simply called Knock by everyone, he was one of the few in his brother's band of idiots who seemed to actually have a brain—that, and he didn't tease him like everyone else. Knock was seated up ahead, behind the controls in the cockpit.

He turned and looked back at Bristol. "Where's your weapon?"

"I guess you're holding it. If someone needs to be shot, go for it ... have at it."

Knock tapped on a touchscreen and the rear hatch slid into place with a sucking thump. He said something into his comms and the little shuttle moved away into open space. Bristol looked out from the rear porthole as the rest of *Her Majesty* came into view. *What an embarrassment*, he thought. The luxury liner was big and clumsy, with cheesy gold scrollwork painted across her outer hull. New armaments had been added to virtually every flat surface—some seemed to point, rather precariously, back at the ship itself. *What a clusterfuck.*

A large section of the wrecked destroyer's flight deck was open to space and allowed barely enough room for the shuttle to clear the outer hull and pass into the mangled bowels of the vessel. Debris was scattered across much of the deck. They eventually found an area clear enough for them to set down. Knock cut power to the drives. They sat there while the cabin vented the breathable atmosphere back into holding tanks. The hatch slid open and, now weightless, Knock pulled himself out of the cockpit and toward the rear of the shuttle.

"Everyone out."

Bristol was the last one to pull himself out of the hatch. In the pitch dark, even their helmet lights did little to illuminate their surroundings. Crossbeams hung haphazardly from above and loose cabling dangled from virtually everywhere. Bristol careened into something and was enveloped into a web of more cabling.

"Careful!" Knock barked from up ahead. The two other pirates, Bristol had no idea what their names were, pulled him free and pushed him down a narrow corridor in the same direction Knock had gone. An HUD warning indicated Bristol's pulse rate was spiking. There was very little he didn't hate about this sort of thing: confined spaces, the dark. Why hadn't he brought a weapon? At least Knock seemed to know where he was going. His helmet light was stationary up ahead. Bristol, moving slowly, was repeatedly pushed and shoved from behind. Timing it, he thrust a leg backward, and nailed one of them in the head. The shoving stopped and eventually Bristol arrived at an opening. Knock was looking at something.

"That it?" he asked.

Bristol pulled himself around the circular compartment. A compartment dedicated to one thing only: housing a toric-cloaking device. Bristol estimated it was twenty feet in diameter and eight feet tall. At the top were hundreds of thick feeder channels, like branches on a large tree.

"Yep, this is it. Looks to be in pretty good shape," Bristol replied, pulling himself around the large device. "You'll need those too," Bristol said, pointing to five large barrel-shaped devices mounted to the bulkhead.

"What are those?" Knock asked.

"They're basically optical power converters," Bristol said,

looking over at the three pirates. "So, how the hell are you going to get all this out of here?"

Chapter 25

Jason was back talking to Billy for the third time in less than an hour. His eyes were still on the display and the three distant side-by-side Mau vessels. Just looking at them made him feel uneasy. The Craing, although cunning, were basically cowards when it came to fighting and squaring off one on one. But now they would be going up against a new combatant, the Mau. Would he be able to turn them as he had the rhino-warriors? Billy's voice brought his attention back to matters at hand.

"Cap, I'm telling you there's simply no way to keep them from killing each other. Truce or not, those two rhino breeds can't be on the same planet," Billy said, exasperated.

"Can't Traveler command them—?"

"Oh no, he's the worst of them all. He just ripped an arm from a Red rhino who was three feet taller and proceeded to use it to beat the snot out of him."

"Do your best, Billy. We'll return as soon as we can." Jason cut the connection and opened a new one to Rizzo.

"Have your SEALs ready to go in five. We'll meet you in the mess."

"Aye, Captain."

Jason stood up from the command chair. "Okay, XO, we should be pretty good at this by now. Once we phase-shift into their hold, jam their communication capabilities. That's crucial if this plan is going to work."

"Aye, sir."

"We'll deploy and get control of their bridge. We all need to remember these aren't Craing. I'm expecting there'll be more resistance. I'll leave you a security team of ten SEALs."

Orion got up from her station and joined Jason; together they left the bridge and headed for the DeckPort. They stepped out onto Deck 2 and quickly made their way to the Gunnery. Ricket was already there, holding his helmet under his arm.

"Good. You're bringing along everything you'll need?" Jason asked.

"Yes, Captain. Although I'm unfamiliar with the technology on that vessel, I'm bringing what I expect will be required."

Jason noticed Ricket had on a stuffed-to-capacity backpack that was nearly as big as he was. "You want me to carry that?"

"I can carry up to twelve hundred pounds, Captain."

"Sure you still want to get rid of that body of yours?" Jason said with a smile, but regretted the comment as soon as he said it.

Ricket didn't answer and didn't seem to be fazed by it. Once they'd finished suiting up and were armed with sidearms, as well as with multi-gun rifles, they headed together to the mess hall. Rizzo and the other SEALs stood at the ready.

"Okay, this drill is going to be somewhat different than how we typically phase-shift into the belly of combatant vessels. Ten of you will secure the LZ and stay put. Before they even know we're there, the rest of us will phase-shift directly onto their bridge and take control. The whole operation shouldn't last more than a few minutes. That's the plan, anyway. Questions?"

Rizzo shook his head, "We got it, Cap."

Rizzo broke the men into two ten-man teams and everyone put on their helmets. Jason hailed the XO.

"Go for XO."

"We're ready on our end."

A moment later everything flashed white and Jason knew *The Lilly* was sitting in one of the vessel's hold areas. The bridge coordinates had been pre-loaded into their HUDs and all that was needed was to select *Activate*. Jason said, "Go," and the assault team of fourteen disappeared.

* * *

His team appeared in an instant and caught the Mau off guard. The bridge was crescent shaped, more long and slender than wide. Jason wasn't sure if the Mau were humanoid or not. They did not move, did not respond to the sudden presence of a team of infiltrators. Jason and the others raised their weapons, even though there weren't any hostile moves. What struck Jason was an overwhelming sense of dread. A dread so profound his emotions were incapacitating him to the point that even standing was difficult. One SEAL, shoulders sagging forward as if holding the world upon his back, slowly dropped to one knee, then onto the deck. Tears filled Jason's eyes, making it difficult to see. Through blurry eyes, Jason got his first look at the closest of the Mau standing before him. His face, all their faces, stared emotionless, mouths drawn open as if in a perpetual scream. Their skin was white, with a deathly blue tint, which was in stark contrast to the utter blackness of their surroundings. Bulkheads, consoles, even the uniforms worn by the eight Mau bridge crewmembers were black or dark grey. Two more SEALs dropped, both curled on the deck in fetal positions. A Mau crewmember drifted over to the fallen men. Slowly he bent over, reached out and touched one SEAL, and then the other. As the Mau moved back, the SEALs flailed and grabbed at their helmets. Jason watched them both die like that, with their hands clutching at their helmets.

Jason felt the heaviness of his multi-gun and the ambivalence of holding it any longer. Why bother? The fight was hopeless. With thousands of enemy warships en route, their destruction was a foregone conclusion. All would be lost. The sadness of it all. And regrets. So many regrets. *Oh my God, Mollie.* He'd been such a failure as a father. Jason dropped to his knees and heard his multi-gun clang across the deck plates. *I'm sorry, Nan, so sorry for everything.* Despair continued to spiral down, pulling him beneath the surface, suffocating him. *Goodbye, Dira, I love you.* He took a breath. Realization spread through him; yes, at least he had that. He really did love Dira. Now able to breathe, Jason attempted to get back to his feet. But the Mau had already leaned in, an outstretched arm and bony fingers extended to touch Jason. Ricket's multi-gun, which was set at the highest plasma-burst level, not only took the Mau's head clean off, but it took off a significant portion of his neck and shoulders as well.

With that, the spell was broken. Jason and his team returned to their feet, no longer feeling that same awful, debilitating, dread.

"Why have you come here?" asked one of the Mau, although his distorted open mouth still had not moved. Jason realized he was dressed slightly differently from the others. Silk-like, the wispy material of his uniform hung loosely over his skeletally thin body. His uniform differed: not black like the others, more like the very darkest shade of red.

"Don't move. If any one of my crew gets emotional in the slightest degree, we'll blow all your fucking heads off. You'll speak only when answering our questions. Is that understood?"

"Yes," he said.

Jason brought his attention to his remaining SEALs. Rizzo was the last to get back on his feet, and from the expression on his face he would just as soon blow the Mau away, right here and now.

"First of all, what did you do to us? What the hell was that?"

"Our kind, the Mau, are a highly empathic race. The ability to manipulate the emotional state of less-evolved beings, especially humanoids, takes little effort."

"Let me show him what a less-evolved human can do to him, Cap," Rizzo said.

Jason ignored Rizzo's outburst.

"All of you, get over there against the bulkhead," Jason demanded, gesturing with the muzzle of his multi-gun toward the back of the bridge.

Ricket stood before one of the consoles. He took off his pack and started to remove the various items he'd brought along.

"Who's in charge here? You?"

"I am the first officer, the one in charge."

"Where is your captain?"

"On one of the other Mau vessels. He commands all three vessels."

"Fine. What is the total number of your vessels among the approaching Craing fleet?"

The Mau hesitated, but began speaking when Jason raised the barrel of his multi-gun.

"There's only these three in local space. More, close to five hundred, still within the Craing Fleet."

"Were you coerced? What made you join the Craing?"

The Mau leader turned to the other Mau huddled together at the back wall, then turned back and faced Jason. "We were not coerced. We requested to join them, and we have allied ourselves with them. It would be foolish not to."

"Terrific, so you're telling me you're no better than they are," Jason said, not expecting an answer, and none was given. "How many on board this vessel?"

"You cannot defeat us. As we speak, our security forces approach. There is not a Mau on this vessel, or on the other two, who does not know of your presence here."

Jason glanced over to Ricket, who momentarily stopped what he was doing and looked up. "What he says is true, Captain. Their empathic capacity carries over. They have a unified telepathic connection between one another. My sensors indicate there are close to two hundred Mau on board each of the three Mau warships."

Jason was prepared for the large Mau crew levels; Orion had scanned the three ships when they first encountered them. But he had hoped to bring forth more of an element of surprise from them.

"Captain, I have configured their navigation, as well as other primary systems onboard this vessel, for remote control by *The Lilly*."

"And the Mau crew is locked out? From any other part of the ship as well?"

"Yes, sir," Ricket replied.

Jason wouldn't be able to overcome two hundred Mau crewmembers. That was becoming obvious. But maybe he didn't have to.

Jason hailed Perkins.

"Go for XO."

"XO, we're all set here. We've taken their bridge and you should have manual control via the remote station Ricket set up there."

"Aye, Captain. I'll have McBride take a look, but we'd do better with Ricket back here."

Ricket stood and nodded his head as if he were somehow able to hear their conversation.

"He's on his way. I'll be joining you shortly as well."

"Captain," Perkins added nervously, "as we speak close to a hundred Mau have entered the hold and encircled *The Lilly*. They don't seem to be armed but our security team has them at gunpoint just the same."

"Yeah, they have a different kind of weapon. Let me know if there's any changes."

Jason cut the connection and brought his attention to the Mau first officer. "I warned you. Have your crew back off or you will be the next one to die."

"I cannot do that. I do not command the crew, the captain does. He is aware of the situation and he will not relinquish this vessel so easily. We are all expendable, our vessels are not."

"Where is he? Which vessel?" Jason didn't wait for his answer. He fired a plasma bolt into the Mau crewmember standing to his right, who grabbed his wounded arm.

The first officer may have gasped, but his distorted, open-mouthed face was impossible to read. He slowly raised a hand, grim reaper-like, and pointed to the bulkhead off to the left.

"Rizzo, hold this bridge while we're gone. If you feel anything out of the norm, anything at all, kill them all."

"Aye, Cap."

"Okay Orion, you're with me. Ricket, load us up with the phase-shift coordinates for that ship's bridge."

"Done, Captain."

"Head on back to *The Lilly*. We'll join you soon."

Orion, Jason, and Ricket phase-shifted off the bridge at the same time.

* * *

Orion and Jason appeared onto the nearly identical-looking bridge with weapons held high. The bridge crew, including the captain, was ready for them. This time it wasn't anguish that gripped Jason's emotions, totally incapacitating him—it was rampant fear. He was face to face with the Mau captain, evident by his midnight-blue robe. *Was it him? Was he the one invading Jason's consciousness?* What Jason felt was beyond anything he had ever experienced before. Abject, total fear: afraid to move, afraid to look into the bleak face before him, afraid to pull the trigger on his multi-gun.

As certain as he could possibly be, Jason knew he was going to die. It was going to happen right now. A foregone conclusion. This was the ultimate weapon and he had no defense against it. One quick glance at Orion and all hope was gone. She too stood paralyzed with fear.

The Mau captain was on the move. Slowly, patiently, coming for Jason. Both his arms rose up, no wasted energy expelled; he'd simply touch Orion and Jason together, end their lives all at once. The paralyzing fright seemed to only increase as Jason's eyes locked on to the Mau captain's elongated, mournful face, his mouth a black abyss of everything evil and forlorn. Jason felt warm wetness as his bladder gave way to the unrelenting terror engulfing him. *Why had he come here without Ricket?* Jason's mind raced, looking for anything, any thought to cling on to. What was he thinking of before? The Mau was upon him, his fingers now encircling the arm of Jason's combat suit. As if his emotions had been magnified tenfold, he felt his heart on the verge of bursting within his chest. Of literally being frightened to death. It would be over soon. *No, he remembered, it wasn't a what, but a who.* Dira. Again. In the fraction of a second it took for the synapses in his brain to conjure up her magnificent image, he again had the familiar yearning. He felt the love. Jason's finger twitched once, twice, then the trigger moved ever so little, but it was enough. The plasma bolt from Jason's multi-gun hit the Mau captain dead center in his gaping, distorted mouth.

Chapter 26

Orion was quick to regain her composure and had her multi-gun leveled on the Mau crewmembers. Jason stared down at the captain's still body. He pretty much looked the same dead as he had alive.

There was no way they could leave anyone alive on the other two Mau warships. He hadn't thought it possible, but these Mau seemed to be as ruthless as the Craing. Their ability to immobilize an opponent through the manipulation of his or her feelings was deadly effective. The problem Jason faced was a big one. Once the ships' weaponry was disabled, and its crew disarmed, they'd still need to deal with this other issue. Would it even be possible to neutralize that kind of weapon? One that six-hundred crewmembers possibly possessed? Which brought up something else ... why hadn't any of the other Mau on board quickly lashed out using the same ability?

Putting two fingers up to his ear, Jason hailed the XO.

"Go for XO."

"We still have one fighter on board?"

"Aye, Captain, the *Pacesetter*."

"Get Lieutenant Wilson prepped and have him phase-shift to open space. But he's not to engage the enemy unless fired upon."

"He's already prepped and ready, sir."

"Good. We also need Ricket back here; tell him to bring the same bag of tricks."

"Aye, Cap."

Jason cut the connection and turned to the Mau bridge

crew. "Who is in charge?" Jason asked the six remaining Mau crewmembers still huddled together.

They looked at one another and eventually one took a step forward. Jason hadn't noticed any difference between them before, but this one was female, which was discernible only by the subtle curves of her body beneath her robe.

"I am now the ranking officer on the ship. I am Ti."

"Okay, Ti. A simple question: do you want to live? Do you want the others on this vessel to live?"

Ti didn't answer, only continued to stare open-mouthed in Jason's direction. Jason brought his weapon up and pointed it in the direction of the others.

Finally she replied, "Yes, but that is a ridiculous question. I want to live. Naturally, all of us want to live."

"Do you all have the same empathic abilities?"

"Of course. We're born with them."

"Why haven't you used them on us, as both your captain and first mate did?"

"Think about it. Even you could probably figure that out for yourself."

Terrific, Jason thought, *a Mau with an attitude*. "Answer the question."

"Can you imagine a vessel with close to two hundred crewmembers manipulating each other's emotions? We do not allow that in our culture."

"But we're the enemy, not your crewmembers," Jason said.

"Let's say three of us attacked you in this way, but came at it differently. One uses the emotion of fear, another anguish, and another insecurity. The combined effect would be a jumble of emotions. There's a problem with that. Some emotions counteract others. For this reason, and others, we have clearly-defined combat protocols, just as you would have for any of your weapons. It's not a difficult concept. Think about it ... can your vessel's cook give the order to fire nuclear missiles?"

Jason almost smiled at that. "So you're the one in charge now. What's stopping you? Why haven't you continued to attack us—or our ship, for that matter?"

"We have evaluated the technology on your vessel. It is Caldurian, yes? Even with three warships, we cannot defeat you. Added to that, twice you personally have overcome *Mon-Ge*, which is what we call our empathetic ability. I may look different than you do, Captain, but I am not stupid."

Jason was somewhat encouraged by the Mau officer's candidness. "On the other Mau vessel, the first officer said the Mau sought the Craing out, asked to join their fleet."

Ti didn't respond.

Jason continued. "Theirs is a fleet that moves throughout the universe, killing all those that oppose them. Billions are killed. That or subjugated into slavery."

"Our planet has not been attacked, our people are untouched. Why do you think this is so?" she asked.

"Because you've preemptively made it unnecessary."

"Yes. We have made the most intelligent decision based on our situation. A decision that has saved our planet."

"And you're okay with that? You can sleep at night knowing you're supporting such a diabolical race of people?"

Ti was quiet for a moment, her expressionless face staring at Jason. "We are not monsters, Captain. In fact, by our nature, we are a caring people."

"I'll have to take your word for that," Jason replied. He wanted the three Mau vessels, but more importantly, he wanted the Mau to willingly join the Alliance side. "I have a dilemma. With close to two thousand enemy Craing vessels headed this way, I have no time to screw around. You're either with us or against us." He was being hailed.

"Go for Cap—"

"The other cruisers are closing on us," Perkins said. "They're at battle stations, sir."

"Understood."

Jason looked at the Mau officer and then at the others. "As I was saying, you're either with us or against us. Join us, join the Alliance and fight the Craing. We'll do our best to protect you, your people."

"I am but a low-level officer. The decision to join the Craing was a political one. A decision that affects billions of Mau."

"Live or die, it's your choice. But it's a choice you'll have to make right now."

Ti held stationary for several long moments, then spoke. "I communicated with the other officers on this vessel, as well as with those on the other two. We choose life."

The Mau bridge crew moved slowly, gliding back to their respective stations. Five Craing light-battle cruisers came into view on the bridge's central display.

Orion stepped in closer to Jason and spoke to him via NanoCom. "Cap, do you trust her? They may be sacrificing their own ships here."

"We could easily have self-destructed at any time," Ti said, turning back in their direction.

Orion made a face behind her visor, evidently not liking her thoughts being read so easily.

The Mau crew moved somewhat more quickly now, and bony fingers tapped quickly at their station consoles. The Mau ship vibrated and Jason saw multiple missiles now targeting all five of the Craing warships. The Craing, without hesitation, fired off salvos.

"Go for Cap," Jason answered an incoming hail.

"You want us to phase-shift *The Lilly* out of here, Captain?" Perkins asked, his voice nervous and several octaves higher than usual.

"What's the ETA on the incoming?"

"Less than one minute, Captain."

"Stay put, but keep this channel open."

Ti moved closer to Jason and put a hand on his wrist. "You fear our missiles won't penetrate the Craing shields and that our own shields are inadequate. But you need not worry."

Jason listened to the open channel audio feed coming from *The Lilly*'s bridge and the excited exchange of verbal commands and updates from the various bridge stations. All the chatter was in stark contrast to the near-silent battle updating on the Mau bridge. Jason watched as they continued to work at their stations. Perhaps what was exchanged in their telepathic relay wasn't all that different.

A second, and then a third barrage, emanated from the three Mau destroyers. Plasma fire erupted from both sides—Craing and Mau alike. One by one, incoming missiles were targeted. Jason listened and watched his HUD. He heard Perkins yell for everyone to brace for impact. Both Jason and Orion reached out and grabbed for something solid to hold on to. The ship lurched as each incoming missile connected with the Mau ship's shields.

"Shields are holding," came McBride's voice back on *The Lilly*, but he'd spoken too soon. The display flashed white; blast debris, with large chunks from one of the Mau ships, flew into view on the display.

Immediately, Jason hailed Rizzo, his heart pounding. Losing the young SEAL would be a crushing, sad, blow. Thinking about it, Jason knew Rizzo and his team were still on board one of the Mau ships. No reply.

Two more flashes. The display showed two of the Craing light cruisers were now mere space dust. Then three more consecutive flashes. All five Craing vessels had been destroyed.

Chapter 27

A security team of three armed SEALs now stood at the back of the bridge. Ti was being adamant and now hovered uncomfortably close to Jason as he prepared to leave.

"Locking us out of our own helm, and other key ship system controls, exhibits bad faith. With our latest actions, haven't we shown we are committed to helping you? Isn't it obvious we've passed beyond the point of no return?"

Although her expression never changed, it was clear to Jason she was furious.

She continued, her frightening white face mere inches from his own: "We have alienated ourselves from our own fleet, from our own people! What more confirmation of loyalty do you need?"

Looking at her, Jason remained calm, wondering how she managed to speak when her mouth was frozen into an opened-wide perpetual grimace. *Perhaps she was communicating through something at the back of her throat?*

"I appreciate that, truly I do. But taking such an action when held at gunpoint is far different than doing so voluntarily," Jason said, really needing to get off their bridge. "Give it time. Prove yourselves."

"How do we do that when our freedom is so restricted?" she asked.

"I don't know. I'll think about it—I promise. But right now I need to attend to my dead crewmembers."

"All six of them? And what about the two hundred of our own lost crew?"

That stopped Jason. He'd been insensitive with regard to the tremendous sacrifice Ti and her crew had recently made. But this was war and right now he needed to attend to the needs of his own crew.

"We won't forget what happened here today. What you have sacrificed. But I have to go. We'll talk later."

Orion and Jason phase-shifted back to *The Lilly*.

* * *

Orion and Jason entered the bridge together. Jason felt the heaviness that came from losing not only a close friend but a valued seaman too. The XO stood and Jason took his place in the command chair.

"So what happened exactly?"

Ricket turned away from the Mau remote piloting station. "The Mau destroyer took multiple nearly simultaneous hits, Captain. First her aft shields went and then the others."

Jason needed to accept the inevitable. Rizzo and the others were gone. At least it was quick, he thought, or fairly quick.

"So, the destruction wasn't really instantaneous?"

Ricket stared, but he didn't comment.

"How long do you think it would take a trained SEAL such as Rizzo to access his HUD's *Return to Last Location* function?"

Everyone on the bridge stopped what they were doing and looked at Jason. Orion furrowed her brow and turned back to her station. As she started to enter something, Ricket moved in, pushing her aside. She moved over to the next station.

Ricket spoke while he worked: "*Return to Last Location* function would not necessarily bring him back to *The Lilly*. With multiple catastrophic explosions, and the fact that both Mau vessels had drifted in space—"

Orion beat him to it. "He could have phase-shifted into open space." She leaned in and continued looking at the display. "Yes! I've got him! Got a signal."

Ricket continued, "We had checked for life signs. None of the team's combat suits showed signs of life, or anything else, for that matter. But checking Nano—"

"Right there," Orion interrupted, pointing up to a new video feed segment on the display. There, among countless chunks of debris, some the size of automobiles, others smaller even than a deck of cards, was a small, man-shaped object floating stationary in space.

"It's intermittent, but Rizzo's nano-devices are definitely showing faint signs of life." Orion got to her feet. "Request permission to take a shuttle out there and pick him up, Cap."

"Granted, but I'm going with you. We'll get Dira on the way."

* * *

Lieutenant Wilson was at the helm of the Caldurian shuttle. Orion, next to him in the copilot's seat, watched out of the forward window. Seated behind them, Jason watched Dira opening and closing her assortment of medical bags, checking their contents, and readying her supplies. She glanced up and caught Jason looking at her.

"You're staring again."

"Nah, maybe I'm just making sure you're doing everything correctly," Jason replied with the hint of a smile.

"Oh, okay. Well, let me know if you see anything amiss," she replied, continuing with her work.

"There he is!" Orion said, pointing straight ahead.

Jason and Dira, both dressed in combat suits, headed aft. Jason took one of the larger medical bags from Dira and waited for her to pass by him into the cramped airlock.

"Cramped in here," she said. "I don't think we'll all fit with Rizzo, especially if he can't stand."

Wilson's voice announced over their comms that Rizzo's body would soon be right outside the airlock hatch.

"Stay in here and I'll pass him in to you. Get to work on him. After the airlock closes, I'll join you."

Dira nodded and watched through the aft porthole as Wilson backed the shuttle in close to Rizzo's body.

The airlock depressurized and the rear hatch slid open. Tethered with a line and pulling along a second one for Rizzo, Jason pushed off. Not more than ten feet away, Jason was upon Rizzo's body in seconds. He reached out and grabbed Rizzo's arm, pulling him in close so he could clip the other tether line onto a metal ring at his torso.

Rizzo's battle suit was badly pitted, which was caused, no doubt, by shrapnel from the ships exploding apart all around him. As he pulled Rizzo back toward the shuttle, Jason got his first opportunity to look into Rizzo's visor: a visor not only pitted, but cracked right down the middle.

"Crap!" Jason said.

"What is it, what's going on with Rizzo?" Dira asked him, excitedly.

"His helmet is cracked. I think moving him is making it worse. Shit! His helmet is breached," Jason replied. He still had several feet to go and even then the airlock would take another minute or two of precious time. He hailed Ricket.

"Go for Ricket."

"I need to phase-shift into Medical ... he has only seconds to live."

"Hold on to him and phase-shift to the coordinates I'm providing."

"Give them to Dira too—we'll need her."

Almost forgetting to unclip their tethers, Jason took a firm hold of Rizzo's arm and phase-shifted to Ricket's new coordinates.

They phase-shifted to Medical on *The Lilly*. Both Jason and Rizzo landed on their sides in the middle of the room and hit the deck hard. Jason moved over to Rizzo and started to remove the latches that secured his helmet to the collar mechanism. Rizzo's eyes came open and he struggled, seemingly unable to breathe. As he jerked and flailed, Jason couldn't catch hold of the last latch. Eyes bulging, Rizzo stared back at Jason terrified. Then Dira was at his side.

"Hold him still!" she barked.

She got her fingers under the final latch and it sprang free. She pulled his helmet up and away from his head and Rizzo sucked in a long breath of air. His eyes closed and his body went limp.

"We need to get him out of this suit and into the MediPod," she said.

Jason was already at work doing just that.

Chapter 28

"This thing was never meant to cloak something the size of a fucking luxury liner," Bristol yelled down from the catwalk. "You should have two, or even three, toric-cloaking devices for this to be done right."

Keeping his eyes on the device, Stalls didn't bother to look up at his brother. "That wasn't my question. Again, will it work?" he asked, while eight of his men continued trying to position the unwieldy device into its designated compartment on board *Her Majesty*.

Bristol shrugged. "It's a crap shoot. Look who you have installing it. I wouldn't want these morons moving a couch, let alone one of the most advanced technological devices ever made."

Stalls temporarily lost his condescending smile and glanced up at Bristol. "Do not disrespect your fellow crewmembers; it's not only rude, it's a good way to get dead."

Bristol realized that several of the sweat-drenched, out-of-breath pirates below were now looking up at him. *Shit*. He really needed to watch himself. He was already hated by most of the crew. He could very well end up with a knife in his throat.

"How long before we can test it?" Stalls asked.

Bristol stood back and surveyed the progress. "Well, the hardest part, securing the micro-webbing around the outside of the hull, is done. The optical power converters have been installed and tested. An interface and control panel has been added to the bridge. So, it's basically up to these geniuses of yours to finish up mounting the device."

* * *

Bristol tried to look disinterested but had to admit that he too was excited to see if the thing would work. He watched his brother growing more and more impatient.

Captain Stalls had changed his clothes for the big event. Now, wearing a buttoned white shirt, with an elaborate ruffled collar and overly snug black trousers, Stalls strutted back and forth in front of the now-installed control device.

"Surely we must be ready to try it out now?" Stalls erupted, first looking at the control panel and then to Bristol.

Bristol shrugged. "How will you know if it's really working? Can you deploy a probe, get an off-ship perspective?"

"Yes, of course we have a probe," Stalls replied, but he glanced at Pike just the same. Pike nodded almost imperceptibly, and returned to what he was doing at his station.

"Good ... okay, we'll send out a probe," Stalls said.

"Captain, we've got an approaching freighter ten light minutes out. Looks to have a full load. Shall we intersect?"

Stalls gestured for Pike to put it up on the display. "What a relic. No, I've been more than explicit. We're en route to Earth. The sooner we can get underway, the better."

"We could disable her, grab her cargo on the way back," Pike suggested.

"Are you all seriously that obtuse?" Bristol chimed in. "Why not try out the device on a real subject?"

Stalls let that sink in for a moment and nodded appreciatively. "Yes, that's an excellent idea, Bristol. Pike, have the rest of the fleet hang back. Set an intersecting course for the freighter."

* * *

The freighter's bridge was dingy and Brian felt claustrophobic. The bridge crew consisted of two guys in dirty T-shirts and Betty, who in any normal situation would have definitely caught his eye.

He wiped at something wet on his cheek and saw a trail of yellowish-green pus smeared on his sleeve. *Terrific*, he thought to himself, *my eye ... no, that's gone—my eye socket is infected.*

"You need a medic," Betty said, dropping a tray of food down in front of Brian.

"What's this?"

"Same stuff we eat," she replied.

"What about him?" Brian asked, nodding toward the hopper.

"What about him?" she retorted, looking at the scaly green alien with contempt. "He's already eaten."

"Yeah, I guess he has."

As foul a creature as the hopper might be, he was the only thing keeping the crew at bay. Brian had even been able to catch a few hours of sleep.

Betty crossed her arms and continued to look at the hopper. "We don't want him on the bridge."

"Then you'll have to get used to it. Where I go, he goes. Anyway, he's not doing anything." Brian looked over at the hopper, who had curled up into a ball, apparently asleep.

"What do you call him? What's his name?"

Brian shrugged. "I don't call him anything. If he has a name, I don't know what it is, or care."

She shook her head in the hopper's direction, then looked down at Brian. "That eye of yours. You'll be dead soon. What are we supposed to do with him then? We all saw what he did to the captain."

"To start, I'd be nice to him."

"Vessel's approaching," the T-shirted guy on the right said.

"It's coming up as a luxury liner.

T-shirted guy number two made a face. "I'm getting significant weapons signatures. If it's a luxury liner, it's packing some major firepower."

"At what point will someone actually pull it up on the screen?" Brian asked nobody in particular.

Betty moved to the nearest station and the front display flickered and came alive. Sure enough, it was *Her Majesty*. He couldn't imagine a less welcome sight.

"Do you have weapons capability on this freighter?"

"Nothing substantial. Nothing that would make a dent in that liner. Why would we want to, anyway?" she asked.

"Because those are pirates. The same ones that captured me—and your captain too, for that matter."

"They're charging weapons."

"Can't you take evasive moves, get us out of here?" Brian asked with urgency.

"We're a freighter, remember? What exactly did you have in mind?" Betty snapped back.

All eyes were on the display when *Her Majesty* disappeared.

"Where the hell did it go?" Brian yelled.

Betty and both T-shirted guys checked their readings.

"She's gone," Betty said, breathing a sigh of relief.

* * *

"They're not seeing us, Captain. As far as they know, we've left the sector," Pike said.

Stalls smiled and looked over to Bristol. "Good work, little brother. You know, with this device, nothing can defeat us. Nothing."

"What should we do with the freighter, Captain?" Pike asked.

"You say she's got a full load?"

"Looks to be some kind of grain," Pike replied. "Probably took them months to accumulate that quantity," was only muttered, an afterthought that would be disregarded.

"I guess it would be a shame to waste it. Could bring us a healthy bounty." Stalls watched the old freighter in silence for several moments. "Go ahead, take out her drives. Make sure her cargo holds remain undamaged."

"Yes, Captain."

Three short plasma bursts targeted the aft section of the freighter; a large explosion followed. The freighter, almost as long as *Her Majesty*, was propelled in the opposite direction.

"What the hell just happened?" Stalls barked.

"We must have hit a propellant tank. The good news is she seems to be heading in our same direction, toward Earth. We can still grab her on our way back."

"Fine. No more distractions. By this time tomorrow, I want to visit a place called San Bernardino."

Chapter 29

Ricket finished retrofitting all three Mau warships for remote piloting and was now back on *The Lilly*'s bridge. Heading back to Trumach, Jason felt they'd accomplished a good day's work. Certainly the Mau were an odd bunch, and not easy to look at, but they were able fighters and the technology on their three destroyers was substantially more advanced than anything the Craing had brought to bear. Getting those other Mau vessels, close to five hundred of them, to join the Alliance could go a long way toward defeating the Craing fleet. A fleet that would be upon them in less than twelve hours.

Jason headed to his ready room; he was due to speak with his father. They would provide each other with updates on their current situations. By the time Jason got situated at his desk in front of his virtual display, the connection had already been made, and the admiral was waiting for him.

"Sorry to keep you waiting, Dad. Did I get the time wrong?"

"No, but we're about to move out and only have a few minutes to talk. I need to bring you up to speed on our readiness and hear what's going on there."

"On my end," Jason said, "the Craing fleet was farther along than we had estimated, almost ready to enter Allied space. We've got them turned around now and heading right for us."

"And where's that?" the admiral asked.

"Trumach, the rhinos' home world. Seven Craing ships are in the area, as well as three ships from a planet called Carz-Mau. They've aligned with the Craing and, unfortunately, have brought the fleet size closer to two thousand warships."

"I know the Mau; scary-looking bunch. What the hell are they doing with the Craing?" the admiral groused.

"Apparently, they figured it was a foregone conclusion that the Craing could not be defeated. They preemptively joined their ranks to protect themselves from attack."

"That does complicate things. Fifteen hundred Craing ships were bad enough."

"Well, we've captured three of their vessels here in Trumach space."

"You did what?" the admiral asked, obviously irritated. "And what about the seven Craing ships?"

"All destroyed." Jason held up his hands as if surrendering. "I know, I wasn't supposed to engage the Craing at this point, but there really wasn't any alternative. The good news is the rest of their fleet is coming to investigate. That'll give you more time to position yourselves in Allied sectors."

"What didn't you understand about not engaging the Craing fleet?"

"Unavoidable, you would have done the same," Jason said.

The admiral stared back at Jason for a long moment. "Tell me about the rhinos."

"Two Craing light cruisers were in the process of offloading several thousand Red rhinos brought in from a sister planet. Traveler tells me they've been at war for as long as anyone can remember."

"Let me guess, you intervened."

"Again, no choice. I'm on my way back to Trumach now," Jason replied. "There's a temporary truce between the Reds and the Greys, but it's tenuous at best. I'd like to get the Reds to switch sides. We'll see."

"Certainly sounds like you've been busy," the admiral said, his brow furrowed. "On my end, things are far less exciting, but good progress has been made. The outpost fleet has assembled and currently sits in space above the moon. Much of the original Craing crew is back on board their ships, but concessions needed to be made."

"Concessions?"

"Namely, they want to migrate. When Overlord Glenn was alive he'd promised them they'd be able to migrate to a small Craing settlement. We need to make good on that promise once we've dealt with the Craing fleet."

"And you've agreed?"

"Of course, what else could I do? I've packed as many Alliance military personnel onto those ships as possible; basically, it's on-the-job training—so we're not left crewless once this is over."

"Sounds only fair," Jason answered back.

"Yeah, well, we didn't have much of a choice. Now for the Dreadnaught, or, I should say, the *Independence*: her repairs are complete. Even the drives are now operational, although they haven't been fully tested."

"And a crew?" Jason asked.

"That was the tricky part. We don't have nearly the Craing crew complement to run all the ship's systems. It's a skeleton crew at best. With that said, we do have three thousand-plus U.S. Army, Marines and Naval troops on board. The military brass in Washington insisted, and I can't really blame them."

Jason didn't respond, but felt a pang of guilt knowing that those boys most likely wouldn't be going home again. The Craing would target that big ship from the get-go.

Jason and his father continued talking strategy and fleet logistics for the upcoming engagement. It was clear to both of them that their efforts would still come up short.

"I've reestablished connections, relationships, with many of the Allied leaders. Not all are willing to join forces again, preferring to keep a low profile and hope the Craing pass them by. Latest estimates have us at close to eight hundred-fifty warships, including the *Independence*. Jason, needless to say, *The Lilly* will have to be the deciding factor here. We'll need the kind of out-of-the-box thinking and good luck that you saw at the edge of our solar system. For that reason, I'm giving you as much leeway as necessary."

"Understood. How much time will you need once you've arrived in Allied space?"

"You'll need to keep the fleet busy for at least another day. You'll also have to stay in one piece so you can help us to hold the line there," the admiral said.

"When are you leaving?"

"As soon as I get off the line with you. We're ready to go."

"Good luck, Dad."

"You too, son."

Chapter 30

Nan and Mollie walked through the double front doors of the now completed pre-manufactured home. Both of their jaws dropped at what Teardrop had managed to accomplish in the time span of less than a week. Teardrop, hovering in front of them, was there to greet them and handed Nan several sets of keys.

"Would you like a review of the home's features and capabilities?" Teardrop asked.

Nan nodded, but was surprised by the drone's use of the word *capabilities*.

"Before we begin, please provide a name for these premises."

"What?" Nan asked.

"Oh, let me! I'll do it," Mollie said.

Nan and Teardrop turned toward Mollie.

"How about Bag End? You know, Bilbo's house. Come on, Mom ... Bag End from the Hobbit movie?"

"Oh. Okay, I guess. Bag End it is," Nan said, sounding somewhat indifferent.

What first caught Nan's eye upon entering the home's expansive great room were the stunning furnishings. She had not specified the furniture and was looking forward to handling that aspect herself.

"How did you decide what furniture to buy?"

"The Architectural Digest and other home magazines in your bathroom. You had made notes and circled numerous items," Teardrop replied, gliding further into the house.

Nan and Mollie looked at each other and smiled. Nan had

to admit it: she couldn't have done a better job furnishing the room herself. Not just the modern, yet classic, pieces Teardrop had selected, but the design treatments as well. There were an abundance of natural elements seamlessly incorporated into the open-concept plan. Wide-plank hardwood flooring was laid throughout. Across the room was a fireplace, surrounded in thousands of inlaid river rocks that reached up toward the forty-foot-tall ceiling. To the right and left were cherry wood shelves lined with hundreds of books, old classics to the latest best sellers. On the ceiling were massive-looking wood beams. Nan guessed they couldn't be real timber. Crisscrossed at the apex of the pitched ceiling, they gave the home an earthy, yet elegant, barn-style feel. Not so unlike Tolkien's Bag End, funnily enough.

Mollie ran, leaping onto a large sectional overly-stuffed leather couch, but her eyes never strayed from what was mounted above the fireplace.

The drone came closer and handed Mollie a complex-looking TV control.

"This is an eighty-four inch, ultra high definition 3D television. The surround sound system and subwoofer have been integrated into the walls and ceiling."

"What's that?" Mollie asked, pointing at the bottom shelf of one of the bookshelves.

"Those are game devices. A PlayStation 4 and an Xbox One ... and those are the most popular games for each," Teardrop said, pointing to the two shelves above the consoles.

Nan was quickly losing her euphoria. "I didn't authorize a budget for any of this extra stuff."

Mollie scowled at her mother and crossed her arms.

"These items, and others we have not talked about yet, were donated."

"What are you talking about? Why on earth would anyone

donate thousands of dollars of electronics?"

"Viewing the respective company's records, I discovered other persons, usually in high management positions, have procured devices without making any payment. I also mentioned their own internal policies, which precluded using that type of activity."

"In other words, you blackmailed them."

"The term blackmail would not be appropriate, since there was no threat, actual or implied. I simply brought the issue to the forefront of their attention."

"Uh huh. Well, let's move on with the tour for now."

Mollie was all smiles again and back at Nan's side.

"Before we move into the kitchen, I'd like to talk about some of the security capabilities."

There was that word again, Nan thought.

Teardrop continued: "Although not easily discernible, you'll notice the small wall panels throughout the house."

Nan hadn't noticed them at all. Only several inches wide each, they matched the wall color. But now that she knew what to look for, she could see dozens of them—some high up, others down near the floor.

"This is one area where it was necessary to utilize Caldurian technology," Teardrop said. "I would like to demonstrate."

Nan shrugged, not sure what he was talking about.

Teardrop moved to the center of the room and said, "Bag End, Intruder alert."

Each of the small panels slid open, their little doors disappearing into recesses in the walls. Small gun barrels appeared, each one moving and tracking Nan, Molly and Teardrop's every movement.

A female voice, emanating from all around, said: "No intruder detected. Property perimeters have not been breached.

Returning to nominal mode."

"What was that?" Nan asked, looking up and turning around.

"That is the artificial intelligence, the one you have named Bag End," Teardrop said.

"Seriously, this house has an AI?"

"Yes."

"She sounds like the one we had on *The Lilly*," Mollie said. "My dad didn't like her much. She annoyed him."

For some reason that made Nan laugh. She thought of Jason hearing that same bitchy voice the first time he walked in the door and laughed even harder.

"It's not funny, Mom."

"No, you're right, it's not." She stifled her grin and followed them into the adjoining kitchen.

The kitchen was large, with thick wood cutting-board counters, all the best stainless appliances, and several things Nan recognized from *The Lilly*.

"Okay, this is crazy. A food replicator too?" Nan asked with exasperation.

"Yes."

"Oh my God!" Mollie loudly exclaimed.

Nan spun on her heels, fists clenched and ready to fend off an attack. Mollie stood at the floor-to-ceiling rear windows pointing outside.

Relieved, Nan actually wasn't surprised. She'd watched Teardrop's construction frenzy in the backyard the previous day. Wanting it to be a surprise for Mollie, she wasn't disappointed in her daughter's over-the-top response. Nan opened the sliding glass door and they walked out onto the back porch. The pool was big and blue and inviting. At its far end the zero-horizon edge gave way to the San Bernardino foothills in the distance. Although much of the scrapyard was still visible from this angle, it wasn't too bad. Either that or she was just getting used to it. Then something else caught her eye.

"What's that Teardrop, at the edge of the property?" Nan pointed at a metallic structure ten feet high—she was sure she hadn't seen it before.

"That is a turret-mounted plasma cannon."

Chapter 31

The Lilly was back on Trumach and parked alongside the three large Mau warships.

Jason, still wearing his captain's jumpsuit, made his way down the forward gangway and noticed several thousand Red rhinos had set up makeshift campsites across the green, open prairie landscape in the distance. It amazed him how similar this planet was to Earth. Billy and Traveler greeted Jason, both agitated.

"All right, what's all the commotion?" Jason asked.

Traveler was the first to speak up. "We must be free to fight the Red beasts and restore honor to our kind. Again, our mates have been raped, our offspring massacred."

Billy held up a hand. "We got here pretty early on and we didn't see much of that sort of thing. But I guess it's possible. On your orders we got a truce going, but they've been chafing at the bit to kill each other ever since."

Jason noticed a large purple bruise under Billy's right eye. "What the hell happened to your face? How on Earth could you get a shiner like that wearing a combat helmet?"

"Removed my helmet for a while, then got between a Grey and a Red. It wasn't pretty," Billy said, lighting up a cigar and letting the smoke envelop his head.

"Let me guess, you took off your helmet in order to light up one of those stink bombs."

Jason turned his attention back to Traveler. "Where are your warriors? I don't see them out there."

Traveler turned and pointed in the opposite direction. "There, we do not mix with the other kind."

Sure enough, a smaller campsite had been erected several hundred yards away.

"The Grey rhinos are uneasy, ready to return home to their mates and offspring. They do not understand why they must wait here."

"That wasn't our agreement. The Craing fleet will be here in less than a day," Jason said.

Traveler looked uneasy. "I cannot hold them back ... their first obligation is to their mates. I, too, have a similar responsibility."

Jason began to walk in the direction of their new camp, and Billy and Traveler hurried to catch up. Over the last few months, Jason had come to know most of Traveler's Grey rhinos and there was mutual respect between them. As much as he'd like to permit them to return to their homes, he needed their help one last time. As they entered the camp, the rhinos moved into a circle around them.

"I'm going to make this short. Traveler tells me you want to return to your homes, your families. That was not our agreement. Our agreement stated that you must first help us defend against the Craing fleet, and only then would you return home. But if returning home is that important to you, you may now leave. Thank you for your help. Good luck." With that, Jason turned to leave.

Traveler stood up tall, hands on hips. "We thank you. We have been proud to fight at your side, Captain."

Jason stopped and looked up at his friend. "Don't thank me, thank the Reds. I'm on my way over to them now." With that said, Jason continued walking away.

"Why would we thank the Reds?" Traveler called after him.

Jason stopped and turned to face the rhino leader. "From what I understand they have agreed to fight at our side, fight the Craing. You can thank them yourself, because they'll be protecting your homes, your mates and offspring, while you cower under your mud domes. By the size of them, they're probably better in battle anyway. Goodbye. Stay safe, my friend."

Jason quickly turned away before any of them saw his smile.

Traveler looked to his warriors, then back toward Jason, who was walking quickly toward the Red rhino camp. Arguing began and loud voices broke out amongst them. Rustling Leaves was the first one to chase after Jason, then others rushed to follow.

"We cannot allow the Reds to fight on our behalf, Captain," Traveler bellowed, also hurrying after them.

Once again, Jason turned to see that half the rhino-warriors were following behind him. The rest were still arguing among themselves. He needed all of them.

Raising his voice so all would hear, Jason asked, "Just curious. How will your mates feel about the Reds fighting on their behalf? Perhaps next time, instead of running from them, they'll be welcoming them into their domes."

Traveler quickly caught up and huffed angrily at Jason's side. "I know what you are doing, Captain. I do not believe the Reds have agreed to fight against the Craing. They certainly have not agreed to defend Trumach."

"Do you want to take that chance? I suggest, Traveler, before I make it over to their camp that you and your warriors return to *The Lilly*. Let the Reds see that you are preparing for battle."

The snorting increased. Traveler slowed and finally directed his rhinos in the direction of *The Lilly*. Glancing at Jason, he snorted several more times and followed the last of the rhinos into the ship.

Billy, who'd maintained some distance, once again walked by Jason's side.

"You're a sly Diablo, mi amigo," he said.

"It worked, didn't it? Now let's see if it'll work twice." They headed off to find the leader of the Reds.

Chapter 32

"Yes, as you just witnessed, the Greys are now on board my ship, readying themselves to fight for the freedom of the rhinos, not only on Trumach, but Mangus as well."

Jason stood before their leader: a Red rhino named Hangs to Ground. He easily stood eleven feet tall and towered over Jason. Around his hips he wore a belt with a variety of trophy skulls that dangled and clanked together as he moved. At least one of the skulls looked to be human. As Jason spoke, the large beast began to pace back and forth, listening to what Jason had to say. Jason's attention was drawn to the Red rhino's maleness, which, in fact, was so conspicuously large that it did at times touch the ground as he walked.

Jason continued. "Traveler said something to the effect that the Greys will be triumphant against the Craing in battle. Later, the Greys will return home proud, for they will have protected their mates, offspring, and the weaker ones of their kind."

Just like with the Greys earlier, the other Reds had crowded around and looked on as their leader took in that information. Their response was no less dramatic. A chorus of loud huffs and snorts, along with bursts of steamy snot, filled the air. They yelled and conveyed their indignation toward their leader. Obviously the thought of Greys fighting on their behalf was unacceptable.

In the end, the Reds took even less convincing than the Greys. Hangs to Ground and his Red teammates agreed to join forces with Jason in fighting the Craing and, by doing so, in defending their home world and all rhinos.

The rest was up to Jason: how to configure the logistics of

transporting over two thousand-plus Red rhinos into an area with enough space. It would be a tight fit. They would have to be split up and squeezed into the holds of the three Mau vessels.

* * *

Jason looked around the ready room at his fellow officers and key personnel. This would be their last chance to meet as a group before going into battle. Ricket, the last to join them, climbed up on his seat and the meeting got underway.

"The Craing fleet will enter this sector within the next two hours. Long-range scans indicate they're coming in force. They've lost ten warships and they're absolutely going to seek our blood. I say good, let them come. Let's finish this."

Billy said, "It seems to me our biggest obstacle will be troop movement, logistics, getting our assault teams where they need to be."

Perkins addressed Billy's comment: "We'll be relying heavily on *The Lilly*, as well as the shuttles and their ability to phase-shift. Our own teams can phase-shift individually or as groups and should be prepared for doing that on a moment's notice."

Dira sat directly across from Jason and her eyes rarely left his. She looked small and withdrawn. As the Craing approached them, her home world was once again in jeopardy. She was obviously worried.

"Captain, would it be possible to snare us several more medical techs? I have a feeling we're going to get overwhelmed in Medical," Dira asked.

"If you have an idea of who you want, go ahead and work with the XO to make the necessary transfers."

"Captain," Orion asked, looking more serious than Jason had ever seen her, "can we beat them? There's so few of us and so many if them."

"Look, everyone, I'm not going to sugarcoat this. We're in for a hell of a battle. Yes, we'll be outnumbered again. Maybe even two to one. But considering how we've managed to beat far worse odds in the past, I'm hopeful. Think about it: the Earth's outpost fleet has a rebuilt Dreadnaught. Our Alliance fleet, on top of the advantage of *The Lilly* and the two new Mau warships, has the addition of one thousand Red rhino warriors. Let's just take it one day at a time." Jason wished he'd been able to paint a brighter picture, but who would he be kidding? The situation was dire. Most if not all of them weren't going to make it. The odds were just too stacked against them.

One by one the officers and section heads nodded, then went about discussing their responsibilities for the upcoming battle. By the end of the meeting they all knew what was expected of them and their respective teams. Jason looked around the room, letting his eyes rest on Ricket.

"You've kept yourself scarce the last few days, Ricket. Anything you want to add? Any updates?"

Ricket didn't answer for a moment, then said, "No, captain, nothing new to report."

Surprised, Jason dismissed everyone else but asked Ricket to stay behind.

"What the hell's going on with you, Ricket? Are you still a member of this team, or not?"

Ricket had removed his baseball cap and, childlike, was fiddling with it in his lap. Something was very wrong and it was affecting his duties. Jason knew he desperately wanted to transform himself, break away from the confines of his two hundred-year-old mechanized form.

"I apologize, Captain. I'm afraid there is something wrong with me."

"Yeah, I see that."

"It is debilitating."

"Obviously."

"What does one do when enveloped in sadness, consumed by it, but the tears can never come?"

"Where have you been the last week? What were you doing?"

"Thinking."

"I don't think we can, I can, defeat the Craing without you being one hundred percent present. You know how I count on you."

"Yes, Captain. Again, I'm sorry."

"How long would the procedure take?"

Ricket looked up. What resembled a glimmer of hope spread across his mechanical features.

"No more than an hour in the new MediPod. But the mortality rate is still fifty-fifty."

"You're no good to me like this, to anyone. If it's truly what you want, then go. Let's go right now and get you whole again."

"Thank you, Captain." Ricket replaced the baseball cap onto his head and Jason stood and waited for him to crawl down from his chair. Together, they left the ready room and headed to Medical.

Something wasn't adding up for Jason. "How is it this procedure, which seems to be incredibly complex, only takes an hour, while Rizzo has been recovering in a MediPod for over a day?"

Entering Medical, Ricket stopped and looked up at Jason.

"What is considered my consciousness—memories, feelings, emotions—will be put into stasis. Temporarily stored. That is the most difficult aspect. This cyborg body will be destroyed in the process, eliminated. Based on my own original DNA, and with the help of billions of nanites, a completely new body will be formed. So there's nothing to repair or heal. That process would take significantly longer."

Dira, as if she'd been expecting them, stood at the side of the largest of the MediPods, its clamshell top already open. Seeing her concerned face brought the full seriousness of the situation to bear for Jason. A tear rolled down her cheek, which she quickly brushed away. A pained smile crossed her face as she helped Ricket climb up into the overly large compartment.

A lump the size of a grapefruit filled Jason's throat. Things were happening too fast. Perhaps he should stop it now, before things went too far.

Again, childlike, Ricket looked up from the MediPod. He'd removed his baseball cap and held it out toward Jason.

"Will you keep this for me, Captain?" Ricket asked.

"Sure. You'll know where to find me when you get out of this thing," Jason said with a reassuring smile.

The MediPod began to close. Ricket shut his eyes as if going to sleep, which Jason knew wasn't the case. Cyborgs never sleep.

The clamshell top shut with an audible sucking thump. Through one of the MediPod's small windows Ricket's face was visible, illuminated by a dim light.

Dira touched Jason's hand. "Ricket's been coming here for days. Sometimes I'd find him where I'd left him the night before—programming this thing, making last minute updates. You wanted to know where Ricket's been? He's been right here."

Chapter 33

"Captain, the outpost fleet will be making their transition to Allied space in fifteen seconds," Perkins reported.

"And the Craing?"

"They'll be within weapons' distance in about forty-five minutes."

Jason sat back in the command chair and watched the display in silence. Everything came down to this moment and he hoped they were ready. The first part of their plan was a simple one: keep the Craing fleet occupied here while the EOUPA and Allied fleets converged on their flank, a mere ten light years away. The second part of the plan would be based on previous confrontations. Offensively, again, they'd be taking the battle right into the Craing fleet, striking their deadly Dreadnaughts from within, with both SEALs and rhinos. *The Lilly* would be constantly maneuvering, dropping off troops and moving into hotspots, as needed. Both shuttles had phase-shift capability. Their newer, larger Caldurian shuttle, recently renamed the *Epcot*, was currently loaded up with rhino-warriors; the remaining original shuttle, named *Oracle*, was packed with Billy's SEALs. Both shuttles would drop off and pick up troops on a continual basis. With phase-shift parameters now expanded to three thousand miles, *The Lilly* and the shuttles would have far-reaching capabilities. The two Mau vessels, which Jason simply referred to as *Mau One* and *Mau Two*, were currently packed with two thousand Red rhinos. Each Mau ship had set aside extra hold space out of which the shuttles would phase-shift.

"Let's go to general quarters, XO."

"Aye, Captain. The outpost fleet are in the process of calling up wormhole coordinates from the interchange, sir."

"As soon as the admiral has made the transition, open a channel to him."

"Aye, Captain," Seaman Gordon said from Comms.

His father's decision to personally command the outpost's fleet, as well as the entire contingent of Allied forces, was of concern to Jason. Selfishly, he didn't want his father placed in harm's way. Sitting as he was there in the Dreadnaught *Independence*, he and his crew would immediately be targeted by the Craing. But he knew his father needed to redeem himself after their devastating defeat to the same Craing fleet months earlier. The truth was, the crew knew their odds of survival were slim. Jason's thoughts turned to Nan and Mollie back home. With their near certain impending defeat here in deep space, how long before the Craing would bring a hell-storm down on Earth?

"The outpost fleet has made the transition, sir. A channel is open to the admiral."

His father's face appeared on the forward segments of the display, but something was wrong. The admiral's attention was on someone else on the Dreadnaught's bridge.

"Admiral?" Jason asked.

"Just hold on," he snapped back, still working something out with his crew.

"Captain, um, we have a problem," Orion said from Tactical.

The admiral's face had turned grey. "Jason, we're still trying to figure things out here, but we're not where we're supposed to be."

"What do you mean? Where the hell are you?"

Orion chimed in again with, "Cap, they're three sectors away, forty-five light years' distance."

"Jason, we're nowhere near where we're supposed to be," the

admiral repeated.

"Maybe you entered the wrong coordinates; try again," Jason said a bit more forcefully than he'd intended.

"You think?" the admiral barked back. "Do you have any other commands for me to follow, Captain?"

The admiral's attention was on someone off-site again. Jason could see his father was close to losing it. "What the hell do you mean we've lost our connection with the interchange?"

The admiral and Jason both looked to each other and said the same thing simultaneously: "Granger!"

"Contact him!" the admiral shot back to someone off screen.

Granger seemed to know whenever we were looking for him, Jason thought. It wasn't an accident he was nowhere to be found.

"I'm betting he already knows about this," Jason said.

"Captain, the Craing fleet—they're splitting into three groups."

"Put it up on the display."

The admiral's video feed moved to the left as a new segment, showing the virtual battle logistics, came alive. In green, and to the right, were *The Lilly* and the two Mau ships. Red icons filled two-thirds of the screen, revealing three distinct groups; two of them were following separate vectors.

"They're attempting to flank us on two sides, Captain," said Orion. A sobering realization hit Jason.

"They knew, Captain," she added.

"Jason," the admiral spoke again, "We're heading your way via FTL. Get out of there. That's an order. We'll fight another day."

Jason, not ready yet to respond, continued to look at the virtual battle logistics. Three groups of Craing warships approached from their front and would soon be alongside; behind them was the beautiful Alcara system, with its three Earth-like planets, two uninhabited gas giant planets and one white dwarf sun. Escaping now would be so easy ... live to fight another day. Jason concentrated on Trumach, the home of Traveler, the rhino-warrior who had endured so much for them, so much for Jason. The thought of the Craing fleet annihilating these beautiful, gemlike planets, with their populations in the millions, was horrific. Did he have a choice? No, not really.

Jason and his father held each other's stare for several moments before Jason slowly shook his head. "Sorry, Dad. Get here as fast as you can."

"I've given you a direct order, son."

"I understand that. But I'm pretty sure if our roles were reversed, you'd proceed similarly. Take a look at what sits behind us. There comes a time when you need to make a stand. Today is that time for me."

Jason watched as his father looked at the same spacial representation of Alcara; he slowly nodded his head in agreement.

"We'll get there as soon as we can. Good luck, son."

Jason signaled to cut the connection.

The Lilly's bridge was quiet, and all heads were turned in Jason's direction. His crew had followed him into battle before, but never had they fought with such terrible odds stacked against them. Well, once again they'd just have to trust him. And, if they survived the day, he would have his revenge. He'd find Granger, follow him into hell itself, if he had to, and then kill him.

Jason sat up straight, smiled back at the faces turned his way, and said, "Who's ready to kick some Craing ass?"

Chapter 34

Causing mayhem, plundering the vessels of the wealthy in open space was one thing, but attacking a planet? Bristol watched as Earth, with its blue oceans and large continents of brown and green, filled the display. This was so beyond wrong! Eston's hatred of one man and the desire for what wasn't his to have had consumed him like nothing Bristol had ever seen.

Pike broke the silence. "Captain, this is strange. Their defense amounts to five Craing light cruisers in upper orbit, and five more of the same lifting off from one of the larger continents."

"So they're aware of our presence. Good. Let's see how they react to two hundred warships encircling their world." Stalls stood up and crossed over to the display table. The five cruisers had merged into a tight formation.

"Smart! When facing insurmountable odds, rally together, pool your resources," Stalls said aloud. "Not that it will do them any good," he chuckled.

"We're being hailed, Captain," Pike said.

"Of course we are. But I'm not in a particularly talkative mood today. Destroy the cruisers. Five nuclear-tipped missiles should do the trick."

"Eston! Just wait a minute; you can't start a war like that," Bristol yelled, getting to his feet.

"I can and I will. And I told you, don't call me that," Stalls snapped back, immediately losing his smile.

"Missiles away, sir," Pike announced.

Bristol watched as the tight missile group moved across space, separating as they closed in on their targets.

"They've countered with a barrage of five of their own, Captain."

Bristol joined his brother at the table and they watched in silence. Three of *Her Majesty*'s missiles were eliminated, but two continued on toward the cluster of cruisers. The remaining missile icons blinked out.

"Missiles ineffective; no damage to the cruisers, Captain."

"I can see that. You see me standing here looking at the same fucking icons you're looking at, don't you?"

"Aye, Captain, I can see you," Pike replied matter-of-factly.

"I'd forgotten about those damn Craing shields," Stalls said.

"Incoming, Captain. Sixty nukes, targeting different ships."

"Well, instruct our fleet commanders to defend themselves. Hopefully they've figured that one out for themselves."

Again they watched in silence. Before the first round of their nukes reached one-third of the way to their targets, an additional barrage, followed by another, was headed toward the pirate ships.

"Why aren't any of our ships firing? What the hell are they doing?"

Pike and two bridge crewmen were on comms, speaking with elevated voices.

Bristol stopped looking at the display table and slowly turned to his brother. "This is what happens when you don't know what the fuck you're doing, big brother," he said.

Stalls whipped a backhand across Bristol's mouth. "I won't warn you again. Brother or not, you will show me respect or find yourself in the brig."

Bristol wiped blood from his split lips and looked at it. He smirked and looked back to the table. One by one the outpost ships' missiles not only found their intended targets, but destroyed them as well.

"We've lost twenty-seven and counting," Pike said.

With the first wave of Craing missiles succeeding, it was clear they were going to lose the battle. Stalls fumed, his face getting redder by the moment.

"Bristol, get the toric-cloak initiated. Pike, put us right in the middle of those cruisers!"

Bristol casually walked to the newly added control panel and tapped in the command.

"We're now invisible. You do realize, though, that once you fire anything, our position will be revealed to them."

"Yes, I know that," Stalls spat back. He then looked over at Pike and said in a lowered voice, "Make sure you hold fire until we're in position."

"Aye."

Stalls looked down to the table. *Her Majesty*'s icon, now a faint yellow, continued on an intersecting course with the five Craing cruisers.

"Load every missile we have—"

"Captain, we'll be in too close, we'd blow ourselves up!"

"Rail-guns then; charge all rail-guns and utilize every plasma cannon we have."

"One hundred and thirty-two of our ships are destroyed so far. We're getting multiple distress calls. There's survivors out there, Captain."

"Well, they'll just have to wait, won't they?"

Her Majesty moved into the middle of the Craing cruisers' formation. Stalls smiled, excitement showing on his face.

"One hundred-eighty vessels lost. The remainder of our ships are deserting, Captain," Pike said.

"Cowards, all of them, cowards."

"Shall we engage the enemy, Captain?"

"Hold a moment longer, let them think they were victorious. Let them put their guard down."

Bristol watched his brother in disgust. They would have not only lost allied ships today, but family members, too ... an uncle, several cousins, and others. Hell, complete clans were wiped out in a matter of seconds. Bristol realized he wasn't alone in his contempt. There was hatred also in the eyes of Stalls' own bridge crew as they watched their captain go totally off the rails.

"Fire! Fire everything we have!"

First, a blaze of plasma bolts, then a continual hail of rail munitions erupted from *Her Majesty*'s impressive array of weaponry. The large ship shook to the point Bristol wondered if it could hold together.

The Craing cruisers were caught off guard. Within seconds, three of their five ships were either dead in space or coming apart at the seams. But the two remaining cruisers were returning fire.

"We're taking damage to decks three through eight. One drive is down and we're open to space at so many locations I can't count them all. Suggest we move out of here while we still can, Captain," Pike said, his easy demeanor completely gone.

Stalls hesitated.

"We need to get the fuck out of here. Now!" Bristol screamed. "Pike, stop firing. Move us out of here and go systems quiet—and pray our toric-cloak doesn't take a shit right in front of them."

Pike didn't wait for Stalls to agree, and he made the course adjustment by engaging the one remaining drive. Slowly, *Her Majesty* moved off into open space.

"Let's just hope they'll stay put and lick their wounds before pursuing us," Bristol said.

Stalls, now somewhat composed, was back seated in his command chair.

"Pike, have my shuttle prepped and ready for flight in ten minutes. Load up coordinates for a location called San

Bernardino, California," Stalls commanded.

He looked down at his shirt and pants and huffed in disgust. "These certainly won't do." With that he was out of his chair and heading off the bridge. "I'll be in my cabin changing. As you were, everyone."

Bristol looked to Pike and then at the others. "You all know he's lost his fucking mind, right? It's not just me; he's totally gone off the deep end, right?"

Although the bridge crew kept silent, they all nodded in agreement.

* * *

In actuality, from start to finish, it took Teardrop close to seven days to complete the construction of the house. As much as Mollie loved the new digs, she protested spending the night there before her father returned.

"Fine, stay in the old house. Let me know how you like the cold shower in the morning. Oh, and try to keep yourself entertained tonight. I'll be in front of the big-screen watching—"

"Okay, okay, I got the point, Mom."

Nan smiled and continued turning strips of bacon in a large frying pan. She loved the new kitchen. She loved the house. She only hoped Jason would, too. He was sentimental in his own way so new was not always better as far as he was concerned.

The sun was setting and an amber glow filtered through windows into the back of the house. A shadow crossed by the large rear windows and both Nan and Mollie looked up.

"What's it doing now?" Mollie asked.

"It never stops. Um, I think Teardrop mentioned something about spraying the external walls with some kind of nanite."

"What's that for?"

"Protective something or other. I don't really know, but it was fairly adamant about getting it completed as soon as possible."

The sliding glass door opened and Teardrop entered.

Mollie turned and smiled. "Well?"

"Hello, Mollie. Hello, Nan."

"Are you finally done?" Nan asked.

"Yes."

"We'd offer you a BLT, but I don't think you eat," Mollie said.

Before Teardrop could answer, the house shook. Immediately, the kitchen and the open family room darkened.

"What's going on, Teardrop?" Nan asked, fear in her voice.

"Security shutters have been engaged."

Sure enough, a metal shutter unrolled, obscuring the outside world.

"We have security shutters?" Mollie asked.

Chapter 35

Jason and Perkins stood together watching as the Craing fleet moved into position.

"Truth is, we don't know how much *The Lilly*'s shields can withstand. Hell, they were damn near impenetrable before," Jason said.

"Still, it's two thousand warships, including three Dreadnaughts, against three ships," Perkins replied.

"Well, if we stick to our plan, we'll be out of sight most of the time."

"And that'll leave the Mau's ships out in the open, like lambs led to the slaughter," Perkins replied.

"That's why we'll need to mix things up a little," Jason said. "We'll have to alter our strategy some. For sure, I could use Ricket's assistance about now."

They continued to look up, turning around to take it all in. Like others on the bridge, Jason was overwhelmed at the sight. Their upgraded wraparound display provided ultra-realism to the scene, as though the top-third of *The Lilly*'s bridge had been opened to space, offering them a 360-degree view of everything around them. The ability to zoom in and out was as simple as making the appropriate hand gesture.

"Change to virtual view," Jason ordered.

The display changed and a logistical representation of symbols and icons took the place of the sun and planets, and a multitude of warships. If possible, it presented an even more daunting viewpoint.

The three approaching Craing formations were a mixture of

heavy and light cruisers, a Dreadnaught, and the Mau warships.

"Why didn't I think of it before?"

"What's that?" Perkins asked.

"The Craing fleet. We know the little bastards force other species to do their fighting for them, like the Serapin-Terplins and those nasty pill bugs we encountered on Halimar that shot shit from their bellies, and the captured rhino-warriors. There must be a thousand more of them on board those ships."

"Probably, and a bunch of other beasts we haven't even encountered yet."

"What if we could turn them?"

"The rhinos?" Perkins asked, not understanding.

"Yes. Turn all those prisoner rhinos against the Craing. But I really need Ricket for this."

"I am here."

Jason and Perkins spun on their heels and turned toward the entrance of the bridge. Dira, leaning against the bulkhead with her arms crossed over her chest, was beaming. Her ear-to-ear smile momentarily stopped Jason's heart. But it was Ricket at her side who'd caught his full attention. Or was it really Ricket? He was the same height, and had more or less the same features, but the mechanical aspects of his visage were gone: he was a cyborg no more! And he was younger, handsome in a Craing-sort of way. And, unlike the modern day Craing and more like the Craing they'd encountered on HAB 12, Ricket had a full head of hair.

"It's about time you got back to work," Jason said, doing his best to keep a straight face.

"Do you have my baseball cap, Captain?"

"Next door, on my desk."

Ricket darted away. Jason met Dira's eyes and mouthed the words *thank you*! She mouthed back *you're welcome* and left, but not before blowing him a silent kiss. Chuckles erupted from around the bridge.

Ricket rushed back in, now wearing his cap. Seeing him again, back with the crew caused several on the bridge, including Jason, to blink away moist eyes. As if on cue, everyone turned their attention back to their stations.

"Are you up to speed on current events?"

"Yes, Captain. I have the same, if not more capabilities than I had before. I've been monitoring communications with the admiral."

"Do you have any idea how we can track down Granger?"

"Granger does not wish to be found, it seems. What is evident is that we never had real control over the installed *interface* communications devices. If I hadn't been so preoccupied I would have—"

"Let's stay focused on the here and now, Ricket. How do we get the outpost fleet where they're supposed to be?"

"Only by working directly with the interface, I'm assuming."

"Can you contact him, or it?"

"No, but I think you can."

"Me?"

"The Zoo, Captain."

"The Drapple."

"Incoming! Multiple groupings ... mixture of nukes and fusion-tipped missiles," Orion exclaimed.

"You know what to do, Gunny. Take them out."

"Aye, Cap."

"Ricket, is there a way to maybe open a channel or something that can go ship-wide? Go out to every Craing ship—Dreadnaughts, light and heavy cruisers, all of them?—and do so simultaneously?"

Ricket contemplated the question, actually chewing on his lip while thinking. "We could get away with it once, Captain;

after that, they'd be wise to it."

"Once is all we need. I need to talk to Traveler." Holding two fingers to his ear, Jason hailed the rhino, hoping he'd figured out how to use his comms by now.

"This is Traveler."

"This is the captain, Traveler. I need to ask you a very important question."

"Yes, ask your question."

"On your home planet, Trumach, I saw the Reds communicating from miles away."

"Yes, Reds and Greys alike do this. It's called—"

Jason cut him off. "I need you now to communicate the same way to all the rhinos on the other ships. The ones held hostage."

"My horn-call will not travel in space, Captain. That is a stupid idea."

Jason almost laughed. "Your NanoCom will be tied to their ships' PA, or public address system."

There was quiet for a moment and then Traveler grunted. "I like this idea. I need to think of what to say."

"Yes," Jason said. "It must be something that will make them revolt against the Craing. That will cause them to join with our forces. You understand?"

"Of course I understand. I know what to say," Traveler replied.

"Let them, Reds and Greys alike, know we're coming. Let them know they will be fighting for their own freedom and the freedom of their home worlds," Jason added.

"Yes, I know what to say, Captain."

Jason looked at Ricket. "Are you set? Can you hook us up, connect us to their ships' PA systems?"

"One moment, Captain." Ricket, working away at the Comms station, added a few more keystrokes and nodded. "I've tied Traveler's NanoCom into multiple channels. As I said, we will only get this opportunity once."

"Okay, Traveler. Do it. Do your horn-call now."

Jason's eyes widened and he put both hands to his ears as the loudest sounds he'd ever heard filled his head. Ricket too held his ears. The horn-like bursts continued and got even louder as Traveler conveyed his message.

When Traveler stopped calling, Jason continued to hear echoes for several moments.

Chapter 36

The Lilly's three rail-guns continued their onslaught, only pausing for cooling at separate and select intervals. With an unlimited supply of JIT rail ordnances, the guns kept up with whatever the Craing threw at them. The Craing fleet, in its current formation, was utilizing only a fraction of their combined firepower and had yet to bring into the fray their three Dreadnaughts. But as Jason watched, the three enormous ships were slowly maneuvering toward the front of the fleet's formation.

Traveler's horn-call didn't seem to have much of an effect. Not at first. It was only when several ships started to fall out of formation that it became evident rhinos were indeed on board a significant number of those vessels, and they were taking Traveler's call to rebel in earnest.

"Cap, at least fifty Craing warships have left the fight," Orion said.

"And with Craing bridge crews killed or in hiding, they've got multiple ships adrift. Several have actually crashed into each other out there," Perkins added.

All this was good news to Jason, but they were playing defense. They needed more ships.

The Lilly's bridge went quiet as Ti's face appeared on the display. Even Jason, who had gotten somewhat accustomed to the Mau, figured he would never fully get used to their unusual appearance.

Jason said, "We've relinquished control back to your helm. The Red rhinos you're transporting should be a reminder that you're only safe as long as you keep to your agreement to fight for the Alliance."

"No need to threaten me. I've already given you my commitment."

"Good. One more thing I need to ask of you, Ti. It's time to let the other Mau within the Craing fleet know what you're doing."

"All that will do is get us killed that much quicker. The Mau don't take kindly to deserters."

"Then I suggest you appeal to their sensibilities, their emotions, whatever it takes. Every warship that flips and fights for the Alliance increases our odds of survival."

Ti's face, as if cut from stone in a perpetual scream, was motionless.

"Is that a yes?" Jason asked.

"Yes, I will try."

As Traveler had done earlier, Ti called out to the other Mau commanders to break away from the malevolent clutches of the Craing. The response back to her was a tangle of back and forth bickering along with overt threats. Jason hadn't expected much success, and was quite surprised when ten Mau warships jumped formation and headed in their direction.

"Let's keep an eye on them," Jason said. "They could just as easily deceive us."

Ti responded to that. "Captain, deception is not possible. All ten vessels have relinquished their command to me."

The Craing fleet began targeting the rogue Mau vessels with plasma fire and missiles. Two ships were struck and exploded. The turned eight ships soon fell in behind *The Lilly* and joined the two original Mau vessels in returning plasma fire at the Craing.

"Cap, one of our rail-guns is showing signs of stress. It's

taking longer intervals to cool," Orion said. "I don't think they can keep up the barrage; it's just a matter of time before all three give out."

Frustrated, Jason stared at the display. It would be so easy to take *The Lilly* into hiding—phase-shift into the hold of another ship. But without her presence here to fend off the Craing fleet, undoubtedly the ten Mau warships would be destroyed in mere minutes—not to mention both Trumach and soon after Dira's home planet of Jhardon would both be annihilated within hours.

"We're not going to defeat their fleet," he mused aloud. "Not with eleven warships, and even with *The Lilly*'s capabilities, we will lose."

"What do you suggest, Captain?" Perkins asked.

"We steal a Dreadnaught. Increase our odds of staying alive until help arrives."

"What about our new Mau friends? It's not like they can phase-shift along with us."

"Maybe not. Ricket, can our shuttles, or even the *Pacesetter*, phase-shift along with a Mau warship to another location?"

"Only the Caldurian shuttle, *Epcot,* and *The Lilly* have the long-distance phase-shift capacity to do something like that."

"We've lost rail-gun number one, Cap. Second one is now faltering," Orion said. "And shields are down to eighty-two percent."

Jason continued to study the display. Three Dreadnaughts—which one ... It really didn't matter.

"How long can you jam communications once we're on board?"

Ricket shrugged. "I don't know. Not long."

"Can you give us enough time to secure the ship, take command of her bridge?"

"Based on the last Dreadnaught we captured, it will take us

quite a while, Captain," Perkins said.

"Well, not this time. I'll do it in less than two hours."

"Shields are down to fifty-six percent and falling fast, Cap. All three Dreadnaughts are in the fight," Orion said excitedly.

Two more explosions flashed white on the display.

"We're down to eight Mau ships. Lost two of the last ones that joined us."

"I can get you two hours, maybe three," Ricket said.

Perkins was on his feet and looked nervous again. "How? Take a Dreadnaught in two hours? I'm sorry, Captain, but that's just not possible. We should cut our losses and phase-shift out of here. That's all we can do."

"No, it's not. What we're going to do is unleash one thousand Red rhinos, along with two hundred-plus Greys, right inside one of those monster ships."

"Shields down to thirty-one—"

Jason raised a palm up in Orion's direction, halting her updates. "We need to move quickly, everyone. XO, get Billy queued up with a thirty-man assault team. Ricket, put what you need together for jamming comms on this Dreadnaught, and Helm, remote phase-shift the *Epcot* into an open area on the first Mau ship—the one commanded by Ti ... Let's move it!"

Ensign McBride at the helm station turned toward Jason. "Captain, there's too many rhinos. I can't find enough free space to phase-shift the *Epcot* into."

"Seriously?" Jason, two fingers to his ear, hailed Traveler.

"Yes?"

"No time to explain, but I'm connecting you so you'll be heard by the Reds in one of the ship's holds. You need to tell them to huddle closer together, squeeze in, and make room for a shuttle."

Seaman Gordon gestured that he'd made the necessary

comms connection on the Mau ship.

"Go ahead, Traveler," Jason ordered.

The horn-call was a short four bursts.

McBride, over the past few days, had familiarized himself with the upgraded point-and-plot phase-shift positioning system. At present, he had all three wireframe virtual models going: Ti's Mau vessel, *The Lilly*, and the Dreadnaught. His hands moved fast as he expanded or decreased the size of the wireframe models as necessary. As he selected internal sections on each ship, colors changed and numerical coordinates hovered in the air. Seemingly satisfied, McBride turned to face Jason. "Seems there's enough room now, but barely, sir. The rhinos are right on top of each other."

"They'll have to put up with it for a few minutes. Go ahead and phase-shift the *Epcot*."

"*Epcot*'s now on board the Mau vessel, sir. Which Dreadnaught are we sending them to?"

"That one there," Jason said, pointing to a Dreadnaught located within the grouping at the left of the screen. "Find an open hold, phase-shift the *Epcot*, along with a Mau ship, and repeat the same process with the other Mau ships. But get the ships holding rhinos over there first."

"Aye, Captain." McBride returned his attention to his virtual models and expanded the selected Dreadnaught frame, zooming in on what looked like a large open area. "The hold area there has the easiest access to the central corridor, Captain."

"Go ahead, Ensign."

Jason saw Orion staring at him.

"Gunny?"

"Shields down to five percent."

"Helm, phase-shift us now, out of range, but stay within three thousand miles of that Dreadnaught. Go!"

"Aye, sir."

The overhead logistical view shifted to coincide with their new coordinates.

"Captain, *Mau One* is secure in the Dreadnaught. I've phase-shifted the *Epcot* to *Mau Two*."

"Keep at it, Ensign."

"Shields are back up to fifty percent, Cap."

"Helm, put us back in front of the remaining Mau vessels."

Chapter 37

Nan recognized the sound: a ship, or maybe a small shuttle, was moving above the house.

"What is that, Teardrop? Is it one of ours?"

"Repeated hails have been ignored. Scans of the vessel reveal it to be a small shuttle, piloted by one humanoid."

Nan and Mollie followed Teardrop into the great room, where the big screen showed six different security video feeds from outside. Three of the cameras tracked the shuttle as it hovered over the driveway, lowered its landing gear, and slowly descended.

Nan noticed a familiar symbol on the side of the craft and took a step closer. "I know that symbol. It's the pirates who took me hostage. You can't let him land. Don't just hover there, do something!"

"I'm scared, Mom," Mollie said, sliding under her mother's arm for security.

Repeated pounding shook the house and the floor beneath their feet.

"Is he shooting at us, is that what that is?"

"No. The plasma cannon is firing at the shuttle," Teardrop replied. "You will need to arm yourselves."

"Arm ourselves? What are you talking about?" Nan asked, incredulous at the prospect.

"We know how to shoot, Mom. Orion showed us, remember?"

Teardrop was on the move again and heading for the hallway leading to the bedrooms. With Nan and Molly close behind, it disappeared into the first room off to the left, a spare bedroom.

"Where are you going? You're supposed to be our security, damn it!"

Teardrop accessed a compartment behind a false panel at the back of the closet. An assortment of energy and other types of weaponry filled every inch of the back wall. Two side-walls also were shelved and contained sidearm belts, ammunition, an assortment of edged weapons, and things of which Nan had no knowledge.

Teardrop handed Nan and Mollie belts with attached sidearm holsters. She had no doubt that both belts would fit them perfectly. Next came small energy pistols, and then, the larger plasma rifles.

The pounding outside had increased.

"What's that?" Mollie yelled above the noise.

"The shuttle is returning fire," Teardrop said, moving out of the room and back toward the great room.

Close behind, Nan and Mollie followed. On the big screen, multiple feeds showed the shuttle maneuvering itself, quickly dodging left and right, as it continued to fire down on the plasma turret in the back yard.

The top of the plasma turret exploded in a shattering blast that shook the house. They watched and listened as the shuttle returned to the front side of the house and set down on the driveway. Moments later, a tall man emerged. Again, Nan leaned in to get a better look. She knew that face, and the way he tied his hair back in a long ponytail.

"That's Stalls. Oh my God, that's Stalls."

* * *

Brian awoke to repeated licking. Not all that unpleasant, he thought to himself, regaining his wits. Wet and sloppy, something continued to lap at him. Opening his good eye Brian followed the action of the hopper's long tongue as it delved deep into his open eye socket. With each penetrating thrust, it came back out with less and less blood and pus. The hopper stopped, noticing that Brian was not only awake, but watching its every move.

Sitting up, Brian pushed the hopper away, figuring it was better not to talk about the licking, at least for now. Betty, slouched down in a chair, watched from across the room.

"I don't think I've ever seen anything quite that disgusting," she said. "Here, take this ...wrap it around your head. I can't look at that open socket another second. And I'll never, ever, be hungry again."

She tossed him a long strip of cloth from where she was seated and turned her attention to the hopper.

Brian did as he was asked and covered his eye socket, tying both ends of the cloth behind his head. "How long has it been doing that?"

"Too long."

"Seriously?"

"You've been out for six hours. The hopper goes at it once or twice an hour."

"Well, nobody said you had to sit there and watch."

Betty shrugged, but didn't say anything.

"I have to admit, I do feel better."

"Saliva. My saliva kills the infection," the hopper added.

Sitting up, he felt a little woozy. Brian looked around the bridge and then at Betty.

"We were attacked. Someone fired on your ship?"

"Yeah, pirates," she answered. "They've gone, but not before destroying our propulsion system. We're now hurtling though space with no way to stop. We're dead, we just don't know it yet."

"Show me."

Reluctantly, Betty unfolded herself from her chair and sat down at one of the consoles. After a few keystrokes she looked over at Brian.

"You want to see, or not?"

Unsteadily, Brian got to his feet and walked over to where she was seated. He crouched down and looked at the small display.

"None of this looks familiar to me. Zoom out a bit?"

Betty changed the view and sat back. Brian recognized several of the star systems now. He looked at her and smiled.

"What? Something funny in all this?"

"Just that on our current course we're headed toward my home planet."

Betty adjusted the zoom level in more and brought the Sol system into view. "Here? That's your system?"

"Yep."

"Well, you can wave as we pass right by it."

"Are you always so negative?"

"No, only when a mountain of shit lands on my head."

"Maybe we can figure out how to slow down, or even stop. There have to be positioning thrusters on a ship like this."

"Of course, but you'd expend the propellant in a nanosecond at the rate of speed we're traveling."

"What kind of shape are the drives in? Any chance of repairing even one of them?"

"Hardware's not my thing. They pretty much look like scrap to me."

"Well, it just so happens I grew up in a scrapyard," Brian said. "Let's go take a look."

Chapter 38

All eight of the remaining Mau vessels were tucked into various holds within the Dreadnaught. Ricket had determined the frequencies used by the Craing fleet and was jamming their local in-ship communications.

Jason placed Traveler in charge of rhinos—Greys and Reds alike. Those that protested, or compromised the mission, would be dealt with immediately; the stakes were just too high for infighting. Communications had been tricky. Traveler, the only rhino with a NanoCom, had managed to work out a system with Seaman Gordon on Comms. His voice, or horn-call, was now broadcasted where needed. Multiple rhino teams were organized, and a captain assigned to each one. Jason was impressed with Traveler's ability to lead with little handholding. Truth was, once the rhino teams were let loose, they needed little guidance. They were told to keep on going until they'd eliminated all adversaries.

The last ship to phase-shift in, *The Lilly* hovered within the Dreadnaught's primary inner corridor, which spanned miles and ran the length of the ship. The corridor's five hundred foot span allowed more than enough room, wing-tip to wing-tip, for *The Lilly* to move forward unhindered.

Immediately hundreds of hover security drones appeared from multiple directions. Plasma fire erupted from each as the small meter-long drones maneuvered defensively, constantly changing location.

As things stood, there was little any outside threat could do to harm *The Lilly,* now moving forward within the confines of the Dreadnaught's main corridor. Her shields, again at one hundred percent, were virtually impregnable from handheld, or drone, weaponry.

"I'd like to go along, Cap," Orion said.

"I want you here, ensuring our rail-guns are getting repaired, and to stay on tactical, watching our back."

"Repair drones are working the guns; should have them back to normal within the hour. I'll watch your back better with a multi-gun in my hand," she replied.

The armory was crowded as Jason, Ricket, and several crewmen suited up. Jason finished locking his helmet into place and opened his visor.

"Not this time, Gunny. Be my eyes and ears on the bridge. I trust you more than anyone else up there. Shouldn't say that, I know, but just the same that's the way it is." He moved out into the corridor and found Billy and Rizzo leaning against the bulkhead.

"Team ready?"

"In the mess. And they're more than ready," Billy replied. He gave Jason a crooked smile.

"Where's Traveler?" Jason asked as they entered the mess hall.

Ricket stopped and accessed his virtual notepad. "If he remembered to put on his belt, he'll be showing up right about ... Now."

Traveler appeared mid-step and nearly lost his balance. He stood up tall and glared down at Ricket. "Let me know when you're going to do that." Bending low he looked closely at Ricket, peering into his visor. "Ricket?"

"It's me."

Traveler huffed and stood back up to face Jason. "Reds and Greys fighting together, I am skeptical. Today is an ominous day, Captain."

Billy's team of thirty fresh SEALs gathered around. "Everyone up to speed? You all know the drill?" Jason asked, making eye contact with each of them.

"Aye, Captain."

Jason brought up his own virtual notepad and a 3D representation of the Dreadnaught's internal corridor. "Billy, Rizzo, Traveler, Ricket, and myself will phase-shift right onto their bridge. Team leaders, the rest of you will phase-shift to perimeter access positions: here, here, and here, with your ten-man teams, and clear any opposition forces. The Craing are cowards, for the most part, so watch out for Serapins and other combatants. Let's get control of this vessel quickly so we can move on to phase two and create as much havoc as possible for the rest of their fleet." Jason then added, "Ricket will be phase-shifting us in force simultaneously. Everyone ready?"

"Ready," came their unified response. Weapons came up, poised for action.

Jason watched as Ricket accessed the necessary phase-shift configurations via his HUD, and with a familiar white flash, everyone phase-shifted out of the mess.

* * *

The Craing apparently were ready for them. An army of fifteen Serapins rushed forward from their sentry positions around the bridge. A sixteenth Serapin lay on the deck. Traveler had unwittingly phase-shifted on top of the creature. With a huff, Traveler kicked at the Serapin's head, sending it skittering across the deck plates.

The Serapins rushed forward from all directions. Jason and the others brought their multi-guns up to bear, firing continuously. Five Serapins quickly went down while the remaining others moved in, jaws opened wide, ready to strike. Jason's team had gotten accustomed to phase-shifting on the fly back on HAB 12, and now each shifted, sometimes mere feet away, with no more than a moment's notice. Jason shifted to his left and fired as the closest Serapin stumbled into the open space Jason had just vacated. With two lethal plasma bursts to its head, the beast went down hard. He had not expected this level of resistance this early on in the mission. An indication he'd need to be prepared for the unexpected moving forward. Turning to his right, Jason saw that three Serapins were converging on Rizzo. When the young SEAL shifted several feet away and then reappeared behind them, Jason and Rizzo fired until the three went down. Now sixteen dead or dying Serapins lay around the bridge. Billy moved from one carcass to another, sending one more lethal shot into each of the Serapin's heads.

Jason headed directly for the raised section at the far side of the bridge, where four medallion-wearing Craing officers nervously stood. Each wore a sidearm, but only one, wearing the bronze medallion, had the stones to pull it. Jason didn't hesitate to shoot him between the eyes. Propelled right off his feet, the Craing officer went airborne into the bulkhead behind. The others raised their hands in submission. Without slowing his pace, Jason grabbed at their medallions and, one by one, tore them from their necks.

"Lose your weapons," he commanded.

The three Craing looked up at him, perplexed.

"Drop your belts—now!"

They did as they were told.

Turning to face his team, Jason was surprised to see Ricket was already at work and seated at a nearby station. No less than twenty-five Craing crewmembers, many splattered with blood from the Serapins, sat stunned at their consoles.

"Captain, security hover drones have been taken offline." Ricket looked up and gestured to the Craing crewmembers. "We'll need to enlist the crew's help to instigate tactical operations against the rest of the fleet."

Jason noticed the Craing crewmembers were taking special notice of Ricket, obviously seeing the resemblance to their renowned past Emperor Reechet. Jason figured he could use this to his advantage.

"Ricket, translate this for me. It's better they get the message in their home language and coming from you." Jason walked along the rows of Craing crew. "I am Captain Jason Reynolds. By now you may have heard of me, and my ship *The Lilly*. The ship that singlehandedly went up against five hundred Craing fleet warships." The Craing obviously had heard as they began to murmur excitedly among themselves. He continued. "Normally, I would kill you and set an example to the rest of your fleet that I mean business. Can anyone here tell me why I shouldn't kill you all, right now? Anyone? Shush! Don't just call out, raise your hands."

Hands shot up all around. "You! Make it good, or you'll be the first to die."

The Craing, who looked remarkably like the others, in Jason's view, immediately pulled back his hand and shook his head. Jason pointed his multi-gun and shot him in the foot. He fell off his chair onto the deck, both hands holding his injured appendage.

"You'll live," Jason barked. Since killing the bronze-medallioned officer, he'd switched to a heavy stun setting.

More hands went up.

"You, why shouldn't I kill you right now?"

"Because we will do whatever you ask. Please do not kill us."

"Good answer. But before I ask anything of you, someone

tell me this: of the three Dreadnaughts, which bridge crew is best? And I mean, which bridge crew kicks ass? This one or one of the others? And remember, I only have need for one bridge crew."

Again, they looked to one another, talking more openly and with more conviction.

"We are by far the most excellent crew."

"Show me. Destroy one or both of the other Dreadnaughts and you will not only live, but will be generously rewarded with positions on *The Lilly*, or other vessels in our fleet."

There was quiet hesitation. The Craing crew knew that any decision once given could not be taken back; they would be committed. Jason wanted a crew who would come to the same conclusion on its own. A crew that would be trustworthy, and not change position as soon as Jason's back was turned.

"I know how to commandeer at least one of the other Dreadnaughts, if not both," a voice from across the room said in excellent English. He was the Craing who'd worn a red medallion, something Jason hadn't seen before.

"Who are you?"

"I am Empire Fleet Commander Han Di."

Billy snickered, but quickly stifled it.

"Okay, Han Di, speak up. I'm all ears."

The figure of speech seemed to derail the commander for a moment, but he carried on anyway. "Dreadnaughts can cluster."

"Explain," Ricket said, jumping from his seat and moving closer to the commander.

"As many as four Dreadnaughts can cluster together, connecting lengthwise. Any Dreadnaught with two or more clustered vessels is referred to as a Meganaught."

Jason was unimpressed. "What good would that do us? Why would another Dreadnaught even consider doing this cluster-thing with a vessel that has been boarded by the enemy?"

This brought a smile to the commander's face. "Two reasons, Captain. First, although there is heightened security within the fleet, your presence here, within this vessel, is still unknown. Second, not only is this the command ship for the fleet, I am the fleet commander. If I give the order to cluster, which is not uncommon, I will not be challenged."

Commander Han Di seemed to know what Jason would ask next. "No, Captain, I cannot command the fleet to surrender. Out there, among the fleet, are three heavy cruisers with dignitaries and overlords present. Ordering Dreadnaughts to cluster is one thing; to surrender a fleet is another."

Ricket now stood before Commander Han Di. "The clustering of Dreadnaughts ... which one would have supervisory systems command?"

"This one, of course," said Commander Han Di. Then he turned to Jason. "I ask one thing in return, Captain."

"You mean above and beyond your life?"

"I ask that I remain in command. Under your orders, of course."

"And you expect me to ... what, simply trust you?" Jason asked.

"Captain, change has been coming to the Craing for some time now. We know you have been to our home worlds; you know of the dissent there, yes?"

Jason shrugged.

"Plundering, killing off complete species, races of other intelligent life forms, with little thought of repercussions—it sickens me. It sickens many."

"There's other ways to instigate change, other than joining the side of your enemy," Jason replied.

"You are not the enemy; our enemy lies within our own

culture. And someday, when things have changed, I will return home."

"You don't want to cross me, Commander Han Di. But for now, this is your vessel. Instruct all hands to put down their arms and do as they're told."

"We'll need to open communications immediately, before there are any more suspicions," Commander Han Di said. "And please return my medallion."

Jason looked to Ricket. "What do you think?"

"There is little we risk by going along with it, and much to gain. I suggest we trust him, for now."

Jason found the red medallion among the others on the floor. He picked it up, looked over at Commander Han Di, and said, "Here, catch."

Chapter 39

Tension was high, but all was relatively quiet on board *The Lilly*, still stationed outside the Dreadnaught's bridge in the vessel's primary corridor. The command to the three Dreadnaughts to cluster had been given by Commander Han Di. Each vessel now moved on an intercept course and would unite with the others within the next hour. Jason put Seaman Gordon on Comms to closely monitor all Craing fleet intership communications. *The Lilly's* presence, and that of the other Mau ships lying within Han Di's Dreadnaught, had not been detected.

Jason sat in the command chair as the same question kept nagging at him. Why had Granger and the Caldurians gone to all the trouble of installing the communications equipment for the interface only to screw with them in the end? Then he thought about the Crystal City: a virtual ghost ship that had used the same interface wormhole-type travel—but how? Who on board had requested the in-and-out points? Everyone on board had died, yet someone had remotely transported it across space ... *but who?*

The logistical view above him showed the three Dreadnaughts moving closer together. From what Jason understood, once clustered together the three Dreadnaughts' central corridors would be opened, thereby creating one huge continuous corridor between vessels. At that point, Jason would unleash the might of the Red and Grey rhino-warriors, the SEAL teams, and *The Lilly* itself. He'd continue using his previous success method of fighting battles from within, and stake claim to the other two Dreadnaughts just as he had this one.

"Captain. We're being hailed. Deep space, unknown contact, sir," Seaman Jeffery Gordon said.

"On screen, Seaman."

Granger's face appeared on the display; this time he wasn't smiling. Sweat glistened from his brow and something seemed amiss about the scene behind him.

"Jason, I do apologize for the unfortunate situation we find ourselves in."

"And what, Granger, is that situation?" Jason asked, doing his best to keep his temper in check.

"You, there, facing insurmountable odds against the Craing fleet—and me, I guess you could say, I've been overruled. There's been a change in policy and I need to adhere to a different set of standards. This is coming from the interface—not from me, and not from the Caldurians. I do apologize."

"Time is short, Granger. What exactly does that mean for the Allied fleet?"

"It means we will no longer provide technology to alien races, namely yours and the Craing. To go against the interface is not advantageous for Caldurians' long-term wellbeing."

"And what about the Craing? They're no longer considered a threat?"

"Oh, they're most definitely a threat. This isn't a one or the other situation. It's both."

"You made promises. Lives are at stake."

Granger did not respond.

"I told you once, Granger, you don't want me for your enemy."

"It's out of my hands. I am not your enemy, but if that is what you want, I can live with that. The chances of our meeting again are quite slim. You wouldn't even know which universe to find me in. Good luck, Jason. I mean that."

"The connection is broken, Captain," Seaman Gordon reported.

Fuming, Jason looked up to see Ricket standing at his side.

"A most unfortunate situation, Captain," Ricket said. "But I think I may have an idea."

"How to find Granger?"

"No, not Granger. How to find, or at least contact, the interface."

* * *

Jason, with Ricket in tow, ported to Deck 2 and together they entered the Zoo. They made a beeline for the Drapple's habitat.

Jack, broom in hand, waved from the far end of the hall. The window portal for the Drapple was among the most dramatic of all the habitats: as if an ocean's width spanned unchecked before him, the crystal-clear aqua water was void of any movement. Jason, feeling checked anger return, pounded on the portal.

"Can I help you, Captain?" Jack asked, looking up from his sweeping.

"How do I get the Drapple to show up?"

"He shows up when he wants. It's not like I can ring a bell and he comes running."

Jason glared at him for a moment before looking down at Ricket. "Do you have any ideas?"

"Not really, Captain."

Frustrated, Jason looked back to the habitat and nearly jumped out of his boots. There before him was the Drapple.

"Can he hear me?"

"If this organism, or whatever they call it, is actually tied to the interchange, I would suspect yes," replied Ricket.

"Are you the one called the interface?"

The bottom portion of the six-foot-long worm swayed back and forth in the water. Slowly the Drapple turned to face Jason, its features serious.

The portal window began to vibrate and, similar to how a radio frequency is tuned in—full of static and weaker at first, but then stronger and clearer, a strong voice emanated into the Zoo. The interface was speaking.

"We are not one, but many. Yes, an aspect of our existence spends time here. This aquatic environment comforts us. But, more importantly, physical existence here among your kind enables us to watch your progress. Humans are such an intriguing species."

"So you are aware of our situation. Our efforts to stop the Craing fleet?" Jason asked.

"Of course. It is an unfortunate one. But such is the nature of wars."

"Will you help me?"

"Your kind, not unlike the Craing, are slowly evolving. Soon you will outgrow the necessity of fighting amongst yourselves."

"Like the Caldurians."

"Yes, the Caldurians outgrew fighting petty wars, killing each other, some time ago."

"Look, we only want to stop the Craing. We're not warmongers here; we're defending worlds from being annihilated—our own world from being annihilated."

"We cannot position ourselves in between your conflict with the Craing. Society is at a turning point—at an evolutionary crossroads."

"Well, that's not happening nearly fast enough. Their fleet of two thousand warships is poised to destroy more planets, complete stellar systems. I'm not going to let that happen. And let me add one more thing: by diverting the Allied fleet, you didn't save lives, you cost them."

The interface did not respond to this, seeming to weigh Jason's words.

"In simple terms, what I provide is access. There are reasons why I don't interface with emerging societies that would use that capability as a weapon. This puts us in a difficult position."

Ricket took a step closer and put his hand on the portal. "I've been told this capability is not unique to the interface. That it's actually quite simple once one knows the corresponding, universal, mathematical properties."

"The word simple is relative. What is simple for one society may be virtually impossible for another. Although the Caldurians have made strides moving about the multiverse, they still do not have the capability to generate unique kinds of sustainable wormholes which would support travel across the universe."

"I don't believe you're willing to stand by while millions, if not billions, of lives are lost. Perhaps, though, you are willing to compromise? Provide Ricket with the basic mathematical properties, the formula, if you will. If we're not advanced enough to make heads or tails out of it, then we're obviously not ready for its implementation, and we'll make the best of a bad situation," Jason added.

The Drapple was quick to respond: "We are not withholding that information. It is not ours to withhold. But we will agree to provide this information. A transfer to your internal memory stores is now in process. We wish you well."

With that, the Drapple leisurely swam away.

Chapter 40

Teardrop was on the move, its energy weapon protruding from the open plate at the center of its body.

"Warning! Outside security perimeter has been breached. Weapons fire detected. Plasma turret has been destroyed."

"Mom! Can't you get it to shut up?" Molly screamed above all the racket. "How many times does it have to say the same thing?"

Nan and Mollie huddled together as they watched the multiple security feeds up on the TV monitor. Once Stalls had walked around the outside perimeter of the house, he returned to his shuttle. Several minutes later he came out wearing a battle suit and holding a large energy weapon.

Stalls moved from one window to the next, pulling and prying at the metal security shutters. Eventually he concentrated on the largest window shutter at the back of the house. Using the butt of his weapon he continued to pound at it over and over. With little impact on the shutter, Stalls took several steps backward and fired; plasma bolts shook the house and left blackened scorch marks. The firing stopped as Stalls moved in to check the damage.

Nan watched as the tall pirate became more and more enraged. He began to use the butt of his rifle again. He stopped, out of breath, and looked up to the roofline. He raised his rifle and fired. Shingles flew into the air, some of them catching on fire.

The sounds from within the house were deafening.

"Teardrop!" Nan yelled. "He's shooting at the roof. The roof

221

is coming apart!"

Teardrop, now behind them, was also looking at the security feeds.

"He will soon find that the sub-roof is covered in metal plating," Teardrop said, moving about the great room and rising up toward the ceiling. "No structural breach detected."

With a large section of the roof shingles blown away exposing the metal plates beneath, Stalls stopped firing and stood back. Then he was gone, heading back toward his shuttle.

"Is he leaving, Mom? Has he given up?" Mollie asked.

"I don't know, Mollie. Maybe."

In seconds the shuttle was back airborne and hovering over the pool. Its primary energy weapon came alive, concentrating its fire on the security shutters at the back of the house.

"Structural breach in process, structural breach in process."

Both sliding glass windows shattered as the security shutters went from a glowing amber color to a bright white. Intense heat emanated in waves into the kitchen and back into the great room. The large metal shutters disintegrated. Nan and Mollie ran for cover seeing the shuttle hovering before them behind the newly exposed rear of the house.

Nan watched as Teardrop moved with amazing speed, taking up a defensive position at the rear of the house. Nan, who had felt unsure if it would be able to defend them against the pirate's shuttle, now felt some hope. Teardrop fired a continual barrage of plasma bolts into the belly of the hovering craft. The shuttle fired back, but Teardrop was so quick, darting from one position to the next, that the only thing Stalls could accomplish was further destruction to the house itself.

Teardrop rose into the air and moved in closer to the craft, concentrating its fire-power on a singular spot on the hull.

The shuttle continued to fire back and Teardrop was struck

multiple times, destroying one of its arms, and then it suffered a direct hit to its energy weapon. Several more energy bolts struck the drone and Teardrop fell from the air into the pool, where it immediately sank to the bottom.

"Mom!"

"I know, I saw," Nan said back, never taking her eyes off the hovering shuttle. Both Nan and Mollie crouched low, hiding behind the wall next to the fireplace.

"What's he want, Mom? Why's he doing this to us?"

"I don't know. He's a bad man. But we're going to show him he can't get away with it, right?"

"AI, are you there?" Nan yelled above the sound of the hovering shuttle.

There was no response.

"Bag End, Mom, remember?"

"Are you there, Bag End?" Nan tried again.

"Yes, I am here, Nan Reynolds."

"What can you do to help us ... to defend us against the intruder?"

"Security deterrents within the premises are active and functional."

"What about outside; is there anything else you can do?" Nan asked, taking another quick peek around the corner.

"With the destruction of the plasma turret, there are no additional external weapons available."

The shuttle was on the move again. Nan and Mollie listened as it moved over the house and landed on the driveway.

Nan reached over and pulled the small energy weapon from the holster at Mollie's side.

"You remember how to shoot this, Mollie? You remember what Orion taught you?"

"I think so. But those were targets, not a real person."

"I know, sweetie, but you saw what that bad man did to Teardrop. We're both going to have to be brave. Can you do that?"

"I think so," Mollie replied, not sounding all that certain.

Crawling on hands and knees they moved back away from the wall to get a better look at the security feeds on the TV monitor. The shuttle's gangway had already been deployed and it took several seconds to see where Stalls had gone.

"There he is," Mollie said, pointing to one of the outside camera feeds.

Nan pulled out her own pistol and ensured that the safety was off and that it was set to its maximum charge. Mollie watched and did the same on her own weapon.

"He's coming around to the back yard," Nan whispered.

"Bag End, as soon as you have a clear shot of the intruder, shoot that fucker. Don't stop until he's dead."

Mollie looked up at her mother with wide eyes and then nodded her head in silent agreement.

"Security defense mode has been set to lethal," the AI replied.

They heard his footsteps before they saw him. It became apparent Stalls was carefully making his way around to the back of the house, not taking any chances.

"He's right there, Mom," Mollie whispered, never taking her eyes off the exposed back of the house.

"Okay, shhhh, be very quiet now."

His shadow moved across the deck like a stealthy black cat. When he finally came into view, he was no longer wearing his battle suit. Nan knew why. He wanted her to see him. His inflated ego had taken precedence over basic common smarts. Wearing snug-fitting black trousers and a dress shirt, he looked ridiculous. His long black hair was now free, falling all the way down his back. He was at the pool and looking down at Teardrop;

she guessed he wanted to make sure the drone was truly out of commission. Satisfied, Stalls stood up tall and turned toward the direction of the house. Smiling, he brushed his hair back one more time and headed for the broken sliding glass doors. Safety glass crunched under the soles of his boots. He hesitated, peered inside and took a tentative step forward.

Nan felt Mollie tense, her breathing had increased and she knew her heart was about to beat right out of her chest. She held a finger to her lips and put her attention back on Stalls. Her mind raced: *why doesn't the AI just shoot him?*

Stalls, now more relaxed, let the muzzle of his rifle drop several inches. Realizing he was on his way into the great room where they would be instantly seen, Nan pointed for Mollie to hurry and crawl backward out of sight. Nan stood and held her weapon at the ready.

He entered the great room twenty feet away and smiled when he saw her.

"Hello, Nan. I am happy, so very happy, to see you again."

She didn't respond, only held his stare and waited for him to get a little closer. She had practiced, along side Mollie, getting better with hitting the center zone of the targets, but ... as Mollie had pointed out ... they were only targets.

Stalls slowly shook his head and said, "Nan, you have no need for that weapon. I could no more hurt you than I could hurt myself. I've gone to considerable lengths coming here. Finding you. I'm hoping my actions speak for themselves. I'm hoping that you realize I love you. That I want to make you mine."

He took another step, and then another. Almost undetectable, dozens of small security panels opened above and below on the walls and ceiling. Stalls' eyes flashed and focused on the multiple weapon barrels moving into position. He dove, but had moved too late. The room erupted into mayhem. Plasma bolts seemed to emanate from everywhere. Nan crouched and found Mollie several feet behind her. Together, they used their arms to cover their heads and waited.

She watched as Stalls, now unarmed and on the ground, crawled toward the kitchen and its smaller family room area. She watched as his body took repeated shots—tensing in apparent agony each time he was hit with another plasma bolt. Numerous black scorch marks peppered his back and upper legs. He had slowed but was still able to crawl, making it out of the great room.

"Bag End, why have you stopped firing?" Nan yelled.

"Security weapons in compartments two and three are inoperable."

Tentatively, Nan got to her feet. She signaled for Mollie to stay put. She checked her weapon settings one more time and slowly walked toward the entrance to the family room. She stopped and listened and heard nothing. She wanted him dead, more than she had ever wanted anything. Another step and she could see his legs. Not moving. Entering the family room with her weapon pointed at Stalls' prone outstretched body, she kicked at one of his boots. No movement. Lying on his stomach with his face turned away, Nan wanted to make sure he was truly dead. Sliding with her back against the wall and keeping as much space between herself and Stalls as possible, she moved into the room.

Stalls moved quickly for a man shot a dozen times. How he had retrieved his weapon Nan had no idea, and by the time she had brought her own weapon up to fire, she had taken a plasma bolt to the top of her forehead. Her last conscious thought was of Mollie, *Oh my god, Mollie.*

Chapter 41

Betty led Brian and the hopper down into the bowels of the freighter and continued aft in what seemed to Brian like a corridor without end. The smell of fresh grain became even more pungent—to the point Brian nearly turned back. He noticed neither Betty or the hopper seemed to have any problem with the strong odor.

Betty stopped several times to tell the hopper to back off, not walk so close behind her. She was already annoyed at the creature, primarily, Brian thought, because it had defecated twice along the way. Brian tried to explain that the hopper's environment did not include the use of toilets, but she'd cut him short, not wanting to discuss it.

"We're fortunate that the internal ship dampeners and artificial gravity wells are still online," she said over her shoulder. "Can you imagine making this trek in zero G?"

"No, I'm having enough trouble just walking," Brian replied, peering beyond her to see if there was any kind of end in sight.

The hopper was clicking and hissing. Turning its head in Brian's direction, it repeated the same sounds again.

"Unless you can eat grain, you're just going to have to wait a bit," Brian responded.

Betty turned and looked at the hopper. "That thing's not going to gouge my heart out, is it?"

"I don't think so, but it's got a mind of its own. As I said before, best if you try to be nice."

She didn't say anything but did her best to smile in the hopper's direction.

"We almost there?"

"Yeah, we're coming to a juncture, then just up two flights of stairs."

Brian and the hopper followed behind Betty as they approached a set of metal-rung stairs.

"Up this way," she said, taking the rungs two at a time.

Brian was content to take them one at a time, and watched her distance herself; she was out of sight when she turned up ahead.

Brian eyed the hopper, which seemed to know what to do. It squeezed past Brian and sprung toward the top of the stairs in one fluid motion. Now, with both out of his line of vision, Brian tried to hurry up the metal rungs, but felt another round of the continual waves of nausea take hold, eventually forcing him to stop climbing completely. Bending over, he felt bile rise up from his stomach. He retched but avoided throwing up. Looking up the stairs, Brian wondered if the hopper had indeed decided Betty's heart would make an adequate snack.

Using his NanoCom's translator he yelled up toward the top of the stairs, "Hey! Don't eat her heart. Or anything else, for that matter."

A moment later the hopper peered over the railing, but no sign of Betty. *Shit,* he thought, they'd need her to get off this fucking freighter. To his relief, Betty peered over the railing and looked down at him from above.

"You all right down there?" she asked, with no semblance of concern in her voice.

"I'm good," he replied and continued on up after them.

By the time Brian made it to the top of the stairs, he was huffing and puffing. Betty and the hopper, sitting against the bulkhead, watched him approach with indifference. Betty got up and entered a code into a greasy, well-used panel at the side of a metal hatchway. There was a loud clanging sound that Brian figured was the mechanical latch mechanism. The hatch sprung open several inches and Betty pushed the hatch forward enough to enter into the next corridor.

The corridor was dark, with a strobe warning sign above another hatchway at the end of the hall. Brian's NanoCom translated the words.

WARNING! HULL BREACH. DO NOT ENTER.

"This is the entrance to Engineering. As you can see, it's open to space. No way we're getting in there," Betty said.

Brian looked at the blinking sign above the hatch and then at several other hatchways closer along the corridor.

"Where do those lead?"

"That one leads to a maintenance area and a bathroom," she answered, quickly glancing toward the hopper. "And the other one leads to our bin lift."

"What's a bin lift?"

Betty shrugged and shook her head as if it was a stupid question. "I don't know; it's like a fork lift thing that moves bins of grain around. It's huge and it makes a lot of noise."

"Can I see it?"

Betty stared at him for several seconds, shrugged, and said, "Be my guest." She entered another code and the nearest of the two hatchways opened. Brian pushed the hatch open with the toe of his shoe and peered inside. As Betty had indicated, the bin lift was enormous. Parked in a garage-type compartment, the yellow vehicle was easily three stories high and as wide as five school buses parked side by side. Thick manipulator arms at the front of the vehicle held a large, rounded, blue bin. A bin, Brian assumed, used in transporting thousands of pounds of grain stores. There were both wheels and thrusters along the sides of the vehicle. Looking up, he found what he was looking for—a small, windowed cab area.

"That where you'd pilot the thing?"

"Yep."

"So this thing transports grain between ships in open space?"

"Or at a space dock. But I know what you're thinking. It moves pathetically slow. You can walk faster than this thing moves. Don't even think about traveling in space with this."

Brian continued to look at the gargantuan vehicle. "Oh, I'm not, but by the size of those thrusters I'm guessing there's mega-horsepower here."

Betty nodded but didn't seem to make the connection.

"Enough to slow or maybe even stop this freighter?"

That clicked for her and she nodded. "I guess we can give it a try."

"You can operate this thing?"

"Easy. Even that thing could do it," she said, gesturing toward the hopper.

* * *

It wasn't as easy as Betty said it would be. She soon began to communicate with someone, perhaps with one of the T-shirted guys back on the bridge. Brian could hear only her side of the conversation. She referred to *eight fifty* a few times and then Brian remembered: they called each other numbers and used abbreviations of those numbers as their names.

The three of them were now huddled together within the tight quarters of the bin lift's cab.

"I still don't know why the hopper couldn't wait in the garage. There's barely enough room for one in here, let alone two plus your hopper. And did I mention its breath is foul?"

"I try not to tell it what to do. Why don't we concentrate on the job at hand?" Brian asked her.

Betty sat behind the controls and was busy configuring settings on a barely-illuminated touchpad display. Holding a comms device to her ear, she again talked to eight fifty. "All right, I think we're set. Go ahead and cycle the atmosphere."

With the disappearance of atmosphere came a welcome silence from outside the cab. Brian hadn't fully registered how noisy it had become in the cab until then. A series of red lights blinked on, then became a steady amber color. He felt a mechanical vibration as two massive doors started to separate. Beyond, open space. The sparkle of millions of distant stars now entirely filled his field of vision.

"Powering on thrusters," Betty said.

The vibration increased as the bin lift rose ten feet off the deck. She goosed the controls forward and the bin lift slowly headed out of the garage toward open space. From an intellectual level, Brian knew the bin lift was traveling at the same speed as the freighter itself, but that didn't stop him from holding his breath as they maneuvered between the open doors and held steady at the aft end of the ship, along its outside starboard hull.

"You know, this idea of yours may not work. In fact, we may get ourselves killed in the process."

Brian only half listened to her, instead watching the hopper continually lick the glass on the side porthole. Betty furrowed her brow and made a disgusted grimace.

The singular drive throttled up, bringing up the sound level again in the cabin. They needed to yell to speak to each other.

"I'm maneuvering to the aft area of the freighter. If we're not perfectly locked on to the exact right location, this won't work."

The hopper began to rifle through an old cooler stowed at

the back of the cabin. It came up with something that, at one time, may have been edible, but was now nothing more than a clump of mold. Not at all discouraged, the creature ate it in one bite, licked its claws, and returned to searching the cooler.

The aft section of the freighter was a mess. There would not have been any possibility of repairing the damage. Gaping, jagged holes riddled the drives and it appeared as if much of the aft section could break away at any time.

"Shit, this won't work."

Brian quickly saw what she was referring to. Nothing was solid on the hull; things would flex under the stress of any resistance introduced from the bin lift.

"You'll just need to find an area that is solid."

"You think?"

The freighter was turned backward in space, with its aft section heading forward. As Betty maneuvered the bin lift around the stern end, now the forward end of the freighter, Brian couldn't help but think about the massive amount of deadweight tonnage lying before them. Both manipulator arms were moving. Carefully, Betty articulated the clawed ends to open, and then close, around protruding sections of the mangled drives. She tried this maneuver several times, and each time sections of the drive came loose and pulled away from the freighter.

"This is useless. Like trying to grab on to sand."

"Up there. Don't try to clamp to the drive. The framework looks to be solid up there," Brian said, pointing to a section thirty feet above.

Betty let out a controlled breath and maneuvered the bin lift higher. Again, she brought up the manipulator arms and articulated the two claws. This time they held fast.

"We're not dead center like I'd like to be, but this might work," she said.

The touchscreen blinked out.

"What just happened?" Brian asked.

"Well, this thing's old. Temperamental. We'll just give it a second to come back online."

Ten minutes later the screen was still dark. Brian gave it a gentle slap.

"Oh, so you're now going to manhandle it? Really show it who is boss?"

"Easy. I'm just seeing if there's a loose connection. You can't tell me you weren't going to try the same thing. There's a rule in the military: the older the vehicle the more bitch-slapping it requires."

"Oh really, you didn't just make that up?" Betty asked, her lips fighting a smile.

Actually, he had, but he certainly wasn't going to tell her so.

"Look, it's coming back on."

Betty huffed, but wasted no time in bringing the bin lift's thrusters to life. She brought up a visual indicator showing that they were still within safe-output parameters.

Back on her comms, Betty talked to eight fifty again.

"Well, if you have any better idea, feel free to get your fat ass out here and give it a try. For now, this is all we've got."

"What was that about?" Brian asked.

"He's just complaining again. Says we'll over-stress the rotary securing mounts at the back of the ship. As if the fucking things are securing anything of importance now anyway, right?"

Brian nodded, although he wasn't really sure what securing mounts were, and that brought up more thoughts of deadweight tonnage.

Betty steadily increased thrust. The cab vibrated and the noise became physically painful in their ears. The hopper stopped rooting around in the cooler.

The drive's temperature level was quickly moving horizontally, from green toward the red side of the indicator.

"Eight fifty says we're slowing."

A new sound emanated below them, from the bin lift's internal drive.

"What the hell's that?" Brian asked.

"What do you think it is?" Betty snapped back. "This thing was never designed to stop a freighter moving in space at close to the speed of light. She'll hold together."

Fully in the red now, the indicator began to rapidly blink on and off. Then everything stopped. The noise, the vibration, everything.

Betty made a few more taps on the screen and turned toward Brian. "That's it."

"What? Did the drive give out?"

"Huh? Oh, no. I shut down the thrusters. We're dead in space. It worked, Brian." Betty looked as if she wasn't sure she should believe her own words. She stood looking relieved and fell into Brian's arms. Uncomfortable with the closeness, he patted her several times on the back. Then, to his surprise, she started to cry into his shoulder.

Chapter 42

The Lilly shook as both Dreadnaughts completed their coupling process. Now, at three miles wide and almost ten miles in length, the Meganaught held its position at the forward apex of the three fleet groupings.

Earlier, Jason and Billy had stood on Han Di's bridge while the final maneuvering adjustments were completing, just prior to the three Dreadnaughts becoming one gigantic vessel.

"There's no way the other Dreadnaughts can separate themselves on their own, is there?" Jason had asked.

"No, that order would have to be instigated by this bridge, an executive-level command," Han Di replied, still seated in his command chair.

"And you've locked them out from detecting our forces, as well as our video feeds?"

"Yes, your forces remain undetected."

Jason continued to watch the main corridor feed. Thousands of small bodies stood motionless. It had taken longer than Jason had anticipated to round up all of the Craing crewmembers and lock groups of three, four, and sometimes five Craing into the cages along both sides of the main corridor. For the most part they huddled together silently, and had put up little if any resistance.

Now, back on board *The Lilly*, Jason studied the display. Billy, two fingers to his ear, was on comms talking to his SEAL team leaders. The forward display showed the main corridor and twelve hundred-plus rhino-warriors poised on three separate levels as they waited for the inter-ship main corridor bulkhead walls to disconnect from each other, separate into thousand-foot-long sections, and recede back along the surrounding hull bulkheads. Looking for Traveler among the rhinos, Jason spotted him at the front of the Greys on the top-most level. Traveler had lost thirteen Greys and four Reds during their previous battle—taking over this, the first, Dreadnaught. Although they had never fought side by side, the level of camaraderie between the Reds and Greys seemed to have improved.

Ricket arrived on the bridge and headed directly for Jason, seated in his command chair. He was disheveled, hair messed, and his jumpsuit rumpled-looking, as if he'd slept in it. Jason watched him approach and tried to read his expression. The fate of his crew, the fleet, and even Earth, could very well hang in the balance, and could depend on what Ricket had to say.

"Captain, I would like to give you an update."

Jason took another quick look at the display and the waiting SEALs and rhino-warrior teams.

"Go ahead, Ricket."

"I believe I have figured it out. But it's not as simple as the Drapple, or the interchange, would have us believe." Both Perkins and Orion came over to hear what Ricket had to say. Jason hadn't thought the interchange made it sound all that easy at the time, but he let Ricket continue.

"I was approaching this from the wrong angle. But once I took into the mix how the Caldurians travel into the multiverse with relative ease, things started to come together."

Jason took another upward glance at the display and hoped Ricket would cut to the chase soon; he had a battle to fight.

"We need to tunnel into the fifth dimension, Captain."

"Okay, go on."

"I found that when two black holes entangle, then separate, what emerged was a wormhole, a tunnel through space and time.

At first, I thought wormholes were held together by gravity. But this concept seemed to suggest that in the case of wormholes, gravity is an effect, but they actually come about from the more fundamental phenomenon of entangled black holes."

"Where is all this leading, Ricket?"

"This led me to quarks, the sub-atomic building blocks of matter. I wanted to see what would happen when two quarks entangled. I mapped the entangled quarks onto a four-dimensional space. Gravity exists in a separate dimension; it acts to bend and shape space-time, thereby existing in the fifth dimension."

Jason was ready to put a stop to Ricket's lecture when he continued.

"To see what geometry may emerge in the fifth dimension from entangled quarks in the fourth, I employed holographic duality, a concept in string theory. While a hologram is a two-dimensional object, it contains all the information necessary to represent a three dimensional view. Essentially, holographic duality is a way to derive a more complex dimension from the next lowest dimension."

"I need to stop you, Ricket ..."

"It gets better, Captain. What we're talking about, again, is holographic duality. I derived the two entangled quarks and found that what emerged was a wormhole connecting the two. So we have the creation of quarks simultaneously creating wormholes. Again, gravity emerges from entanglement. Thus, the geometry, or bending of the universe, is a result of entanglement—such as what happens between pairs of particles strung together by tunneling wormholes. Captain, we will use the phase-shift capabilities we employ all the time. Entangled particles can be phase-shifted!"

Ricket held up his hand, holding Jason off from stopping his monologue.

"Using the formula, mathematical properties from the interchange, I've created micro-wormholes in my lab on 4B." Ricket took a breath and seemed pleased with himself.

"So, are you saying you can do this? Create wormholes in space?"

"Yes."

"And we can bring the Allied fleet here?"

"No, not all at once, anyway."

"Ricket!"

"I apologize, Captain. It seems we were not given the entire formula. *The Lilly*, with its phase-shift capability, can, in fact, manifest the necessary in-and-out points for spooling a wormhole. And could, subsequently, travel through that wormhole. What we cannot do, at least not yet, is provide this ability unilaterally to anyone else. In effect, *The Lilly* needs to be the one spooling the wormhole."

Jason said, "So, we'd need to communicate coordinates, go ahead and spool a wormhole, have them enter it and arrive back here in the Alcara system. Is that correct?"

"Partially. The wormholes are a finite size and stay open a finite length of time. I estimate only one or two other vessels could make the transition. They misjudge this and they'll be destroyed in the process. At least at first, it may be better for *The Lilly* to play escort."

Jason was exhausted just listening to Ricket. Although this new development was incredible, its application wasn't what he'd hoped for. *The Lilly* needed to be here, not jumping back and forth between distant sectors.

"Can the *Pacesetter* do this?"

"Actually, yes, as well as the *Epcot*, the Caldurian shuttle.

Both would need to cycle back into *The Lilly* to recharge their power banks after each round trip. One more thing, though: to make a wormhole large enough to allow for the size of the *Independence*, we'd need to utilize *The Lilly* for that round trip."

Jason looked at Ricket and nodded. "What you have accomplished is nothing short of incredible, Ricket. Thank you. XO, get on comms and inform the admiral of this development. Orion, I want a viable strategy proposal for bringing the fleet here piecemeal. Present this to both me and the admiral as soon as you have something."

"Aye, Cap," both replied, and they headed off in separate directions. "Ricket, get whatever is necessary to retrofit the *Pacesetter* and the *Epcot*."

* * *

His third NanoCom communication within the last hour with Traveler ended, and Jason was relieved to see Orion and Perkins back with their reports. Traveler and his rhinos were impatient to get underway. They were still waiting for Jason's command to open the inter-ship's main corridor bulkhead that kept separate the first of the two Dreadnaughts. The third Dreadnaught would remain closed off from the others until the rhino forces had successfully secured the second one.

"What do you have for me, XO and Gunny?"

Perkins spoke up first. "The admiral is encouraged. He'd already given the orders for what remained of the Allied fleet to make their way to the Alcara system. We should expect the arrival of four hundred warships within several hours. The outpost fleet, along with the *Independence*, is underway, but will be several days out with the limitations of FTL."

"Thank you, XO. Gunny?" Jason asked.

"I've come up with several approaches and worked through them with the XO. Logistically, moving the outpost fleet here will take a full day. If we can move two ships at a time, obviously that cuts the time in half. I've contacted Ricket and he's working on it."

"So we're looking at six hours minimum before we can instigate any kind of attack?" Jason asked her.

Orion gestured to the overhead display. "Let me show you. If we go with two flanking group attacks, the first being a combination of EOUPA and Allied vessels on one side, and the Mau ships, *The Lilly*, and the Meganaught on the other, we hem the Craing fleet in on two sides."

Jason watched as the scenario played out with icons on the overhead display.

"I don't see how we can maintain a perimeter around them that way, Gunny. Three, or better yet four, flanks would keep them from running—keep them in the fight."

"Agreed. The second scenario provides for four separate attacking flanks," she said, nodding toward the display again. "As you can see, the admiral and the *Independence*, with a small complement of heavy cruisers, will hold the rear quadrant. We'd position the Allied forces here on the left quadrant and the outpost fleet there on the right quadrant. *The Lilly*, Mau ships, and the Meganaught hold steady where we are at the forward quadrant."

"I like it; show them both to the admiral and let him decide. But there's little doubt he'll see things the same way we do."

Jason looked up to the display again and shook his head. "None of this works unless we can take the other two connected Dreadnaughts. Give me the corridor feed again, Gunny."

Jason hailed Billy.

"Go for Billy."

"Your teams ready?"

"Yes, sir."

Jason hailed Traveler.

"Yes, Captain?"

"Be ready."

"Yes, Captain."

"Seaman Gordon, contact Commander Han Di. Ask him to open the first corridor bulkhead."

Chapter 43

Her Majesty was running quiet with the toric-cloak miraculously still operational. Pike stood at the display table while Bristol paced nervously at the back of the bridge, scratching at the pimple on his nose—his fingertips coming away bloody.

"They know we're here, Bristol."

"You really think so, Pike?" he retorted sarcastically, wiping his fingers on his pants. "We're venting atmosphere from multiple locations, and radiation levels around us are through the roof. They know exactly where we are. I'm just not sure why they haven't finished us off."

Bristol joined Pike at the table. He looked at the five remaining outpost warships and at planet Earth beyond. He said, "What do we have left in the way of weapons?"

"We have a lot of missiles. Rail-guns are shot to shit. We have four plasma cannons still online." Pike's eyes held on Bristol, glancing at the blood on his nose. Self-consciously, Bristol wiped at it and returned to his seat. He thought about their predicament.

"How many pirates do we have on board?"

"Few hundred. Not all are fighters ... you know, the cook staff, all the whores on the lower deck ..."

"Fighters, how many fighting pirates?" Bristol barked.

"Hundred and fifty, give or take," Pike replied looking up, his interest piqued.

"Listen, Pike. I'm not the fucking captain here. So you don't have to do what I say. But you have to realize we're not going to defeat those Craing battle cruisers. There's just no way."

242

"So what do you suggest?"

"We board one of them, take the helm, and make a run for home."

His comment evoked disbelieving stares from the entire bridge crew.

Smiling, Pike stood up tall and crossed his arms over his chest. "Why don't you keep quiet until you have something to say that makes sense."

"Look, if you can get one of those cruisers to come alongside *Her Majesty*, I can get a team into their bridge."

"*You* can?"

"Fine, then Knock can lead the team. But I can breach her hull."

"You have one of those devices? One of the ones we used to board *The Lilly*," Pike mused, more as a statement than a question.

"I have one that was defective. I think I can fix it. So, can you come up with a way to bring one of those cruisers alongside us, or not?"

"Sure, we can surrender."

"Whatever. Give me an hour to debug the optical substrate on the device."

Pike, obviously not knowing what Bristol was talking about, shrugged and leaned back over the table.

* * *

Testing of the small phase-shift device went surprisingly well. Bristol had found a location on board *Her Majesty* where there was a large enough area not to expose the ship to open space. Given that she was a refurbished luxury liner, Bristol knew there were large areas, such as theaters and swimming pools, but the expansive mid-ship dance floor turned out to work best for his needs.

Similar to the devices he had used on board *The Lilly,* this one had a simple timer mechanism that would allow Bristol to set the duration for phase-shifting to a constrained area in the multiverse. If placed correctly, the subsequent void left behind would later provide access from one ship onto the other.

Bristol placed the device onto the large two hundred square foot dance floor. He rechecked his settings—and ensured the device would stay activated for exactly ten seconds. Running backwards, Bristol got all the way back to the dancehall's outside bulkhead. With the small remote transmitter in hand, he took one more look around. *Perfect.* He pressed the activation button.

As expected, a section of the dance floor disappeared. Four seconds into the test, things went terribly wrong. He'd set the radius too wide, maybe by fifty feet. The sound of rushing water only confirmed his worst fears. The pool, one level up, and of equal dimensions to the dance floor, was quickly emptying into the now open void and into the dance hall. When the timer elapsed, the missing dance floor returned from the multiverse, but thousands of gallons of water, albeit only knee-high, remained in the dancehall space around him.

Bristol smiled. "Fuck it. The test worked."

* * *

With the toric-cloak taken offline, *Her Majesty* was visible again. Their surrender came via a hail to each of the outpost vessels. Pike took on the negotiations and, to Bristol's surprise, put on an excellent performance. Pike balanced just enough indignation, along with trepidation, to sound convincing. He agreed to all their terms with one exception: the ship's personnel leaving via life-pods.

"Although we do have adequate pods available, release of them would be impossible. Too much damage, too many interface mechanisms destroyed," Pike said.

"Fine. You will constrain your crew to one area of the ship. We see one weapon, you die," the stern voice commanded over the broadcast comms channel.

Bristol watched the display as three of the Craing battle cruisers moved across space and saddled up close to the liner's broad starboard hull. It was Bristol's cue to head on down and join the assault team, and the rest of the crew waiting close behind.

Wearing his battle suit, Bristol carried the phase-shift device in his open palm. On comms, Pike had relayed to him the position of the most forward battle cruiser. It was situated at one of their larger mid-ship hatchways.

An explosive charge shook the ship.

"What was that?" Bristol asked.

"They didn't even wait, they blew the hatch wide open. We're being boarded. You better move it along, Bristol. And don't even think about leaving me behind," Pike warned.

Bristol cut the connection and concentrated on finding Knock and the rest of the team four levels down. He heard Knock's voice over his comms. "I see you. Keep coming, we're up ahead."

Heavily armed and wearing battle suits, Knock and ten other pirates stood at the outermost bulkhead.

"Where's everyone else?" Bristol asked.

"Close by in an air-locked compartment. This better work, Bristol. I wasn't in favor of this whole surrendering bullshit—just so you know."

Bristol, now at Knock's side, looked at the bulkhead behind him.

"You're sure this location is forward, close to the bridge on the cruiser?" Bristol asked.

"Yeah, I'm sure."

In the distance there was another explosion, along with the sounds of multiple energy weapons being fired.

"I thought there wasn't anyone left up there except Pike," Bristol said.

"Not everyone went along with your plan."

"Whatever; stand back. No ... further ... ten yards minimum," Bristol said, shooing the pirates back with both hands. "Okay, that's good."

Finding a flat section halfway up the bulkhead, Bristol affixed his phase-shift device onto the metallic surface. He stood back and appraised his work, then joined Knock and the others further down the hallway.

"Ready?"

"Just do it," Knock replied, irritated.

Bristol pressed the activation button on his remote. The bulkhead disappeared and the surrounding atmosphere immediately began to escape out into space between the two vessels. Knock and his team rushed forward, pushing Bristol into the opposite wall. Once they had passed, Bristol followed. At the opening, he stopped mid-step. He'd have to leap over the expansive void to the walkway within the cruiser. *Shit!* Bristol was not particularly athletic; he took several hurried steps backward and then ran for the other side, realizing only half of a walkway remained within the Craing cruiser. One foot made it across, the other slipped off the edge. With nothing to grab on to, no handholds, Bristol started to fall backwards into the void. A hand reached for Bristol and caught one of his flailing arms.

"What the hell you doing? We don't have time for this!" Knock yelled, as he pulled Bristol all the way into the cruiser. "Stay behind us."

The team moved forward up ahead and Bristol stayed close behind. Looking back over his shoulder he activated the device again, closing the void.

Knock was right. He'd positioned them perfectly and the team was already moving into the cruiser's bridge up ahead. The last to enter, Bristol was surprised to see so few crewmembers manning the bridge. From his early days as a seaman aboard *The Lilly*, he was well aware that these outpost ships would require at least some Craing crewmembers. But he was still surprised to see human and Craing working together. One of the two humans, wearing a captain's jumpsuit, was out of his chair and, like the others, had his hands up. He looked young to be an officer, let alone a captain.

"You won't get away with this," the captain said.

Bristol moved to the front of the team. "I think we already have. Get over there with the others." The pirates disarmed the captain and then the other human.

"We are taking this vessel. Resist and you'll be killed," Bristol said flatly. "Order everyone still on board to get off the ship. Do it now or you all die."

"And who will pilot this vessel if you kill us all?" the captain shot back.

"I will. Now do it." The captain and the other human Bristol assumed was the first officer looked at each other.

"He won't be able to help you, Captain." Knock took two long strides and coldcocked the first officer with a fist to his jaw. He fell to the deck in a heap.

Reluctantly, the captain opened a channel to his crew.

"All hands, this is the Captain Gould. The *Bright Star* has been boarded and the bridge has been taken. You will not surrender. I repeat, you will not surrender under any circumstances. Fight, take back—"

Knock fired a plasma bolt into the captain's head, killing him mid-sentence.

Neither Bristol nor the other pirates were aware that a detail of eight Outpost Marines had made their way to the bridge's outside entrance. It was only when four flash grenades hit the deck that Bristol turned to see what was happening. Their battle suit helmet visors were not sophisticated enough to shield them from the painful, piercing glare. As hands flew to cover their eyes, the Marines moved in, weapons raised. Bristol staggered and fell backward to the deck.

"Drop your weapons, do it now!" yelled one of the Marines.

Knock and the other pirates dropped their weapons and were quickly kicked or pushed to the deck. Bristol, without even thinking about it, ran from the bridge as plasma fire erupted behind him. Still half blind, he followed the same route they'd used earlier. He had a small lead but he heard running behind him. Bristol picked up his pace.

They were gaining on him. Up ahead there was nowhere to run. Bristol fumbled for the small key fob-sized remote and pressed the button. A ten-yard-wide void took the place of the hallway and outer bulkhead. Plasma fire flew by inches from his helmet. In one running stride, Bristol leapt into the void. He grimaced.

Chapter 44

"Damn it!" Jason was on his feet, furious. "Didn't I make myself clear? Why the hell is he opening both corridor bulkheads?"

"Han Di's not responding to repeated hails, sir," Seaman Gordon said.

Billy was hailing him.

"Go for Captain."

"You didn't order the cages to be opened, did you, Cap?"

"Cages? What are you talking about? No, of course not."

"Then we have a problem, Cap," Billy said, sounding out of breath.

Jason watched as the teams of rhinos, stationed on three levels, and Billy's SEALs charged forward into the second Dreadnaught. Sure enough, the cage doors on both sides of the main corridor, on each of the eight levels, were open or in the process of opening.

"Captain, our security team on Han Di's bridge is not responding. And we've got major hostiles coming out of those cages," Orion said.

Jason took several steps closer to the forward display feeds. "What the hell are those?"

Orion, now also on her feet, zoomed in the forward video feed.

"Pill bugs. Hundreds of them," Orion said, making a face and sticking her tongue out. "They're truly disgusting."

"XO, get our pilots prepped, I want our fighters out there providing support for our teams along the corridor."

"Aye, Captain, they're ready to deploy now."

"Captain, we have Serapins coming from the third Dreadnaught—more than a thousand of them, and on all levels," Orion said.

Jason watched the display in shock. This was no accident. It was planned. *Granger.* Jason wasn't sure how, but he knew this was the work of Granger.

"Massive casualties reported, sir," Orion said. "Pill bugs are squirting that acid shit on our guys. We don't have a defense against that stuff."

Paralyzed, Jason continued to watch the inevitable happen. It was a slaughter in process.

Orion pounded a fist down on her station. "Sorry, sir. Hydrogen cannons. No less than ten of them along the corridor have been deployed. They're targeting our fighters."

"Hydrogen?"

"They're used for short-range combat. Highly effective, they pummel targets with sub-temperature bursts. Similar to rail munitions, but it melts prior to hitting key hull areas."

"Have our fighters target the cannons."

"Shields are failing on all fighters, Captain. We don't have an adequate defense against those things."

"Bring the crew back in, at least until we figure out a new plan."

"Captain."

Jason tore his gaze away from the display and found Ricket looking up at him.

"Captain, I haven't fully tested it yet, but I think I've managed to make it work."

"Managed to what?"

"Start generating stable wormholes—to bring the outpost fleet here."

"You have perfect timing, Ricket." Jason made a fist. "Finally some good news!"

"Thank you, Captain."

"Okay, Orion, which outpost fleet vessel has our largest complement of ground troops?"

Orion checked her console and looked up. "The admiral's Dreadnaught, the *Independence*. It has over three thousand Marines, and close to two thousand Army Rangers."

"Then that's the first ship to come over."

"That's not what the admiral specified, Captain. He wanted—"

Jason cut her off with, "Well, things change, Gunny. We need those ground forces and we need them now."

Perkins shook his head. "How will you get them in here, on board the Meganaught, sir? It would take hours shuttling them in from open space."

Jason thought for a second. "There's room for one more Dreadnaught to cluster, right?"

Perkins looked unsure, but Orion nodded.

Ricket said, "Yes, but you'll need executive command access for that. You'll need to take back Han Di's bridge."

"That's right. We need to move fast, everyone. Orion, contact the admiral—let him know what I'm proposing. He won't disagree, I promise. Have him get his ground forces ready for an assault. XO, I need a special team assembled ASAP in order to take back Han's bridge. Unfortunately, they'll be even more ready for us this time."

"What team, sir?" Perkins asked.

"I'll need Billy, Rizzo, Traveler, and you too, Orion."

Perkins was flabbergasted. "You're taking team leaders out of action, sir?"

"No, I'm not, if you'll let me finish. Give the order for all teams to fall back. Get as many of them into *The Lilly's*—into her holds, whatever. Do it as soon as possible. Shuttle all others into the Mau ships if necessary. Any place safe."

"Sir, I don't see how retreating—"

"We'll live to fight another time, XO. And question orders again on my bridge and you'll be confined to quarters until you're later brought up on charges. Am I making myself clear?"

"Aye, Captain," Perkins replied.

* * *

Traveler, Billy, and Rizzo phase-shifted directly into *The Lilly's* mess and joined Orion and Jason. With two fingers to his ear, Jason was on comms to Dira.

Dira said, "Jason, dead bodies are stacked up outside along the hallway. The injured, far more than we can handle, are close to a hundred rhinos and twenty SEALs. What happened out there?"

"We've been outsmarted at every turn. Simply put, they were expecting us."

"Jason," Dira said, hesitating, "is everything okay? The crew, all of us, are scared. Stupid to ask with the world obviously falling in around us, but—"

"Yes, we've had some setbacks, but we're getting back on track." There was another pregnant pause. "I have to go—"

"Yes, of course—me too. Take care of yourself, Jason."

They clicked off and Jason turned his attention back to his team. Billy and Traveler looked tired and both had multiple bandages covering an assortment of minor injuries over their bodies. Rizzo looked a little better, but he too had a bandage on his left ear.

Orion was passing out fresh multi-guns when Ricket entered

the bridge, wearing a battle suit.

Jason said, "You weren't specified to be on this team, Ricket."

"Yes, Captain. But if Han Di refuses to relinquish command-level control, you'll need me to hack into the Dreadnaught's systems."

"I thought of that, Ricket, but it would only take a second to phase-shift you in once we've cleared the area."

"Yes, Captain. The strange thing is now that I'm mortal I want to be in the fight. To personally do everything I can to stop the Craing."

Jason didn't respond, trying to weigh Ricket's request with what was best for the fleet. The truth was Ricket was too valuable to put in harm's way. But hadn't he chastised him in HAB 12 about the same issue—that time for not fighting?

"Do your best to stay in one piece. Keep low, and toward the middle of the team. We can't afford to lose you. Understood?"

"He can't get much lower profile than he is, Cap," Billy said with a smirk.

"Yes, Captain," Ricket replied.

Jason saw relief and something else on Ricket's newly expressive face. Appreciation.

"All right, everyone, we've done this before. I want zero casualties. Stay aware and be prepared to phase-shift at a moment's notice. They are expecting us, so safeties off."

All helmet HUDs began counting down for a synchronized phase-shift into the Dreadnaught's bridge. Jason watched as his team readied their weapons before everything flashed white.

They phase-shifted onto the Dreadnaught's bridge, only to find it totally deserted. Overhead lighting was dimmed and row after row of console displays were dark. Offline.

"Captain Reynolds," came the familiar voice of Commander Han Di.

Jason turned to see the Craing fleet commander's face on the central bridge display.

"Did you really think we would make things easy for you?"

Jason had less interest in what the Craing commander had to say than where he might be physically located. Ricket, now seated at a nearby station, moved his fingers quickly over the input device.

"Captain, this Dreadnaught has been slaved to one of the other Dreadnaughts. Actually, the third one." Looking up at the console display, Ricket saw Han Di. "He's on that bridge right now."

"How can you tell?"

"There's no activity coming from Dreadnaught Two, Captain. Both one and two are slaved."

Jason turned toward the display again. "I'm coming for you. I'd suggest you hide, Han Di, but you won't have time."

Ricket nodded, confirming he had loaded the team's HUDs with the third Dreadnaught's bridge coordinates. With that, the assault team phase-shifted together.

* * *

Fifty mutants. It had been a while since Jason had come up against the human-looking Craing soldiers. Encircled by two rows of twenty-five, the inside row were down on one knee, while the outside row stood behind them. They fired as soon as Jason's assault team arrived.

Jason felt plasma fire hitting his battle suit with such force that staying on his feet was nearly impossible. Immediately, HUD warnings indicated suit integrity failure was imminent. Firing back was not an option, so a quick phase-shift to an alternate location was imperative.

Jason phase-shifted right into the fray, displacing the space of two mutants—turning them to soupy, disconnected body parts—the bloody mess falling to the deck around him.

Traveler was the last to phase-shift, his body already blackened with scorch marks. But he, too, phase-shifted and, like Jason, displaced a number of the encircling mutants. The firefight lasted less than a minute. Confused, and not wearing comparable battle suits, the mutants went down in a dramatic barrage of plasma fire.

Han Di, his red medallion setting him apart from the other officers, stood on the raised officer's platform at the far end of the bridge. Before Jason could start in his direction, more combatants filed in from several perimeter entrances.

"Ricket, get on one of those stations."

"Yes, sir."

Billy was at Jason's side. "Cap, have I mentioned I really hate these little fuckers?"

"Once or twice," Jason replied, watching a hundred-plus armed Craing soldiers pile in.

"I can't believe it—Craing actually coming to fight their own battle," Orion said.

Dressed in dark-green battle suits, the small warriors didn't hesitate to fire. Within moments the bridge was nothing less than chaos.

"Damn, their suits are pretty good," Rizzo said, not having much luck taking down a grouping of twenty Craing in front of him. As the Craing steadily moved forward, Rizzo was pushed back. He phase-shifted to a position behind them and fired into their backs. Soon enough, they'd turned and were pushing him back again.

"Suit's about had it, Cap," he said, "and I'm all out of phase-shifts."

To everyone's surprise, Traveler phase-shifted into the middle of the Craing fighters. Displaced by Traveler's bulk, eight Craing ceased to exist.

"Thanks, Traveler," Rizzo said, now taking cover behind a console.

Billy and Jason had better results phase-shifting into a bunch of Craing than they did trying to pick them off one by one. But, eventually, they too ran out of phase-shift options.

Orion, finding something wrong with her multi-gun, flipped it around and swung it like a bat at the head of an attacking Craing. Jason put a couple of plasma bolts into the Craing's helmet, dropping him at her feet. By the time Jason and his team had wiped out the majority of Craing, the rest were running from the bridge.

"Now that's the Craing I remember," Billy said.

"Captain, this bridge has taken too much damage," Ricket said, getting up from his station.

Jason, just now able to assess the situation, was speechless for several seconds.

"Holy shit," Billy interjected.

The bridge was a shambles: any remaining consoles were nothing more than scorched scrap.

"Were you able to get us back in command?" Jason asked Ricket.

"The only thing I was able to do before my station was destroyed was to slave this Dreadnaught back to Dreadnaught One. From there, I should be able to finish what I started."

The bridge was empty; no sign of Han Di or anyone else. Moving slowly, Traveler was a mess. Jason thought he'd be hard-pressed to find even one inch of unscorched hide anywhere on his body.

"Hang in there, big guy; you're definitely due for some time in a MediPod," Jason said.

"I am fine, Captain."

Once again, they phase-shifted onto Dreadnaught One's deserted bridge. Ricket went right to work, hacking the Craing security firewalls and then accessing the Meganaught's executive-level systems.

"Done, Captain," Ricket said, taking a deep breath.

"And we can bring on, or cluster, the *Independence* when she arrives?"

"Yes, sir. But we'll need to maintain control of this bridge. That is essential from this point on."

"Traveler, get yourself to Medical. Return in an hour with your best team of rhinos. As Ricket says, we can't lose this bridge again."

"Yes, Captain."

Traveler flipped-open his wristband, but Ricket stopped him, reaching a hand up to his.

"The coordinates have already been uploaded to your device; just press the activate button."

Traveler stood up tall and shifted away.

Chapter 45

With the flight deck doors fully retracted, Jason and Billy stood on the deck's platform looking out at the carnage. Jason brought up his virtual notepad and a multi-feed segmented view of the three Dreadnaughts' bridges. Traveler and six other Greys and, surprisingly, two goliath Reds, were keeping sentry on the first Dreadnaught's bridge. Similarly, the other two bridges had their own complement of rhino sentries. Additional sentries were set to cover revolving shifts outside the entrances of each bridge.

What concerned Jason the most, though, was the obstreperous nature of the situation on the main corridor. A thousand or so Serapins, plus pill bug creatures, and too many other vile species to count, were roaming the Meganaught unhindered. Since Jason had pulled back his troops, and without the Craing providing them their allotted daily meals, the varied creatures were turning on each other. It was utter mayhem out there and Jason felt partially responsible. At least before, as captives, they hadn't been killing each other.

The Lilly was moving again, slowly making forward and aft revolutions of the corridor. Each of the sub-temperature energy cannons had been taken out during the ship's first pass.

"What do we do with them?" Billy queried.

Jason shrugged. "Killing combatants in the course of battle is one thing, but I'm not in the extermination business. What we need to do is get them back in their cages."

"Sounds like a good exercise for the ground troops aboard the *Independence*, once she gets here," Billy added.

Jason had to smile before turning his attention back to the increasing noise behind them on the flight deck.

"So what's the plan, Cap?" Billy asked, taking an extended puff on his freshly lit cigar.

Jason had to yell over the noise: "Five fighters will resume their patrols of the corridor. Maintain order, and positively ensure any remaining Craing are kept far away from all three bridges. *The Lilly* will phase-shift to open space and use what Ricket figured out to instigate a wormhole to this location for the outpost fleet."

"So what's the problem?"

"The problem is finding open space. Even with our extended three thousand mile phase-shift capabilities, the fleet surrounding us is composed of more than two thousand warships. They have encircled the Meganaught. The secret's out—they know we're here; they just don't quite know what to do with us. Eventually, they'll have to attack. But our imminent problem is getting out to open space. The radius of the Craing fleet extends to fifty thousand miles."

"Just make multiple phase-shifts, what's the problem?"

"The problem is *The Lilly* can't make fifteen or sixteen consecutive phase-shifts without stopping periodically to recharge. We do that, and we'll be engaging the enemy in open space. Defeats our purpose."

"Where's the Allied fleet in all this? I thought they'd be here by now."

"Close. Probably too close, and I'm sure they've been detected on the Craing's long-range sensors. They've held up somewhere waiting for the outpost fleet to arrive for a unified attack."

Jason looked down at his virtual notepad and the Rhino teams moving about the Dreadnaught bridge.

"Why do I need open space?"

"What do you mean?" Billy asked.

Jason gestured to the video feed. "Remember earlier, when Traveler phase-shifted into that group of Craing combatants?"

"That was pretty foul. Really disgusting."

"One of the unique properties of phase-shifting is that the thing *shifting* takes space precedence, or ownership, over the space into which it phase-shifts. We've seen that time and time again. Whenever *The Lilly*, or even one of us, phase-shifts, we displace matter when we complete the shift."

"Yeah, we know that," Billy said, making a face that said *well, that's obvious.*

"I'm just saying we can phase-shift into space anywhere. Any Craing warship that happens to be in the way will be destroyed."

"So what are we waiting for?"

* * *

It was time for battle, the most important battle of his life. Jason wanted to make sure everyone was on the same page. The captain's ready room was filled to capacity. Traveler, too large for a standard chair, stood off to the side. Ricket, to Jason's left, looked stronger and more confident in his new body than ever before. He also looked younger, less frail. The others—Orion, Perkins, Billy, Chief Horris, and the rest of the command team—didn't look quite as sure of themselves. Looking around the table, he missed seeing Nan there, and having Mollie nearby. He wondered what they were doing at that particular moment, back home safe in San Bernardino. His eyes stopped on Dira, who looked tired but, as always, lovely. He wished they had had more time to cultivate their burgeoning relationship. Would it ever be possible to someday do so? How many at the table would still be alive in the hours ahead? He looked across the table again at Dira and gave her a quick wink. He brought his mind back to the present moment.

"So, in review, let's go over it one more time," Jason said. "As agreed to by Admiral Reynolds, the *Independence* will be the first warship to come over. That will be *The Lilly*'s first order of business once a viable wormhole has been produced. Soon after that, the *Pacesetter* and the *Epcot* shuttle will introduce smaller wormholes and bring back two warships per cycle. Over the past hour we've been maneuvering the Meganaught, attempting to reposition her to the outer fringe of the Craing fleet, with the overall intention of surrounding the Craing once the EOUPA and Allied fleets arrive. Any questions?"

No one spoke up, then Orion nervously cleared her throat. "Can we do this? I mean, can we actually win, Cap? It just seems so overwhelmingly lopsided."

All eyes were on Jason. He knew they needed him to be a positive voice: assuring them with ultra-conviction, that, yes, they really did have a chance to succeed in the upcoming battle. A battle fought not only to ensure their own survival, but the survival of their home worlds, their loved ones.

"You give me your all today, each and every one of you, and we'll hammer a stake in the hearts of the Craing. Today is the day we drive them from Allied space, the day they realize their empire is vulnerable. Yes, Gunny, we can—and we will—win, if you all do your jobs."

Jason stood and, one by one, looked at each of them. "We all may not survive the day. Sadly, some of us will fall in the coming battle. So look to one another ... do so right now. You're fighting for each other—fighting to ensure that the warriors next to you will survive the day. Will you fight for them? Will you help bring them back to this table?"

The room went still and quiet. They looked to one another.

Dira reached out and grabbed the chief's hand on her right, and Billy's on her left. In turn, Billy and the chief did the same with those next to them, and it continued around the table. Jason sat down, joined hands with those next to him and completed the circle. Traveler stepped forward and placed a heavy hand on Jason's shoulder. No one spoke. No one needed to.

Chapter 46

Mollie froze, her heart ready to leap out of her chest. The noisy gunfire had stopped. What had happened to her mother? Biting her lip and fighting back tears, Mollie slowly, quietly, crawled from the great room toward the kitchen and the smaller adjoining family room. Ever so carefully, Mollie peered around the corner. The bad man's legs lay sprawled before her, a mere two or three feet away. Not moving. *Was he dead*?

She inched forward, now able to look further into the family room. The bad man, the one her mother called Stalls, was on his back and had been shot; big black spots, some oozing blood, covered his entire body. Stalls' eyes were closed. He looked dead.

Mollie's eyes went to her mother, her body in a heap next to Stalls. Her forehead had a black mark on it. Keeping her voice low, Mollie said, "Mom... Mommy?"

Movement. Stalls' eyelids opened and he looked at the ceiling. Mollie froze, and stopped breathing. His chest rose and a groan came from his lips. His head turned and he looked at her mother. Slowly, he reached a hand out and touched her arm. Mollie felt something she had never felt before. Certainly not to this degree. Hatred. She wanted to kill him. Kill the person who had taken her mother's life.

What was that? Mollie was afraid to hope. There it was again. Her mother's eyes fluttered. Not opened but fluttered. Stalls kept trying to get up on one elbow, but he was having trouble. Mollie, ever so carefully, crawled backwards out of sight. Feeling safe for the moment, she considered her options. There was no way around it. She had to kill him.

But the rustling whisper from her slightest movement seemed to be amplified. She didn't think he was aware of her presence in the house. That was one thing in her favor, she thought. Again, she moved her arm and carefully withdrew the small energy pistol from its holster on her hip. It made a noise as it cleared the rim of the holster. He had to have heard that, she thought, now becoming still again. She leaned sideways and watched his legs. No quick rush to see what was around the corner. No, he definitely hadn't heard her. Mollie looked down at the energy weapon. It was similar to the one Orion had showed her how to use. But not exactly the same. This one had a trigger. There were several other small knobs, and a slider-switch-thingy near the barrel. *Do I have to do anything with those?* Mollie wondered.

Stalls moved again and, after several tries, made it to his feet. He was making a lot of noise, groaning and moving around. Mollie felt confident that she could safely get to her feet as well. She brought the energy pistol forward, steadying it with her other hand, just as Orion had taught her. Peering around the corner, Mollie saw Stalls crouching at her mother's side. He was gently touching her face, moving her hair off her forehead and inspecting her head wound. Again, the anger welled up inside her. Mollie brought up the pistol and aimed it at Stalls' head.

"Don't touch her."

Stalls froze. Quietly, almost soothingly, he said, "I should have figured you'd be around here somewhere, Mollie."

"Stand up, slowly! I have a gun and I know how to use it."

Stalls slowly got up, trying to straighten his body, but having difficulty. He brought both hands up.

"I'm sure you do, Mollie. Don't do anything crazy, little girl. Look, I'm not armed," he said, his words sounding somewhat slurred.

He turned to face her. "I didn't come here to hurt you, or

your mother. You have to believe me."

Mollie was surprised to see that the big pirate had taken numerous shots to his face. Two large black scorch marks pocked his skin, one almost severing part of his lower lip, which hung loose, looking ready to fall off at any moment. A continuous stream of bloody drool flowed down onto his ruffled shirt.

Her mother groaned, then stirred. Mollie turned in time to see that her mother's eyes were open and she was trying to say something. She tried again, and the words were inaudible, but Mollie knew what she said.

"Shoot him."

Mollie understood. She looked back to Stalls, but he was already moving. In a blur, he slapped the gun from her hands and reached for her neck. Mollie ducked below his outstretched arms and ran, quickly getting tangled up in her mother's outstretched legs. Stalls came at her with surprising speed, and only by crab-walking backward was she able to avoid his grasping hands.

In quick pursuit Stalls too tripped over Nan's legs. Mollie got to her feet and walked backward toward the broken back windows. From behind her came a strange sound: *flipflap, flipflap.*

Stalls was no longer hurrying to catch her. Mollie took a glance back and realized she could probably outrun him. He was an adult, but he was injured. She hesitated too long.

"Why don't you leave us alone?" Mollie asked, tears coming to her eyes.

"Leave you alone? Why would I do that? No, you will soon come to think of me as your father. You will be a princess in my castle. Your mother ... a queen." Stalls smiled, causing the dangling section of his lip to finally fall free. He brought his fingers to his mouth and said, with a wet slur, "Shit."

Flipflop, flipflop.

Stalls heard the sound and looked beyond Mollie to the porch outside. Mollie's eyes grew wide as she watched her mother rise up behind Stalls, holding the pirate's energy rifle. She shot him in the back and watched as he fell to the floor. She smiled reassuringly toward Mollie, but quickly wavered, then crumpled to the floor herself.

Mollie jumped over Stalls to her mother's side. Not knowing what to do, she pried open an eyelid with two fingers. Her mother brushed Mollie's hand away, looked up at her and said something in a whisper.

"What, Mom? I'm scared."

Barely conscious, Nan said, "Get help, Mollie. Hurry." Her eyes shut as she lost consciousness.

Flipflop, flipflop.

Mollie stood. *How do I get help?* "Hello, Bag End? Are you there?" She waited for a response, but heard nothing.

Flipflop, flipflop.

Annoyed, she spun around. "What is that stupid sound?" she asked aloud.

It was coming from outside ... at the edge of the porch? *No! In the pool.* Mollie ran out through the ruined sliding doors and onto the deck. The pool was littered with bits and pieces of the house's framework and shingles from the roof. Then she saw it: a claw slapping at the water trying to grasp the edge of the pool.

"Teardrop!"

Down on her knees at the pool's edge, Mollie reached under the water until she felt the drone's metal arm. She pulled it up toward the surface. Using both hands now, she put her back into it and pulled harder. Teardrop was just too heavy to pull free from the pool. Frustrated, she looked around for anything that could possibly help. Teardrop's claw was opening and closing, as if trying to grab at something, at anything. Scooting back, Mollie pulled again; this time she brought the claw right to the pool's edge, where it immediately clamped down on the rim. Teardrop then rose up out of the water and hung there, between the pool and the deck for several moments. The muzzle of a weapon hung limply out of a cavity in its chest. Faint at first, sounds emanated from the battered, one-armed drone, but were too garbled for Mollie to understand. She wondered if it had shut itself off. Then Teardrop began talking much more clearly.

"Mollie Reynolds, intruder alert, intruder alert—"

"It's too late for that. He's already dead. My mom ... She's hurt. She needs a doctor."

Teardrop, seeming to come back to life more and more by the second, hovered above the pool. The drone spun around once and moved forward into the house.

Mollie watched it as it hovered above Stalls' body, then over her mother's.

"Immediate MediPod attention is required. Death is imminent."

"My mother's dying?"

"Yes. Your mother and the intruder require immediate MediPod attention."

"No, no, no ... Can't you help her? Wait, what do you mean the intruder?"

Teardrop hovered back over Stalls' inert body. Stalls' hand twitched once, then a leg. Mollie's eyes widened.

"What's wrong with him? For heaven's sake, why won't he just hurry up and die?"

Frantic, Molly hurried inside and helped Teardrop lift, or more like drag, her mother. It was awkward; Mollie was off balance and nearly dropped her.

"Hurry! We need to get her away from him. Can't you see he's waking up?"

Stepping around his not-fully-conscious body, Mollie paused. Remembering what Orion had taught her in self-defense class, she pulled back her leg and let loose the kick of all kicks straight at his face. Stalls fell back on the floor.

Teardrop and Mollie hurried out the back of the house and headed to the side yard. "We need to get her to *The Lilly*. You need to take us to my father, to *The Lilly*."

Teardrop lowered Nan and then hovered over the pool for several seconds.

"What are you doing? We need to go!"

Teardrop was back in the pool and heading toward the bottom. Mollie stayed at her mother's side. Her eyes were fluttering again; at least she was still alive. There was movement in the house. This was a nightmare, like the movies she'd seen where the bad guy unbelievably kept coming back to life long after he should have been dead. She squinted her eyes. Was he ...? *Oh no, he's getting to his feet.*

Teardrop was back, hovering over the pool.

"Where were you? You need to help me, right now!" Mollie screamed in the drone's direction. Teardrop had reclaimed his other arm from the pool. It wasn't working perfectly, but at least it was attached.

Back at Mollie's side, Teardrop lifted Nan's body into the air on his own. "We must proceed to the subterranean base." The drone headed off into the scrapyard. Before following, Mollie took one more glance toward the house. Her heart stopped. Teardrop's distant voice was now harder to hear: "Mollie Reynolds, we must proceed to the subterranean base."

Stalls was not only standing, but he was holding his rifle. Appearing to have problems walking, Stalls leaned against the doorframe. He smiled down at Mollie—his lower teeth showing through the ragged gap along his lower lip. Then the smile was gone.

"You little bitch." His gun came up, the muzzle pointed at her head.

"Please don't kill me?" she said, slowly getting to her feet.

"Sorry, but if you're this much trouble as an eight-year-old—"

His words were drowned out by a low-frequency rumble. Then a vibration—a vibration so intense the ground shook. Mollie lost her balance and fell to the ground. *An earthquake?* Then she saw it coming from above. Yellow, and as big as a barn, it was falling fast toward Earth.

Screaming, Mollie scooted backward, trying to escape an unidentified falling object she was sure would end her life. Then, in the blink of an eye, the ground shuddered and the new house, along with Captain Stalls, was flattened into something no thicker than a pancake. The huge ensuing dust cloud rose high into the air, making it impossible to see anything. Mollie, unsteady, got to her feet and wiped at her eyes. As the air cleared, she now saw what was towering above her. It was some kind of monstrous-looking vehicle, with tires the size of a man and a big, blue container-like thing behind it. A hatchway opened in its glass-paneled cab area. A man swung out, precariously holding on with one arm. He looked down at her.

"Mollie? Is that you?"

"Uncle Brian?"

Chapter 47

"I thought we weren't using that thing," Jason said, hovering over Ricket's shoulder.

The white communications cube seemed dissimilar to the one installed by the Caldurians on *The Lilly*'s bridge. Just opening it required special tools brought down from Deck 4B. With its cover off and its sides hanging loosely open, Ricket's focus was on modifying the main circuit board.

Jason asked again, "What is it you're doing?"

"Even with the formulaic precepts figured out, we still need to contact the interchange, provide it with in and out coordinates, and spool the wormhole into existence," Ricket replied, now looking up at Jason. "This cube, like all the others installed within the outpost fleet, was configured to talk to the Caldurians, not the interchange. But it still utilizes a highly advanced, remarkably fast communications technology to which I'm surmising the interchange will be receptive."

"So you don't really know if this is going to work. I thought we were past that, Ricket?"

"We will know soon enough, Captain. It is ready." Ricket moved to his right and started to type something on that station's console.

"So you're just going to leave it open like that?" Jason questioned him, looking down at the opened box with its ripped contents of tangled wiring harnesses and added components, some parts precariously dangling over the sides of the box.

"For now, Captain."

"But this looks like a hobbyist's experiment gone bad. We're entrusting people's lives with this ... whatever it is."

"Yes, Captain. It is important we test it and ensure it actually does what it is intended to do. Although I have done virtual modeling of it on a smaller scale on 4B, I am ready to initiate contact to the interchange to request the spooling of a full-sized wormhole. As an added benefit, our communications to the outpost fleet will no longer require FTL transmissions. Through this device, they will be instantaneous."

With time quickly running out before the Craing commenced an attack on the Meganaught, or perhaps even split up their forces and sent warships to deal with the unprepared Allied fleet, Jason knew he needed to get things hurried along.

As much as this was a test, as Ricket put it, once they commenced spooling wormholes, all hell would break out. They would be committed.

Jason had selected Lieutenant Wilson to pilot the *Pacesetter* and Lieutenant Grimes to pilot the *Epcot* shuttle. Both were prepped and ready within *The Lilly*'s flight deck. The five other fighters would be phase-shifting the Mau warships into open space. With their three-mile phase-shift limitation, this part of the plan was dangerous. The Mau vessels would need to come out fighting and make their way to their predetermined outer perimeter positions.

Ricket stood and turned, backing away from the station, and said, "We're ready, Captain."

"AI, sound general quarters," Jason ordered. "Contact the interchange, Ricket."

Ricket, who'd prepared a data script ahead of time, tapped only one virtual key at the station.

All eyes went to the overhead wraparound display. It started with a distortion, a blurring effect two thousand miles off the Meganaught's port side. A kaleidoscope of colors, in prismatic flares, emanated out from a growing black void. Jason didn't realize he'd been holding his breath until he and the rest of the bridge crew collectively exhaled.

"Wormhole's stable, Captain," Ricket said.

Seaman Gordon excitedly added, "I have confirmation from the *Independence*; the wormhole is there, sir."

"XO, order Lieutenant Wilson to phase-shift."

With those words, Jason knew the battle of their lives had begun.

The *Pacesetter* reappeared fifteen hundred miles to their starboard and quickly moved in the direction of the wormhole.

"Three Heavy Cruisers and a destroyer-class warship are maneuvering to intercept the *Pacesetter*, Captain," Orion reported.

"Helm, put us there. Phase-shift *The Lilly*. Put us in between the *Pacesetter* and the Craing." *So much for our plan*, Jason thought.

The Lilly phase-shifted in time to deflect plasma fire from two of the cruisers.

"Ricket, get working on spooling new wormholes for *The Lilly* and the *Epcot*."

"Gunny, deploy rail-guns, JIT munitions."

The *Pacesetter* was closing in on the yawning wormhole, but the Craing destroyer was in close pursuit.

"Captain, the Meganaught is taking fire ... from all sides," Orion reported.

Like frenzied bees around a hive, Craing warships were attacking the Meganaught. Pinpoint flashes danced across her shields, indicating she was able to deflect the brunt of the Craing onslaught. But Jason knew the shields could hold up only so long. No matter how large the Meganaught was, it was only one vessel attempting to fight off thousands of Craing ships.

"Time for you to get over to Dreadnaught One's bridge. Good hunting, Gunny."

Orion stood alongside two other crewmembers; each of them wore a battle suit and a phase-shift belt. Once their helmets were securely latched into place, they disappeared in a white flash.

By the time Jason returned to his command chair, the Meganaught was already firing its massive plasma cannons. Jason looked up to the video feed coming from the Dreadnaught's bridge. Appearing among the roving rhino sentry guards were Orion and her tactical team, already seated at consoles.

"*Pacesetter* is coming up to the wormhole, Cap," Perkins reported, now seated at Orion's vacated seat at the tactical station.

The *Pacesetter* closed in on the new wormhole while taking fire to her aft shields. The fighter deployed her own mini rail-gun and fired back at the pursuing destroyer. Then the *Pacesetter* neared the entry to the wormhole; it hesitated there, and then was gone. The Craing destroyer followed, plasma bolts firing non-stop from multiple cannons.

"Comms, let the *Independence* know the *Pacesetter's* bringing along company."

"Aye, Captain," Seaman Gordon replied. A moment later he reported, "Both the *Pacesetter* and the destroyer have emerged from the wormhole. The *Independence* has destroyed the Craing vessel. Admiral Reynolds says to hurry up and get his fleet into the battle, sir."

Ricket's LA Dodgers ball-capped head was nodding. He gave an exaggerated final tap on his key and said, "Done."

Two more wormholes, one significantly larger than the other, were taking shape. The display above them showed the *Epcot*, which had phase-shifted from *The Lilly's* flight deck, near the smaller of the two wormholes. It held steady there until the wormhole stabilized. Then, just like the *Pacesetter*, it was gone.

The XO turned toward Jason. "Captain, our fighters have phase-shifted into five of the eight Mau vessels. They're ready to move to open space on your command."

Jason didn't like the idea of Mau vessels thrown into the midst of battle without *The Lilly* there to provide cover. Another change of plan was needed.

"Have the pilots hold tight until we return with the *Independence*."

"Aye, Captain," the XO replied.

"Helm, phase-shift us in close to the larger wormhole."

The Craing fleet was mobilizing into two uneven-sized segments. The larger of the two units continued their attack on their former Meganaught, while the smaller segment, close to five hundred warships, made headway toward *The Lilly* and the two newly formed wormholes.

"Take us in, Helm," Jason said.

The Lilly crossed into the mouth of the wormhole, held there, and then felt inertia as *The Lilly* was pulled into complete blackness.

Jason waited for the logistical view on the display to reorient itself. Sure enough, the outpost fleet was there. The *Independence* was less than ten thousand miles from their current position.

"Both wormholes closing, Captain," McBride said from the helm.

The admiral's face appeared on the forward segment of the display.

"What's the situation in the Alcara system, Captain?"

"Good to see you too, Admiral," Jason said, with a wry smile. "We need to move fast; the Meganaught, the vessel that used to be three separate Dreadnaughts, is pretty much on its own against the Craing fleet."

"Well, what are we waiting for?"

Jason looked over to Ricket, who was still entering something at his station. There it was again: a final exaggerated key tap. "Done and done!" Ricket said.

Two wormholes began to take shape.

"You're first, Admiral. We'll be coming into a shit storm, sir."

"Understood. Going general quarters. Just keep bringing my fleet over as quickly as possible."

"What about the Allied fleet?" Jason asked him.

"They've been instructed to attack as soon as the *Independence* shows up. Anything else you can tell me before I get there? I'll be directing the battle and overall fleet command. This should free you and *The Lilly* up to cause as much mayhem for the Craing as possible."

Jason saw that the *Independence* was already moving toward the newly formed wormhole.

"No, I think you know the situation. I've also forwarded everything we have on the Mau. I suggest you contact Ti—she's turned out to be a key ally in all this."

"I'll do so as soon as I have a free minute."

"And Dad?"

"Yes?"

"Good luck," Jason said.

"You too, son."

Chapter 48

With the arrival of the *Independence* into the Alcara system, the Craing fleet wasted no time attacking. Two hundred light and heavy cruisers split off from the huge Craing fleet and bore down on the *Independence*, and in turn she brought her own powerful guns to bear.

Jason gave the order for his fighters to go ahead and phase-shift the first five Mau ships into open space. Within minutes, three of the dark red fighters phase-shifted back into the Meganaught, into the holds of the four remaining Mau ships, and then phase-shifted them back out alongside the others. Their small force was back to eight ships.

Jason hailed Ti, the Mau officer. Her startled face appeared before him on the display.

"Just wanted to wish you well, Ti. As you can see, the Craing are mobilizing; you've got fifty-six Craing warships en route to your current coordinates."

"We see them, Captain. We will do our best to hold our position."

"You'll also be hearing from the Fleet Commander, Admiral Reynolds. Like the rest of us, you'll now be taking directions from him."

"Understood," Ti replied, and she broke the connection.

Jason watched as the nine horseshoe-shaped Mau vessels broke into a tight formation of groups of three. In unison, the Mau's plasma guns fired into the oncoming Craing ships.

"Captain, Orion on the Meganaught is hailing," Seaman Gordon said from Comms.

"Shields are starting to fail, Captain," Orion reported. "We've destroyed three hundred ships, but our shields are faltering and we're seeing hull damage to Dreadnaught Three."

"You'll need to hold them off a while longer, Gunny. Our new Mau friends, along with our fighters, are engaging the fleet in quadrant four. The *Independence* is moving through quadrant three and will cluster with you shortly. The Allied fleet is moving a bit slower than we would like, but they'll divert a good amount of attention into quadrant one when they arrive. I'm guessing in ten minutes. We're still moving outpost ships in as well, so try to hold on a while longer."

"Aye, Cap. We'll hold them."

Jason looked up to see Ricket signaling, trying to divert his attention toward another display segment. "Wormhole is ready, Captain."

As *The Lilly* moved toward the newly created wormhole, Jason saw the *Epcot* emerge with two outpost warships following close behind.

"Ricket, is there any reason the *Epcot* and the *Pacesetter* ... and *The Lilly*, too, for that matter, still need to traverse back and forth? Haven't we pretty much tested this thing?"

"Agreed, Captain, as long as all the ship commanders are updated with new wormhole coordinates and realize they need to move quickly. The wormholes stay open only a finite amount of time," Ricket explained.

"Fine. We'll continue to spool wormholes while staying here in the fight."

"Yes, Captain, and I should also mention we're spooling somewhat larger wormholes than I originally determined possible. If brought into tight formations of five to ten warships per grouping, the timeframe to bring over the entire fleet will be significantly decreased."

"Keep at it, Ricket—you and McBride work with the remaining outpost fleet commanders. Come up with formations that will get them to the Alcara system in the least amount of time."

"Helm, we're changing direction. Set a course for the Meganaught; deploy rail-guns and plasma cannons."

The Lilly jolted and Jason needed to reach for the back of his chair to remain on his feet.

"Report, XO."

"Nukes, with more on the way, sir."

Jason knew from experience the Craing seldom, if ever, used missiles in battle—preferring to use their far more economical plasma cannons. If they were now resorting to missiles, things were definitely heating up for them.

"Phase-shift out of here, Helm."

"Captain, we have one hundred and twenty incoming nukes. They're targeting the Meganaught, not us. Orion says they won't withstand that barrage level."

"Get us in front of them, then. Do it, now!"

The bridge flashed white.

The Lilly's three rail-guns and four plasma cannons fired continuously at the approaching onslaught of Craing nuclear-tipped missiles. One by one the Craing's icons disappeared from view on the display. All but seventeen of them were destroyed.

"Incoming!"

The Lilly shuddered with violent jolts as the nukes careened into her shields.

"Shields are down to two percent, Captain," Perkins shouted, getting up from the floor. "Shields are starting to come back online, Captain."

"Two of the Mau ships just exploded, Captain," Perkins added. Seeing Jason's questioning expression, the XO shook his head. "No, sir. Ti's ship is still in the fight."

The *Independence*, now abreast of the Meganaught, had an encircling cloud of Craing warships pounding at her shields from virtually every angle.

"Captain, the Allied fleet of eight hundred and fifty-six ships has just entered the fight!" Perkins exclaimed with excitement.

Scanning the logistical display above him, Jason could see light at the end of the tunnel. The six remaining Mau ships, along with *The Lilly*'s fighters, were holding their own, destroying most of the Craing warships they came into contact with. The Allied fleet began to pull Craing firepower away from the *Independence* and the Meganaught—a needed reprieve for both vessels. Jason knew it could still end up being a battle of attrition.

"XO, let's get the numbers up on the screen."

With a glance at the display, Jason was surprised to see the Craing fleet reduced to eleven hundred ships, almost half its original number. And some of those ships were floundering in space, with rampant rhinos on the loose, which Jason was sure were causing untold mayhem. Five hundred-plus attributed kills. The Meganaught, with Orion at Tactical, had become an overwhelming foe for the Craing to contend with.

Now, as more and more of the outpost fleet moved into the battle, Jason watched as their outer perimeter closed in around the Craing. The noose was definitely tightening.

This was a pivotal moment; Jason had felt it before. Like in high school, when playing football. The defining moment when you know your team is going to win the game; drive the opposition team into the ground and, maybe, get to have a cheerleader sit on your lap for the bus ride home.

"Captain, the Mau are changing sides!" Perkins yelled excitedly.

"Ti? No, that's not possible."

"No, sir," Perkins replied, at first confused. "The other Mau ships—the ones with the Craing. They're joining Ti's forces."

Jason's eyes flashed to the dynamic counter on the display and realized they now outnumbered the Craing fleet by one-third.

"Captain, I have a repeating message coming in from deep space. It's from a drone," Seaman Gordon said.

"I think we have more important things to worry about right now, don't you think, Seaman?"

"Yes, sir."

Jason watched as the *Independence* methodically moved into position to cluster with the Meganaught.

"Captain, that drone is being persistent. Insists that I connect you on comms."

"I told you—"

"Its location is Earth, sir."

"Connect to my NanoCom."

Chapter 49

Jason stood and put two fingers to his ear. "Identify yourself. Who are you?" Jason commanded.

Teardrop's humanistic voice started to reply, "Drone allocation 724," but it was quickly interrupted by another voice.

"Dad!"

Jason froze. "Mollie? What—"

"Dad, Mom's hurt. She needs to go into a MediPod."

"What happened? Where's your mother now?"

"The bad pirate ... Stalls. He shot her in the head."

Jason was having a hard time connecting the dots. How could Stalls possibly shoot her? Nan was back on Earth. Then he realized the pirate had somehow tracked them to where they lived.

"Where's your mother now. Is she breathing?"

"I think so. Teardrop says she doesn't have much time."

"Teardrop? Who's—"

"The drone, Dad. Hurry! She's unconscious."

"Where's Captain Stalls now? Is he after you? Are you safe?"

"Yes, he's dead. Uncle Brian dropped a bin lift on him."

"Uncle Brian?"

"Yes, and now he's putting a bandage around Mom's head."

Jason closed his eyes, trying to make sense of what he was hearing.

"So where exactly are you now, Mollie?"

"In the cavern below the scrapyard. In the shuttle."

"Okay, Mollie, we're going to get Mom help. I need to talk to the drone."

"This is drone allocation 724—"

"Stop and listen. Can you pilot that shuttle?"

"Yes, I can pilot—"

"Hold on a second ..."

Jason turned his attention to the bridge. He needed Ricket. Thankfully, Ricket appeared at his side.

"Ricket, can you spool out a wormhole as far as Earth? Can you do it immediately?"

"I believe so, Captain." Ricket darted toward his station, climbed onto his chair and started inputting information.

"Helm, phase-shift us away from the battle. Multiple phase-shifts, if necessary."

"Aye, Captain," said McBride.

The display changed, reorienting itself several times, then held steady.

"We're twenty-one thousand miles outside of the battle zone, sir."

Ricket turned to Jason. "I'm relaying the coordinates—where the wormhole will appear—to the shuttle, Captain."

Jason was back on his comms. "Okay, listen to me, drone. Did you receive the coordinates to a wormhole yet? You'll need to phase-shift from beneath the ground and set a course to those coordinates outside of Earth's orbit."

Jason heard a commotion in the background. Mollie was yelling for everyone to sit down and for Brian to make his hopper stop breathing on her. *What's a hopper?*

"Captain Reynolds," came the drone's soothing voice, "we have completed the phase-shift and are now en route to the designated space coordinates."

"Good. Keep me updated on your status. Let me know when you're close."

Jason waited. How does someone survive a shot to the head?

Dread filled his thoughts. *Oh God, Nan, please don't die.*

"We are now five hundred miles from the designated coordinates, Captain Reynolds."

Jason gestured for Ricket to go ahead and spool the wormhole. A moment later he saw it taking form off the port side of *The Lilly*.

"Anomaly identified. Proceeding into wormhole," the drone said.

Jason was about to ask what the hell had happened when the shuttle emerged from the center of the wormhole.

"Ricket, provide coordinates for them to phase-shift into our flight deck. Someone get Dira to prep a MediPod and have her meet me at the shuttle.

* * *

Jason sprinted onto the shuttle's flight deck and was at the hatch when it opened. Expecting to see Mollie, he was startled to see something large and green brush past him.

Dira, several paces behind him, screamed. She was pinned to the rear flight deck bulkhead. Before her stood a scaly-skinned, lizard-like creature—easily as big as a man. Jason pulled for his sidearm and aimed for the creature, but he had to move sideways to avoid hitting Dira by mistake.

"Dad!"

Jason kept his energy weapon trained on the creature and stole a quick glance toward Mollie.

"Don't shoot it. It's friendly."

Jason took another look at the creature, now sniffing at Dira's feet; its long tongue licked at her boots.

"Could use a little help here," Brian said, emerging from the shuttle. Nan's limp body lay unconscious in his outstretched arms.

Jason hesitated as he took in the sight of his older brother. Dressed in strange clothes, Brian had a crude bloody bandage encircling the top of his head, covering one eye.

Jason ran forward and took Nan's body from him. Her forehead was bandaged and her face was white, almost blue, and lifeless. Mollie was at his side, hugging his legs, and looking up at him.

"Don't let her die, Dad."

Jason, with Nan in his arms, turned and headed out of the flight deck. He reached *The Lilly*'s nearest DeckPort in three strides and they emerged on Deck 4. Moments later he placed Nan's body into an open MediPod. Dira, out of breath, joined him at his side. She checked Nan's pulse, then moved to the MediPod's small control panel.

The top of the MediPod started to close as Mollie ran into Medical. Tears brimming, she looked up at Jason, and then at Dira.

"Will she be okay?"

Jason looked to Dira for an answer, not knowing what to tell his daughter.

"I think so," she said.

A virtual representation of Nan's body was now displayed above the MediPod. They kept their eyes riveted on her chest area, where her heart would register a beat.

Jason reflected that it wasn't so long ago he had watched Mollie as she lay in the same MediPod: stone cold dead from a plasma shot to the heart. She'd survived. Now he stared at Nan's slowly turning virtual representation, willing for her heart to start beating.

"Come on, Nan!" Jason yelled, startling both Mollie and Dira.

Soon they were all yelling for Nan to come back to them.

"Come on, Nan!"

"Don't give up—come back to us, Mom!"

Jason noticed his brother was leaning against the entrance to Medical. If what Mollie had said was true, he had saved her life. Perhaps there was hope for him after all. Some woman, unfamiliar to Jason, stood at his brother's side.

"I saw it beat!" Mollie screamed.

Jason looked back to the display. Nothing.

"I saw it, Dad. I did."

He gave Mollie a reassuring smile, but wondered if she had only hoped she'd seen something.

"I saw it, too," Brian said, now standing at Jason's side.

Then Jason also saw it. Nan's heart was beating. Mollie screamed, then Dira screamed. Brian casually lifted a hand up in the air and Jason high-fived his brother. Jason held his arms wide open. Mollie, still jumping and screaming, leapt into her father's arms.

Jason was hailed. He ignored it for several seconds, then acknowledged the XO.

"Go for Captain."

"We have a new contact, Captain."

* * *

Jason entered *The Lilly*'s bridge and made his way to the command chair. "Put it up on the display. Zoom to full screen."

McBride let out a long whoooo. "Thing's as big as a dreadnought."

"Captain, we've seen that ship before," Perkins said.

"Yes, we have. It's Caldurian—the *Minian*."

Again, Jason was struck by the vessel's similarity to *The Lilly*. The same sleek, elegant lines, but it was a much larger-scaled ship.

"Captain, the *Minian* is charging weapons. She's firing on us."

Jason barely had enough time to sit down before teeth-rattling jolts rocked *The Lilly*.

"Shields are gone, Captain. Damage reported on all decks."

"Phase-shift us into the *Independence*. Now!"

To be continued...

Thank you for reading Space Vengeance. If you enjoyed this book and would like to see the series continue, please leave a review on Amazon.com – it really helps! To be notified of the soon-to-be released next Scrapyard Ship book, **Realms of Time***, contact markwaynemcginnis@gmail.com, Subject Line:* **Realms of Time List***. I truly love hearing from the readers of my books—again, thank you...*

Acknowledgments

First of all I'd like to thank my wonderful wife, Kim, and my mother (again) for the support and encouragement to write these books. Thank you to my amazing editors, Lura Lee Genz, Rachel Weaver and Mia Manns—the many hours invested are so very appreciated. Much appreciation to Bethany Kraft for your research and helping me keep aliens, spaceships and rhino-warriors all straight in my mind. Thank you to Lura and James Fischer for your continued support, it really means a lot to me. I'd also like to thank the many subject matter experts and others who supported, contributed, and reviewed this book, including Eric Sundius, David Brock and the many others that selflessly gave their time to this project. Thank you to the gang over at Mojo's Café Shop where I sometimes find a quiet corner to write. I'd also like to thank the fans of this ongoing saga, I read every one of your emails and enjoy your comments.

Made in the USA
San Bernardino, CA
25 July 2014